UnVeiled Voices

UnVeiled Voices

a my.thology

Dr. Sandra Walton Wilson

atmosphere press

Dear Reader,

Everyone has a story to tell. Some are shared. Others are hidden. *UnVeiled Voices* introduces investigations, experiences, and thoughts, secreted by insecurities and/or preferences. This book of historical fiction is punctuated with quotations by noted thinkers.

The details and actions in the presentations can be true. However, there is also a mixture of actual events with a touch of imagination. *UnVeiled Voices* is a conglomeration of different writings, essays, short stories, skits and poems that are meant to touch a heart and offer a look beyond the norm.

I label this work as a MY-THOLOGY, not an anthology. It is a series of writings generated from one author, offering expressions of a multitude. Watching Rod Serling's *Twilight Zone* television show may have influenced me more than I realize because I envision each unveiling as a corralled episode that is finally uncovered. My appreciation for the works of Octavia Butler and Stephen King seeped into the design of some characters and/or plots. Hopefully you will be able to grasp each moment.

Historical notes, paintings, and photographs follow in a dual Appendix at the end of the book. They are included to enrich each piece by offering proof of research.

All of the writings are about unique women whose stories are no longer swept up into nothingness. Each chapter introduces challenges, dreams, encounters, and temperaments to encourage discussions. *UnVeiled Voices* is a "shout-out" of unique viewpoints. Listen to the pages. They are not meant to be a quiet read.

There are invitations to different journeys. For instance, two young ladies living in different time periods are on the run. A survivor of war shares memories. Meet passengers on a sinking ship; the first woman in a historical job; and someone who lives in a refrigerator box. A queen saving her people, a caretaker of the elderly, and keepers of secrets speak of hidden challenges.

One story takes an imaginary look at a woman who is mentioned only twice in the Bible. Her story is not told there. Here she is given a story. On the other end of the spectrum are episodes that deal with second chances with choices but in different time periods. A look at an old way of dealing with the environment; a misspoken word; a conflict over a skirt; a trip to a new world; a first job crisis; and a strange kiss try to explain life's lessons. A widow creating a new life after her first trip to a junk yard and the respect for a pipe-smoking icon offers a rare look at aging. Competing and not competing in the Olympics; a meeting in a cemetery; and adventures in a couple of hospital rooms cause unexpected moments.

Reoccurring dreams and a snorkeling dilemma contrast reality and fantasy. A "Choose Your Own Ending" concept derived from an idea for children's books provides an example of the unexpected. Aggravation can be felt in Spam Calls, COVID provoked situations, unethical medical procedures, and a parent/child battle!

Finally, there is music. Each poem is meant to flow like a melody. Creating these poems was like conducting an orchestra that emits a concert of movements. Just like beautiful music encourages listening to new and different compositions, here lies, rhythmic pinnacles building to surprising finales designed for an audience. A melodic touch flows throughout childbirth;

the historic entrepreneurial spirit of laundry; the essence of a line dance; an introduction to an insect; the problem of classification; and what could have been Eve's conversation with Adam.

Get to know each character. They pay attention to the manners, social conditions and elements of different eras. Each piece is designed for exploration for a better understanding of how individuals might responded in different environments. Hopefully getting to know them will cause you to feel and come away with a new concept about life.

Sincerely,

Dr. Sandra Walton Wilson

> *Our goal is not so much the imparting of knowledge*
> *as the unveiling and developing of spiritual energy.*

– Maria Montessori

*The only way to find your voice
is to use it.*

– Jen Mueller

Table of Contents

Chapter 1: Historically Speaking

Chapter 2: Theatrically Speaking

Chapter 3: Personally Speaking

Chapter 4: Relatively Speaking

Chapter 5: Poetic Speaking

Appendix A: Notes of Interest

Appendix B: Paintings & Photographs

Chapter 1
Historically Speaking

– Maya Angelou

The Finale (1864)

A tiny woman sat alone on the edge of a cliff. The unborn baby that she had carried for eight months pushed a foot against her skin, seeking comfort. She placed her small hand tenderly on the moving lump and rubbed until the unborn rested. Although her legs and arms were covered with scratches and her feet were blistered and bloody, she ignored the pain and rested. She was lost in the woods after days of traveling.

The distant, angry barking of dogs competed with the beauty of the fall leaves for her attention. The creek below offered the music of water slapping against the sides of the rocks, proving that the water level had swollen after yesterday's rain. As she watched an orange, yellow, and black butterfly light on a honeysuckle flower, she appreciated nature's way of painting a memorable picture. She stored it away in her mind for a smiling time. The sweetness of the honeysuckle filled her mouth as she tasted its juices. She never had the time or freedom to revel in the serenity of such beauty. She wanted to share this moment with someone, but there was no one. She protected these miracles of nature by promising to remember.

Although the hostile sounds grew nearer, songs of her childhood began to fill her spirit. She remembered a song that she was told that could help runaway slaves. This small essence of a lady covered in dirt and rags began to sing the words in her mind.

"Steal away. Steal away. Steal away to Jesus. I ain't got long to stay here." She never liked that song. It didn't have a happy beat fit for dancing. Yet it was a catchy tune and she would use it to get to a safe place. She wanted to sing it out loud but she knew that too much time had passed and not enough ground had been covered. There seemed to be no safe place. She was tired.

Aunty told her that, as a slave, she was worth money. As a pregnant slave she was extremely valuable, but as a human being, she had no significance. Touching her stomach, she thought, "Dis here babe ain't gonna be no slabe!"

Hannah always knew that she was intelligent because her mother said she was. She was tired of pretending to be dumb, but it was her way of outsmarting the enslavers. Even as a child, folks said that she was too smart for her own britches and she had better be careful. It worked. Her mother told Hannah to act ignorant and it would save her life. By pretending to be slow-witted at times, she avoided attention. Especially when the new Master came.

Hannah was only six when her mother died. She never knew what had caused her mother to die and no one spoke of it. Aunty Sissy stepped in to mother the child. Aunty guarded her and the master protected her when there was a problem. However, the master's wife and some of the other slaves

File: Slaves cutting the sugar cane - Ten Views in the Island ...
Copyright: Public Domain, from the British Library's collections, 2013

treated her with contempt when he wasn't around. Then the master died and things changed. The mistress remarried and a new master was in charge.

Hannah had covertly learned to read and write from one of the master's children. Little Missy Anne loved teaching her all that she knew. It was their secret because if anyone found out, they both would be in trouble. Hannah loved sneaking into the room filled with books and hiding one in her dress to read later. Knowing how to read was both an asset and a threat.

Then there was Hannah's skin. It was a problem that she couldn't hide. There were times when she just wanted to scrub it off. She was not dark enough to be accepted by the slaves in the cabins and therefore was thought of as privileged. She was not light enough to be embraced by the white folk in the mansions and was treated as property. Some—blacks and whites—said that she thought she was better than the other slaves. They said that she was the child of the old master and a threat to the master's wife. She couldn't figure out how she could be a threat to anyone.

One day a wagon filled with shackled people drove up the long trail to the big house. It wasn't unusual. Traders came to the plantation now and then. This time she saw that a male and a female slave were dropped off. After money changed hands, the wagon pulled off. She was amazed at the size difference between the two slaves. The male was the biggest, blackest being that she had ever seen. The other slave was a little yellow girl. Mable, who took care of the young children, was called to take the little girl to the nursery cabin.

The male saw Hannah staring at him and glared at her. She turned quickly and headed up to the big house. She didn't want any attachment to him because she knew what was going to happen to him. She wanted to get away from it.

The overseer hitched the shackles to his horse, forced the new slave into the barn, and closed the door. At first there were sounds from a whip hitting flesh, and finally screams. Hannah knew what was going on. She had seen it before and had no desire to see it again. When Aunty was called, she knew what that meant, too. There was blood. Finally, the torture was over for the time being and Aunty's job was to use her medicine to help with the healing. Masters seemed to know how much punishment to issue so as not to destroy his property but to instill fear. Hannah was almost glad that she had too many chores to do to keep her mind off of that barn.

Everybody was talking about Big Black. That is what they called him in the slave quarters but he was given the name Solomon. Solomon was sent to the fields from morning until noon and then into the shed to learn carpentry. At night he was introduced to getting honey from the beehives. He slept in the barn on a palate in one of the stalls and stayed to himself when he wasn't working.

About a month later, Little Tissy overheard the master say," "I'm going to mate Hannah with Solomon. Those two could make a sturdy crop of pickinnies." Little Tissy ran to tell Aunty.

When Hannah heard the news, she felt like throwing up. She was not attracted to Solomon, but she knew that this new master had saved her for a "time such as this!" She heard that said at a church meeting and thought it fit her situation.

That is what the preacher read from the Bible. "A beautiful woman named Esther was married to a king and she said that she was there to save her people for a time such as this." Every time she heard that sermon, she wished she could save her people, but that was just daydreaming. She said, "I ain't gone be no field cow. Esther became a queen. I am a queen. Why we got to be pregnant all da time, makin' babies to work da land and feeding dere childrens?" She didn't know how to handle her predicament, but she knew it was coming. This was the first time that she thought about running.

One night after Hannah had worked all day and half the night, she was so glad to get in the bed. She went to sleep right away. Aunty quietly slipped out of their cabin. Hannah awoke to find two figures standing over her bed. It was dark except for a lantern in her face that was blinding her. There stood that big black slave, Solomon, and the master behind him. She knew what was going to happen but couldn't see any way out of it. Not a word was spoken.

She took off her clothes and laid back down as the master watched. Solomon couldn't contain his joy physically at seeing her curvy body and tossed his rags to the side. Surprisingly, he was gentle. It was like he knew that she had never received a man. It hurt like hell! She screamed after the fourth thrust and could feel the blood running out of her body. Solomon continued as gently as possible. It was evident that this was not new to him. His excitement produced a natural lotion that eased her pain...somewhat! Then he came to a thrust that felt like it reached her throat. She screamed and he moaned. Master left the cabin. No one spoke.

She felt the sweat of Solomon's body and she could swear that a drop had fallen from his eye onto her shoulder when she cried out. Could he have shed a tear for her? While he dressed, he spoke words that she had never heard before and then said, "I am sorry!" She guessed he had apologized in an African language. She could hear the sorrow in his voice.

As soon as he left, Aunty ran in with a basin, some rags, and some herbs that she had pounded into a powder. She washed the crying girl and rubbed her privates with herbs. As Hannah sobbed, Aunty said, "You are gonna have to get used dis here business. Dat's what it is, business. Dis here's what happens to the womens. You'll get used to it." Hannah didn't think so. She didn't want to get used to it.

"You's a pretty gal, healthy too. Old Massa didn't let nothing happen to ya, 'cause you kin and all. Dis one gone make the most of it. I's been wondering when dey was gone start."

Hannah cried while Aunty was attending her, but then she began to think about Solomon. There was something about that big man that made her want to know more about him.

She was too sore to walk up to the big house that morning. Aunty reported, "Hannah'll be better soon. She just needs to soak in the river and take some of her medicine and she'll be good as new." Aunty knew just what to say. She had a lot of experience with this kind of situation. She was respected for her health skills and called on for the slave quarters and the big house.

As Hannah was sitting in the water, she saw Solomon walk by. He didn't look her way. She knew that it was intentional, and she was glad because she didn't know what to say to him. At the end of the day, she was feeling better but she couldn't get this man off of her mind. There were boys on the farm who were attracted to her, but she always flirted just enough and let them know that she was not interested in getting into a mating situation with them. It was her intention not to have babies, ever!

Hannah began to pay attention at night. Just as Aunty had

said, it was going to happen again. About a week later, she pretended to be asleep and heard Aunty quietly leave the cabin. Hannah wanted to leave too but she was aware of the repercussions for that. So, she lay there pretending. Sure enough, the two men entered the cabin. She went through the procedure of undressing. This time she was aware of Solomon's body and she trembled. It was smooth on her skin. She dared not touch his back because she didn't want to feel the scarring that she knew had to be there. This time he put his arms around her for a moment and she calmed down.

The master yelled out, "Will you get to it? I ain't got all night." Solomon was ready and proceeded to use his fingers to get her lubricated. He gently began the process of entry and she lay there studying every movement. It was still tight and hurt a bit but not as much as the first time. Before, she felt like she was on fire, but not this time. As she listened to her body, she smelled a fragrance of flowers that came from his hands. He must have used some kind of salve to make the entry easier. He took his time and she began to enjoy what was happening. When he made that final thrust, she did too. She thought, "What was that?" She didn't know, but she liked it.

Then the master walked out the door, saying, "Good grief, this doesn't have to take forever. I've got business of my own to take care of."

This time, when Solomon began to rise, she pulled him back and they clutched each other. She gently rubbed his scarred back as they both lay silently on the narrow cot. It wasn't long before the closeness led to another time of discovery and, before they knew it, the cock crowed. Aunty must have slept somewhere else because she did not return to the cabin that night.

Hannah began to appreciate his gentleness and she looked for him on the plantation. She knew that Solomon had fallen in love with her and enjoyed his duties as a stud assigned to only her. During the day he had learned to be a carpenter, so she knew exactly where to find him when she wanted him. She knew that he went to the carpentry barn every day. This was her first time feeling something special for a man and he courted her openly. Master was fine with it and he no longer came to the cabin.

Then one Sunday after a church service, they "Jumped the Broom." They were doing just fine until it was whispered that the master needed money and he was going to sell some of his slaves. They were sure they would not be sold because of their value to the workings of the plantation. She was pregnant and looking forward to sharing this baby with the love of her life. Surely, Master would never sell either of them. However, Solomon caught the eye of a trader visiting on his way south. He must have brought a fortune. Solomon was chained and loaded into a wagon headed south. They both knew there was no need to fight. This was a lost battle.

Hannah thought her heart would break. She told Aunty, "How could Massa do dat? Here I am almost ready to birth a baby! It don't make no sense!? He know that we could have more babies!"

All of her pleading and crying was in vain. Aunty grabbed her and whispered, "No need to carry on. It ain't gone make no difference. Master must be in bad shape to sell Solomon. You don't wanna lose dis here babe. Carrying on won't gettcha nowhere."

Hannah hated the master already. This just made it worse. She hated living close to the mansion because her work was all day and some nights. She prayed to work down in the fields where some slaves could grow crops of their own on a small patch of land next to their shacks. They could even hunt for their own meat. She ate the scraps from the table in the big house and although they were the best, she found no joy in that. The slaves said the house folk ate "high on the hog" but the field workers were just fine with the lower parts. When she would go down to Sunday celebrations, they dined on dandelion wine, chitterlings, raccoon or possum stew, and cressy greens. Aunty said that cressy greens were always mixed with some other greens because they worked excellently for passing food.

Hannah had listened intently to the women talk about the different herbs that they gathered in the fields and their uses. Periodically, she gathered some of the herbs down by the water to use in flavoring the food she cooked. She watched Aunty as she made concoctions for healing and asked questions.

If there was any illness that the doctor couldn't fix, she had saved many folks. She was called when all hopes were gone. Aunty didn't like going up to the big house, because if things didn't work, her life was on the line. Since Hannah was trained as a cook at an early age by the head cook, Luttie, she knew how to create the best-tasting foods for miles around. Luttie was getting old, so Hannah took on the major cooking chores. Her reputation was known throughout the county. Too often, the master's friends or family would visit to partake of "Hannah's Delectables." That is how they described it. Honey was her secret ingredient in her desserts. It just added an extra rich taste. Every time she went to the hives, she and Ben would talk about Solomon. Ben always talked about Solomon.

"Yes Mame, Miz Hannah, I sho do miss Big Black. He was a good worker, good man and I liked him a lot!"

She would always leave old Ben with a hug and he always gave her some extra honey for herself. The workings of the plantation continued as usual.

However, Hannah realized that she filled a contradictory space and she hated it. She couldn't do anything about it. On one hand, she earned the respect of her people because she could read. She would secretly report information about the white folk's business and conversations. On the other hand, she was rewarded for her fine cooking, being obedient, and acting submissive. Her life was bewildering, complicated, and filled with misconceptions. By the age of twenty, pregnant and without her husband, she decided that she had endured enough. She did something about it! She ran!

So, there she was, standing proudly, like a phoenix rising from the ashes. She raised her hands to the sky and spoke with a soft, determined voice.

"I's bone tired, bone tired! Where be the freedom land? Where it be? I can't explain this feeling that I has here inside of me." She pounds on her chest. "I's real, ain't I? Miss Ruth Ann say I should be proud she pick me to work up in the big house. She say she only picked the bestest Negras to work up dere. If'n she left me out dere in dem fields, I don't see no difference! I still a slabe. What nerb she got telling me I's lucky. Hitting me every chance she get.

"Every night she lay down and it be with her man. Where mine be? De done sold him off, they does! We done jumped the broom and eberything. Oh, I hear 'em talking about how after this here babe dey's gonna to mate me up with 'nother buck. They say they bought him just for me. We be big money makers. I heard dat story befo! Well, I say sometin' now. Dis here ain't what I deserb. I da cook. I impotent. I had to do sometin'. I spit in da food. Then I grind up glass real fine like with some herbs. I put in some real tasty honey and I mix it in da food. Den da mistress, she got real sick with the stomach miseries. The doctor, he come to the kitchen questioning me 'bout what she was eatin'. I pretend like I love da people so much that I could never do 'em no harm. Dey's good peoples. I kept right on cooking my special food for dem. Folks would say, 'Dat Hannah, she be the bestest cook in the county.' I just smiles, kinda silly like. Den one day, Massa, he started feeling poo-ly. Blood started coming up out of his'n mouth. One day Little Ticey, she come running down to my shack. She say Sally tell her de comin' fo me and de crazy mad. So, I runs! Forgive me Lord if'n I did sin. I's sorry but I rather die and go to hell den stay here!

"Slabes keep talkin' about liberation. There's gonna be a big o' fight and we'uns gonna be free. Dey don't know what das talkin' bout. Got me out here looking for da freedom. Dese peoples says they ain't neber gonna let us be free. Dey fight 'til dey die. So, it's time now...my time. I say when! I hear dem dogs gettin' closer. I ain't running no mo! I take my freedom now!"

She thought about trying to go down the hill and using the water to cover her scent from the dogs again. She could wade through the stream until she found a resting place. She wondered if it was worth it because her energy was long gone and now her desire to find freedom in this hell seemed unreal.

A mild wind caused the trees to rustle on this bright fall day of October 1863. The trees were graced with the bright colors of fall. This was her favorite time of the year. The air was cool. It smelled of fresh rain. She thought, "This is a perfect time."

Suddenly, the moment was disturbed. She could almost feel the vibration of heavy feet as they mashed the beauty of the autumn leaves. A stench invaded the freshness of the air and she knew that a change was too close. As two snarling, unleashed dogs advanced toward the cliff, Hannah welcomed being blinded by the sparkling sun, still able to see bits of worn brown boots and dirty hands reaching out to grab her wrists. At that moment, Hannah stepped backward, looked down lovingly at the busy water below, and calmly but softly declared, "Now! I takes it now." Her words echoed serenely against the rocks as she stepped from the cliff and was cradled in the safety of the water. "Now! Now! Now!"

***

Afternote: President Abraham Lincoln issued the Emancipation Proclamation on January 1, 1863, as the nation approached its third year of the Civil War. The proclamation declared "that all persons held as slaves within the rebellious states are and henceforth shall be free." Hannah was legally free before she jumped.

The Trip (1912)

(Based on the life of the Laroche family)

(Juliette and Joseph Laroche and their two daughters Simonne and Louise. Courtesy W. Mae Kent, Public domain image)

I will always remember the day that Pere came home with tickets for what was to be our first big family trip. He was so happy because not only was it to be a new adventure across the big water, but he would be moving back to his home, Haiti. He shouted that bringing his family with him made it even more wonderful.

He ran into the house that day calling our names. He kissed Mere, grabbed my sister Simone in a bear hug, and picked me up, swinging me around. We were excited. It was to be a cruise. I had never been on an ocean cruise. We had been on a boat, but this was going to be different.

Pere had told us all about his parents and the tropical island that was their home. It sounded so different from France. I envisioned it as beautiful. Pere said that it was always warm, the fruit was so fresh and sweet, and the people were kind. I questioned him about why he had left such a wonderful place.

Pere's parents had sent him to France to study engineering. They thought that an education abroad was best for him. Once he met Mere, he decided to stay in France. They married and moved in with her parents and had us. Racial discrimination prevented Pere from obtaining a fair-paying job in France. Although he was an engineer, he struggled to find work, so they lived with Mere's family. Her parents were not happy about the marriage at first, but later accepted it. There was no doubt that they loved my sister and me and I could tell that they loved Pere, too. I know this because I heard my parents talking quietly about it one night. I was the child that listened to everything. Sometimes I spoke before thinking, though, and had to be corrected. However, I was smart enough to never speak about this topic.

I was only a year older than my sister. I was born in 1909 without any problem. She was born prematurely and needed special care. It was expensive and a challenge to pay the bills. When they found that Mere was going to have another baby, they decided to move to Haiti for the sake of the family. They did not want to go through the problems that they experienced at the hospital. That was one of the reasons their plans changed from visiting Haiti to living there.

Pere thought he could get a good job back in Haiti and buy a beautiful home. As a gift for moving back home, Pere's Mere purchased first-class passage tickets for us on the steamship, the *LaFrance*. Mere was excited and a bit sad. She was leaving her home but promised to return periodically to visit. Pere said that he would purchase tickets for my grandparents to visit with us once we were settled. He also said that their trip would be memorable.

Mere was pleased with the first-class tickets, although she felt that it wasn't necessary. Pere said, "If you can't go first class, then no need to go at all." When Pere found out that the ship had a rule that children had to dine separately from their families, he decided to make a change.

"We are a family," he said. "We always dine together. I will not allow my children to be away from us, especially on such a long trip." The last time he had been on a ship was on his travels to France to study. He said that traveling could be dangerous, but people were doing it every day.

He traded our first-class tickets for second-class tickets on a newer ship that he had read about. He called it a historic experience. The ship had been advertised as the greatest ship ever built. It would leave from a dock in England. Traveling to England was not a problem for us. We had gone to London for a vacation once. He was excited because he had read about this brand-new ship that was praised as the best voyage ever. "Unsinkable" was what the newspapers spouted. Mere didn't care what class the tickets were. She was excited to visit New York on the way to a brighter future.

Mere was about a month pregnant with my brother and she wanted to take the trip while she could still get around easily. This was the perfect time. They had not been satisfied with the care she had received at the hospital in France when she gave birth before. She did not want what happened in the hospital to happen again.

Since Mere was French, she was treated fine until they found out that her husband was Haitian. She didn't quite know how to handle it. It must have been awful. I remember seeing her trying to hide her tears about the way Pere was treated at his job also. Pere said, "I am a good engineer but it is difficult for a black man to make a living here. I can provide a better life for us in Haiti. My uncle is the president of the country and my family is well established. They have already found me a job as a math teacher. That will get us started."

My parents were looking forward to the move. However, I knew from Mere's actions that she was going to miss her parents. She would hug and kiss them more than ever before. We would be near the relatives I had only heard of. I looked forward to being in a big family, but I never thought about the loss that Mere might experience leaving her home.

At night, I would dream about living in a paradise. Who knows, maybe one day Pere might be the President of Haiti. What would I be then? I might be a princess! I kept that to myself.

I was even more excited when I heard that we were going to New York first. My grandparents talk about going to the United States. They had been saving for a trip there for years. I hoped that they would come to visit us in our large home in Haiti.

Mere wrote a letter to Pere's cousins in New York so that they could meet us at the dock. That would be the first stop on our trip. She read it to me just to make sure she had said everything that she wanted to say. I guess she just needed someone to listen. I was too little to be of any help with her writing.

When she received a letter back, she said, "Cousin Eloise said that the New York newspapers are reporting that there will be a huge crowd waiting to see the new ship when we arrive." Evidently, the new ship was getting a lot of attention around the world. Eloise said that they will wave a Haitian flag so that we can see them on the dock. I can't believe that we are going to stay a week in New York and sightsee. This was beyond my imagination. We were going to see the United States and then on to Haiti. What could be better?

I was finally going to meet my Haitian grandparents.

However, I was going to miss my French grandparents. They were special to me. That took a little excitement away from my longing to go. I will miss all of their hugs and kisses. I know that sounds selfish because I couldn't imagine what they were feeling. Mere's brother had just married and I was going to miss him too. Pere said once we were established, he would make sure that we would come back to visit.

My Haitian grandparents always sent beautiful dresses, jewelry, and money. I thought of them as being the nicest people in the world. This was going to be the best trip ever, but I hoped my grandparents would visit and maybe someday I would come back to see them in France.

The day before the trip, Pere said to Mere, "I just want to provide the best life possible for you and the children."

Mere kissed Pere on the cheek and said, "You're right. I am fine with going. You don't have to prove anything to me. We can always come back for a visit now and then."

With bags packed, everyone dressed, and tickets in hand, we headed for the docks for the first leg of the trip, —England. Mere said, "I am so happy that our important things are already in Haiti. At least I don't have to worry about that."

After arriving in England, we headed to the designated dock to board the ship to America. It was bigger than anything I had ever imagined. People were busily trying to board. I heard strange languages but the registration was done in English. Smiling, Mere quietly pointed out some people she said were from China. She had seen Chinese people in books and was delighted to see them in person. This was a fascinating place.

Father was amazed at the size of the ship. Although he had been on a large ship when he came from Haiti to France, he said, "This is the largest ship I have ever seen." Children were running around, dogs were barking, the air smelled like the fish market, and everyone was talking. It was a little scary but exciting.

Mere whispered in my ear, "Once on board, we will relax, enjoy delicious food, the music, the people, the theater, and the beautiful suite." When we reached Check-In, I noticed uncomfortable glances from some. I didn't like it.

Pere spoke English, so he took care of getting us checked in. Once the tickets were recognized, my parents walked with dignity onto the deck, guided by a baggage carrier. It was interesting to see his frown turn into a smile once he received his tip. The suite was beautiful. My sister and I screamed with delight in our stacked beds and danced around our parents' bed. Then we enjoyed some fruit, nuts, honey, and drinks in our sitting area.

Glancing around the suite, Pere looked at Mere and said proudly, "Only the best for my girls. Enjoy this. It wasn't easy getting these tickets on the very first trip of the *Titanic*."

Mere said, "Thank you, *Ma chere! Joyeux anniversaire! Sante!*" They toasted with the fanciest glasses I had ever seen. As they sipped their wine, Simone and I touched our teacups. "*Sante!*"

The Queen (1626)

(Based on the life of Queen Nzinga of Angola)

The queen finished her prayers just before daylight ended. Her moonlit visits to the troops were meant to encourage them. She wanted to let the warriors know that their leader cared about them and was dedicated to the fight. This visible commitment endeared her to her men. Many of them had military training and were ready to protect themselves from becoming abducted and taken away on the big boats. Farmers and hunters also joined the troops. They seemed to learn quickly and worked just as hard as the trained warriors.

It was also important on these walks to visit the injured. She made sure to enter their shelters to spend a meaningful moment with as many of the injured as possible. Sometimes she wanted to cry for them, but she knew that an endearing and strong presence was more meaningful. Crying might show a sign of weakness, so she held their hands, hugged some, and made eye contact that showed pride and concern. One dying soldier said on his last breath, "We are one people. I am proud. We must keep up..." He did not get out the last word.

The queen was trained to handle stressful situations. At birth, the wise woman of the tribe loudly pronounced that Sousa was designated for greatness. Her every move was watched. She was tutored and learned quickly. Her aptitude for defusing crises proved to be an advantage even in childhood. The tribal leaders recognized her strengths and intelligence and made sure that she was mentally and physically ready to lead and to handle any challenges to her position.

As queen, she felt it was her duty to be strong and smart and to lead with dignity and intelligence. Her reputation as a strategist and warrior was renowned and proved necessary in creating a bond among the tribes.

Often her beauty was a point of discussion among the villagers. Her unique physique exuded strength. An aura of power surrounded her. Due to long legs, the warmth of a smile, and lashes as impressive as a camel's, her appearance became legendary. She was a winning combination of strength, wisdom, and beauty.

In 1624, the queen became the ruler of her country. The kingdom was under attack from the Portuguese and neighboring African aggressors. The queen realized that, to remain viable, the country had to figure out a way to not be a supply zone in the slave trade. To achieve this, she attempted to ally her country with Portugal. Her plan was to acquire partners in the fight against tribal enemies and end Portuguese slave raiding.

Her attributes proved important when she became an ambassador to the Portuguese Empire, representing numerous African tribes. She was amazed by the size of the ship on which she traveled and how far it was to their port. She took strong-bodied men with her to present an aura of power. She donned colorful garments and sandals that laced up her legs. With rings encircling her neck, lower arms, and ankles, she presented as one of wealth. However, she wasn't sure if that would be an incentive or bring on a feeling of respect. She was taking a big chance coming to the country. She said to her officers, "Know that this is a dangerous mission. This enemy is unpredictable. They may take us, and if so, we will fight. The weapons are enough to put up a battle, but we cannot win. I will work to represent something that they want more than just us and the dancing girls. My gift of beautiful clothes and beads will not let them know how rich our land is...although they probably already know that."

The chief of the Bantu spoke. "My Queen, should we speak in their language or our own?"

"Speak to them in their language. That will show them that we are intelligent people. When we speak to each other, we will speak in our language. In that way they will not know what we are saying. If they have some of our people around helping, that is different. Speak in their language. They may be spies. Do not feel angry with them because I am sure they are not here because they want to be."

The queen presented stately at the court. Tall, strong, and stunning, she was an attraction. People crowded the docks upon their arrival. She ordered four guards to go out first in full regalia. The dancers followed with the drummers. Next came the gifts, a huge rug, exquisitely woven, boxes of cloth, and a carved wooden box holding clay beads. The queen was next, guarded by two soldiers in front and two in the back. She was carried while reclining on a beautifully carved, blue and white wooden plank. Her female servants walked behind the queen.

When she entered the courts, she was amazed by thick cloth hanging from above, large openings in the walls, and the gold carvings on the huge chairs that sat in a room that was a size beyond her imagination. However, the chill in her sleeping area was different from the heat of her land and she had to wrap up to be warm.

While in Portugal, she was treated with respect and took advantage of the opportunities to evaluate them. She was dutifully taken care of in the palace and seemed to be respected as royalty.

She astutely decided to be baptized into their foreign religion to encourage alliances. This was by no means a sign of surrender or approval. It was a strategy to save her people from a destiny of servitude. It only stopped their assaults for about one year. Her assessments proved valuable in preparation to ward off their next strikes to gain control of land and acquire slaves. In spite of the promises that were made, she knew the fight to remain free was not over.

The queen was respected and loved by her people. It was whispered that the queen "walked where leopards tread and laughed with the hyenas." The leopard, the strongest of the big cats, is astoundingly agile, adaptable, and difficult to trace. Hyenas are skilled, intelligent, and aggressive hunters. Queen Sousa, like both animals, had no problem using her ability to recognize friends from foe and to negotiate social hierarchy. Her presence represented a rare blending of power, toughness, and battle agility, interspersed with undeniable charm. In the minds of the warriors, this was an unusual combination, especially for a woman.

At thirty-seven years of age, the queen was as tall as most of her men and could be seen towering over some of them on her important strolls about the military grounds. With wide hips swaying, her strong shoulders erect, a body hugged by colorful garments, and "sandaled" feet intentionally directed, she covered a massive territory of tentative military shelters, calling many of the men by name. That show of respect mushroomed among the armies. The troops were like a large family unit although they belonged to different tribes. With determination and courage, they learned each other's languages. After all, they were fighting to stop the Portuguese from taking their people. Being able to understand each other was important. Interpreters were on hand to help those struggling with learning languages.

Armies joining together was rare. It was uncommon for many armies to be directed by one chieftain, much less a female. Leading such an army could present a challenge for any leader, but she was able to handle it!

The fish-belly-colored men that came from the water were unrelenting foes. However, they underestimated the queen. They had never battled against such a challenging mind. Although surprised by her leadership, respect developed when negotiating. She had made a pact with her God that as long as she lived, she would never allow enemy rule over her people. Although there were rewards for her capture—dead or alive—it was not to be.

Her control seemed infinite. To bolster martial power, she offered sanctuary to runaway tribesmen who had been captured, as well as Portuguese-trained African soldiers. It was known throughout the land that she moved about reaping converts along her way. It worked! News of the enemy's locations reached her early enough for her to outthink them. Therefore, her armies swelled as she moved about the land. Her undying determination frustrated the enemy. They could not find her. She seemed to disappear.

One tactic was to wait until the intruders felt secure and then swoop down with one army, circle with another, and have one out of sight as a backup. These tactics changed so that it was difficult to figure out her plans. Since her goal was to stop slave marketing, the challenge meant killing or being killed. Her shrewd, calculated decisions triggered admiration from both her followers and her enemies.

The meeting before this night's walk was a gathering with the tribal leaders. She made sure to speak seriously, caringly, and sometimes with a bit of humor. This was where her tutoring was important. Her command of the tribal languages allowed her to communicate and was one admired.

The queen opened the meeting with, "The enemy is like a colony of annoying driver ants. Always popping up in different places. Their bites are painful and it is difficult to remove an attack once they've latched on. It is up to us to capture them like we do the ants and use some of them to close the wounds they inflict. When they return empty-handed, their own leaders will be angry."

The tribal leaders listened intently, bobbing their heads in agreement. "We have to stay awake like the night creatures and be like the fly," she continued. "Those eyes see everything and then they move quickly. Jaga Chef, I need you to bring me some of your Ogiek Honey. It gives me strength."

The Jaga leader spoke up. "Yes, my Queen. It will be here. May I speak?"

She swirled her finger in a movement showing approval and inviting him close.

"The invaders think that you are a mystical being. That is a good thing. I want them to use all of their power and weapons fighting what they think is a spirit. When they lose, they will better understand our power."

The queen approved with a nod. He asked for permission to leave for the honey and backed out of the gathering.

She envisioned herself as the savior of her people and she never took that status for granted. At every chance, she would give praise.

The leader of the Bankongos stepped forward and declared, "They are confused that a woman could outsmart them, outfight them, and travel faster than they can." All of the men shouted joyfully! They also thought there was something special about this woman and they thought it was of God. It was obvious that each leader was proud and ready to follow her. She knew that her reputation with her men was positive. With the enemies it was questionable. She liked it that way.

The leader of the Mbundu tribe asked to speak. "We are the uncaptured. They can't figure us out. They once thought that the leader was really a man dressed like a woman until they met you. They are surprised that a woman could keep them at bay. It is said in their camps that you are ageless and at night they have seen you rise to the sky to sleep with the moon and then return again with the sun to fight another day."

Laughter rocked her body when she heard these words. She thought that it was good that their people had these beliefs. It could be a means of protection. Imagination might be useful for survival. She and her men understood that such pronouncements could be valuable.

That night as she took her expected walk among the warriors, an emissary approached the camp. He was stopped by guards and taken to a secret location until she was able to return to her private quarters for an audience with him.

The flap of her domain flew open and the guards entered. "Oh Queen, we have a messenger from the slave catchers." They paused for a moment.

She asked, "Is he alone? What is he wearing?"

The answer was, "He is alone and he is wearing their clothing?"

She asked, "Is his clothing well kept?

"Yes."

The queen allowed the entrance. The messenger moved in meekly, bowing. When he was halfway to the royal chair, she spoke sternly. "Stop! Why are you here?"

Looking at the ground, he answered respectfully, "Oh, Queen Sousa, the Portuguese sent me here. They want to request an audience. They want to sit down with you to talk."

She remembered how they had not provided a seat for

her in the Portuguese Court. Without hesitation she ordered one of her men to bend over so she could sit on his back. She refused to be demeaned among these men trying to prove their power over her by refusing to honor her with something as menial as a seat. She showed them her power by snapping her fingers and it was done.

Queen Njinga meeting with Portuguese Governor Joao Corria de Sousa, 1622 (Public domain image). Snetgen J. (2009, June 16) Queen Nzinga (1583-1663) BlackPast.org. https//wwwblackpast.org/global-african-history/queen=Nzinga 1583-1663/

He waited for her hand gesture to continue. Looking up slightly, he said, "They say to tell you that they have some things to talk with you about that will be of interest to you."

Her feelings about this traitor grew strong. This pretense of humility was distasteful. She wasn't sure if he did not look her in the eye out of fear or respect. In any other circumstance she would have him punished because he was helping to enslave his own people. More than likely, he was a tracker, too. Fortunately, for him, she would make him a puppet.

The queen knew that this was supposed to sound like a peace agreement or a compromise. She wasn't confident about this message because she had been down that path before and trusted no longer. There could be no compromise, now. She accepted the truth, finally. This was war.

After a dramatic pause, she finally spoke, "Go back and tell them that the queen agrees. It is time for us to have a serious talk. I will come there for tomorrow's early meal." She did not ask for their location on purpose. She knew that once they got the message, they would believe that she was aware of their whereabouts. She continued, "My men will escort you safely out of this camp. Go!"

Walking and bowing backward, he left with two guards at his side. This was necessary because, dressed as he was, her men would tear him apart.

The queen was calmly disturbed. The enemy knew the location of her encampment or they would know when the messenger returned to them. She had to regroup. Once her men had made sure he was gone and that they were safe, she ordered the officers to gather the men and pack up to move out right away. Emergency plans were in place.

The queen refused to be a victim of any more deceptions. She prayed that night while traveling, "God of the Universe, as long as I live I will lead the fight to maintain freedom, even if I have to do it alone. Please be my guide and give me strength."

Her God must have heard, because she fought for independence for thirty-seven years and became a historical figure. She is remembered for her intelligence, her political and diplomatic wisdom, and her brilliant military tactics.

The queen died peacefully in 1663 at the age of eighty-one. As long as she lived, freedom reigned for her people. Some say that they saw her rise to the sky one night to sleep with the moon, then the next day she was seen walking toward the sun. A tiger and a hyena followed her along the path.

One day, just before the sun goes down, if you look into the clouds carefully, you just might see the queen taking her walk.

A Survivor (1945)

Aki Ito, sat alone by a pond. A pink water lily nestled in her lap. This was her remembering place on peaceful days. She cherished the times spent there. It had been a safe place. With eyes closed, she remembered family gatherings filled with laughter and food.

Too often she recalled a blasting sound that caused her body to vibrate. It left her deaf in one ear and pain all over. She was told that the sound came from a huge mushroom cloud that took away her parents and a troublesome little brother. She survived deep in a hidden cave, a secret place where she and her friends had played as children.

When Japan went to war with America, the Sachiko family rushed to secretly prepare the cave for them to live in. It seemed strange but exciting. Her father said that something bad was going to happen and he wanted to be prepared. Aki was only eighteen years old and couldn't see how the family could live in a cave. It was fun to play in it but living there was quite a different story.

They stockpiled food, water and other necessities. At the back of the cave was a stream where she and her brother studied the animals that lived there. With flashlights they found fish, lizards and insects that were clear or white. To their surprise some of the animals had no eyes. Her brother explained that they didn't need eyes because they lived in the dark. It was a fascinating place. They looked forward to exploring all parts of the cave.

Although it was a wonderful place to play, it was always cold. Mother suggested that they include blankets that Aki's grandmother had made.

On the day they were moving furniture into the cave, her father, mother and brother headed back to pick up a few more things.

Aki Ito lingered to make sure that she had everything she needed. Finally, she decided to go home to get the cage with her canary. She had put that off for last because she did not want her pet to be cold in the cave. Since her father had dug a fire pit for heat and stacked wood and stones she knew that the cave would be warm.

As she approached the opening of the cave there was a noise. It was louder than any sound she had ever heard. When she looked toward the opening, she noticed that the sky had turned white. She began to move to the back of the cave. Suddenly she was knocked off her feet. Aki had no idea what had happened but immediately thought about her family and then her world became dark.

Aki awoke in a tent filled with people rushing about trying to help those who were lying on cots. She could faintly hear people talking about a mushroom cloud. It was then she realized that she was having trouble hearing. When she strained, she overheard a nurse saying frantically, "Why did they drop a bomb on us? It destroyed everything."

Aki whispered to herself, "Yes, why would anyone do such a horrible thing? My father was right. He was worried."

As a nurse injected Aki with something, the nurse replied, "Because we attacked them. This was how they paid us back. War is a terrible thing." With tears streaming down her face, Aki Ito went back to sleep.

Now twenty years had passed since that terrible day. Aki remembered as if it had just happened. Aki felt that she would never understand man's inhumanity to man as she sat by the beautiful pond, caressing a delicate flower. She smiled as she lifted it and inhaled the sweet scent. It was difficult to hold it steady with only four fingers.

Her family had been victims of what she read was Japan's decision for a preventative war with the United States. She wasn't sure what that meant. She decided that war was not the way to peace. She wondered if there was ever a right or wrong side of war.

If it weren't for her father, she might have physically suffered more or been among the missing like the rest of her family. Aki was told that there was an area in the back of her cave where the bomb did not reach. Luckily, she had been blown by the force of the explosion into that space and it had saved her life. No one seemed to know who or how she was found.

Today she enjoyed the waterlilies. They helped her to remember how lovely life had been around the pond once upon a time. The women in her family always claimed ownership of the pond. Friends gathered there to sit, talk, dance, sing, and laugh. They ate her mother's delicious honey sake cakes at the pond. Everything was discussed by the pond. Laughter abounded there.

Even marriage was discussed for Aki and a chosen one at the pond. Her life was filled with joy. A date was set. Arrangements were made. Invitations were sent and she had the dresses for the day. It was an exciting time.

However, now she sat alone assuring herself that her selected mate was fine. She had waited for him to come back. Maybe he was waiting somewhere for her too. She knew they were destined to be together.

Like a miracle, the pond was still there, at least she thought it was the same pond. It must have taken lots of work to bring it back to its full beauty. Orange blossoms still circled the water and the smell was divine.

As the wind blew through the remains of the white silky wisps of hair that nestled upon her scarred scalp, she closed her eyes and imagined the feel of warmth from her husband to be stroking what used to be her long dark tresses.

Aki lifted the flower to her face again to feel how delicate it was. The crevices in her hands were deep and the skin was tough but her cheek was still soft. To her skin felt the same as when she was young. Her mind protected her from reality. Her mind fluctuated between the present and the past.

Each day she called out to her mother, "HaHa, HaHa!" There was never a reply at least one that others heard. She often seemed to be having conversations but no one else was there. She could feel her mother holding her hands and hear her father's voice.

"Fly away little canary, fly away." That is what he called her, his little canary. He said that he loved her voice. It reminded him of listening to the beautiful singing of a canary.

A bell rang to announce tea time and a nurse appeared. Aki pressed the flower between her trembling hands, put it where her lips had once been and kissed it for the last time.

The nurse smiled at Aki and made sure she was secured in her wheelchair. Although Aki wanted to walk inside, she realized, once again, that her legs were no longer there. She had accepted her plight many years ago. As the chair was pushed from the pond she tossed the flower lovingly into the water. A light wind helped it to drifted away. Aki Ito watched it leave and whispered, "Goodbye, Little Flower!"

Suddenly, as they left the pond, a canary flew above them singing sweetly. Aki had read that only male canaries sing. She thought, "Could that be my father, looking for his little canary?"

She murmured, "Hello Father. I am just saying goodbye to our pond. Your little canary is on the way. I am coming to see you all again very soon!"

Not Quite a Bible Story (100 BC)

The name of Asenath is one of more than 100 women mentioned in the Bible (Genesis 41- 50). Women speak only 1.1 percent of the time. The name is Egyptian and means "She who belongs to her father" and "gift of the sun god." The only details about her are related to the men in her life.

<u>Genesis 41:45</u> - Pharaoh gave Joseph the name Zaphnath-Paaneah. He gave him Asenath, daughter of Potiphera, priest of On, to be his wife.

<u>Genesis 46:20</u> - And to Joseph in the land of Egypt were born Manasseh and Ephraim, whom Asenath, the daughter of Potipherah, priest of On, bore to him.

There are questions about who this woman was and why she was mentioned in the Bible. Why was she chosen to marry such an important man? What was her background? What was her life like?

She needs a story. So here is a possibility. The spelling of her name has been changed to create her as a new character. If she could speak, she might share this story.

***

The Marketplace

I loved going to the marketplace in the city of On. It bustled with activity. Delicious smells of cooked food blended with the odors of sheep and goats for sale. People came from all over to purchase items like goat's milk, olives, honey, and pomegranates. All kinds of cloth could be found there. Some folks said that the best wines in the land were sold in this market. To me, the pomegranate juice was even more delicious and could cure pain. At least that is what I was told.

Men in the practice of medicine race to the flax tents and toward anyone selling honey. It was known that flax and honey were medicines that would never spoil. The merchants bartered loudly and constantly. Musicians punctuated the streets. Beggars nestled right outside of the market square. The merchants shooed them away from their stalls. They screamed, "Get away! You are bad for business. Find your own place." Soldiers usually paraded about to make sure that there was no trouble. The market was a busy place. I loved it.

My sisters and I would take turns going to the market with mother when we were little. My younger brother was never assigned that chore. I asked him why he didn't want to go. He said, "That's women's work. I am a man. The servants could do it." He was not a man. I laughed at his prideful display of masculinity. My sisters were not really interested in the task either. So, I didn't mind taking their turns. I usually brought them something special back. Since they were younger, they wanted to stay close to home and play with their friends.

I looked forward to searching for items from foreign lands. It was exciting to find jewelry and clothes that looked different from anything made in our country. Although I gathered the food from my mother's requests, my eyes were everywhere. Captives were brought into the city for sale. It was normal to see them on the auction block. Most of the time I didn't pay attention to them. I was so busy looking for new and different items. The loud bidding usually drew buyers from everywhere. The noise was annoying and the selling did not interest me. Then one day that changed.

The Boy

On that day, I watched as slaves were pulled by ropes through the city and forced into a pen in the middle of the market square. They were tired and dusty. They smelled awful as they passed by me, followed by insects. It was the smell that caught my attention. Their lips looked dry and wrinkled. As I walked away, something caught my eye. One slave was wearing pieces of a ragged outer garment. I could faintly see that it had been dyed different colors, but only a bit that clung to his neck and shoulders. I wondered what had happened to the rest of it. It must have been a beautiful, expensive garment at one time. I had never seen anything like that garment and wondered where he was from.

Our clothes were usually only one color. I remember thinking that I would love to have something like that. Even at twelve, I had a keen eye for quality. I thought, "If I can get close to him, maybe I could ask him where he was from."

When I looked up from the garment, I lingered on the face of the slave. I had never done that before. It was a young male, maybe a little older than I. The sadness on his handsome face touched my heart for a moment and I wanted to help him. However, there was nothing I could do. His hands and feet were cobbled so tight that I could see swellings and bits of blood protruding from his wrists. I felt his fear. The boy must have seen me watching. He glanced in my direction. He looked away quickly after a whip slashed his way.

I went to the well near my father's friend's carpentry shop. Sitting on the bench was a dipper in a barrel of water. Every market day I would get a drink from it to cool off. I went over for my usual drink and made sure no one was watching me. Then I dipped into it for water and headed toward the slaves. My intention was to offer the slave a nice cool drink of water.

Just before I approached the slave line, the carpenter grabbed my arm and ushered me back to the well. I faintly remember him saying, "Your father would not be happy with you today. You can't go over there. Those people are dangerous." I wasn't sure who he meant...the slaves or the people selling them. The slaves were shackled. There wasn't too much they could do. At that moment, I was frightened of the carpenter. It must have shown on my face. However, I knew he was right. My father would not be pleased.

"Get busy and finish your shopping and be careful! Go find your mother!"

Feeling ashamed, I walked away to finish my errands. While I was wondering about my predicament, my mother appeared, carrying a basket of food. She looked in my basket and saw nothing.

"I can't believe that you have nothing. Asinath, go over there and pick out the best figs and some olives for dinner." My mother took pride in selecting the finest. She didn't trust our servants to be as particular. She went off looking for a certain kind of honey to make the honey cakes that we all loved. Then I saw the carpenter calling out to her. I knew that I was in trouble.

The Auction

I was not concentrating on food. Curiosity had gotten the best of me. For the first time, I watched what was happening around the slave block. I wondered how I would feel if I was on that block. It must be awful.

I wandered to the olive cart. It was close enough to hear what was going on with the auction. One of the handlers whispered to another man, "Put HIM in the back." He pointed to the boy in the colorful cloth. "I am saving that boy for last."

The other man nodded in agreement. "Yes, we can get good money for that one. I'll wipe his face and shake out his rags, so they can see that he is handsome and strong! That rag around his neck will let them know that he must come from a wealthy family. That is why I let him keep it. We'll get a good buy on that one. The rich people are looking for class in their slaves! Glad his brothers wanted to get rid of him."

I couldn't spend all day watching, so I picked out the best olives and went on a search for the figs. I didn't want my mother to know I was paying attention to the slave sale. That would add to what the carpenter told her. She would question me and I didn't have any explanation. I thought about suggesting that she buy that slave, but we already had four servants. That was all we could afford. Plus, my father had servants at the temple. So, there was no need. However, there was something about the boy that was special.

The auction went on while we were shopping. Then I heard, "Go get that boy!" The other man pulled the ropes tied to the boy's wrists with such force it made me feel sick. The boy's fear was obvious through his washed face. Although missing some of the dirt now, he was picking up dust as he stumbled to the block. He finally stepped onto the block.

As the men had predicted, a number of interested bidders, who had been at the back of the crowd, stepped forward. As soon as the auctioneer opened his mouth, the bidders were energized. It was difficult to understand what they were saying because of their competitive shouting.

Unexpectedly, soldiers pushed through the crowd to form a wide space. People in the way were pushed aside. Others moved on their own. A soldier announced loudly, "Make way for Potiphar, the General of Pharaoh's Guard."

Quiet hovered. All eyes were centered on the scene, even my mother's.

Although I had never seen Potiphar before, I recognized him by his dignity and style. A giant of a man walked through the aisle toward the block. Potiphar stepped forward, raised his right hand, and talking ceased. The two slave traders stepped back, quivering. Potiphar's military garb was made of thick material that glistened. The brightness of the sun did not deter the dark purpose of his weapons that hung from a strap around his waist. Even his shadow dominated the scene.

"I am here to purchase that slave." He nodded to one of his men to step forth. He looked slowly around at the crowd as if daring anyone to move. A muscular man in battle attire stepped forward to inspect the slave. He motioned to another soldier to march forward.

My mother was now at my side, watching. We were far enough away to speak and not be heard by the soldiers. I leaned over and whispered, "Mother, do you know him?"

"Your father does," she responded. "He is powerful but is known to be a fair man. You see how everyone moved out of his way!"

With dignity and strength, the soldier presented what he said was a bag of coins to one of the slave holders. He gently took the bag and respectfully handed over the boy. One of the guardsmen cut the dirty ropes that tethered the boy, replaced the wrist shackles with a leather strap, and marched off with their purchase trying to keep up. Potiphar led his men away. Dust from their march clouded the ground as they paraded away from the market. The crowd began to move about as potential slave buyers began to leave.

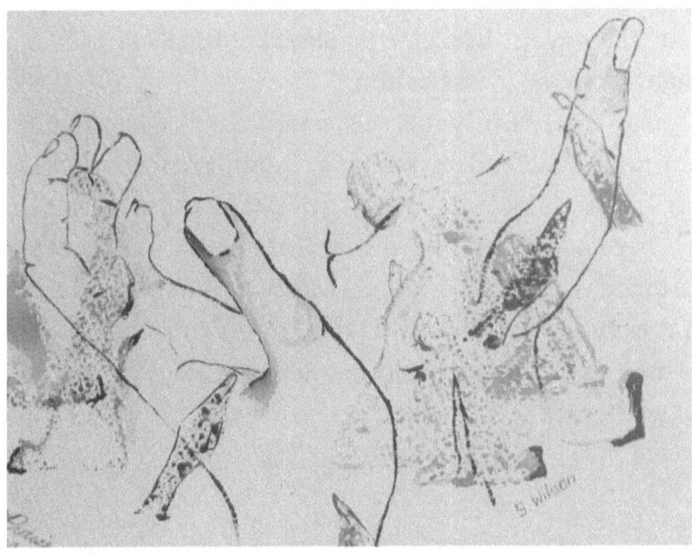

My mother looked intrigued. She touched my arm and nodded for me to follow her as she headed home. I did not have enough time to shop for myself and my sisters, but I didn't care. I guess my expression showed my confusion. We always made sure to go to the temple to pray before heading home, but not today.

As we walked, my mother looked at me with her serious face and said, "So, my dear, what did you think of that?"

I started to say, "What?" However, I answered honestly, "I am not sure, Mother. I never paid attention to these things before." That was the truth. I had trouble lying, especially to my mother. She was respected in the family and the community for her good counsel and I knew to listen to her.

"As you get older," she said, "you will begin to observe more. Some things will be good and some not so good. It is not your responsibility to get involved but to learn."

We headed home with the olives and figs in my basket and my mother's purchases of ground meal, a fish, and beer. I thought that talking about dinner and a necklace that I was saving for would take her mind off my reactions to the activities of the day. It didn't work. She asked me again about my thoughts. I knew it was coming.

I answered, "Everyone was watching, not just me." I felt that I had to defend myself and I didn't know why. I tried changing the subject to some fabric that I thought was lovely and a piece of jewelry that she had admired. It seemed to work but I knew that this discussion was not over. She didn't mention the water incident. I was quietly praying that she would not share the information that she had gotten from the carpenter with Father. I wasn't ready for this Daughter Talk, at least not yet.

Future Planning

It seemed like two years flew by, but I would remember that experience. The day after my fourteenth birthday, my parents invited me to discuss my future. I had dreaded this moment and was able to put it off for quite some time. As the oldest daughter in the family, I had to be the first to marry. My time had come.

My mother began with, "All women must have a man to take care of them. You know that!"

My father chimed in with, "I am not going to live forever. Then what will you do? Your sisters and brother will have a family of their own. The plans for your sisters are almost settled. Although your future as a priestess would give you status, you still need a husband to care for you and you need sons too. All you do is study. That is a good thing, but you have to take your head out of the book sometimes and think of your future!"

I groaned in my mind, never out loud. It took all of my strength to not speak. There was no need. A question had not been asked.

Mother continued the conversation. "There are families interested in you, Asinath. Plans are already in process for most of your friends. Why do you keep holding this up?"

It was true. Most of the girls I knew were interested in a particular boy. I had not gotten to that point. My brother, who was hiding under the table, jumped out, laughing, and ran out of the room.

Once, my seven-year-old brother had said, "I am going to take care of Mother whenever it is needed, but I am not taking care of you, unless I am Pharaoh."

I came back with, "I will take care of myself, thank you." I wasn't sure how I was going to do it, but it sounded good.

A week later, at the marketplace, my friends were discussing how excited they were about their matches. I was happy for them. They thought it strange that I was not ready for that stage yet. I didn't care what they thought.

This was my life. They knew that my parents had been approached by a couple of families who said that I was growing to be beautiful and strong and I would probably be able to have lots of boy babies. I resented that but I also was a bit proud about it. However, I was not looking forward to having babies. Especially after hearing women screaming during childbirth. It scared me.

A number of boys were my friends, but I couldn't envision being with any of them for the rest of my life. Yet, the process had to begin. I was adamant about who I did not want to be with and was told that my strong will was going to give me no chances of having the top picks.

Mother said, "Quite a few of the boys are already promised. You are going to get the leftovers. This is important, Asinath. You are not always going to be young and beautiful forever. You will need sons to care for you in old age." Although they were working diligently on the mating process, I tried to put it out of my mind.

On each visit to the market, I looked to see if the slave would be there. I hoped that I would see him again. Then I thought, "Why would he be there? He is a slave. Maybe he would be the one to go on errands." A couple of times I thought I saw him, but I was mistaken. This was ridiculous for me to think about him. I never did that for any boy before.

Flirting

About a year later, I thought that I spotted him again but I wasn't sure. I continued on my mission. Finally, I glanced back and realized that it was him. I was fifteen years old and was a bit bolder. He looked grown up, and was no longer a skinny, scared, ragged, dusty boy. I moved close enough to get a good look. His shopping basket was full. Dressed in what looked like rich garments and sandals that laced up his lower legs, his appearance was so different from when I had first seen him. His dark, curly, clean hair caressed his handsome face. I couldn't help smiling. A flutter ran across my chest. That had never happened before. I casually walked over near him and pretended to look at fabrics. It took all of my courage to pretend to bump into him with my basket. When he turned to see who caused the jolt, his concerned face turned into a smiling one. I apologized humbly. He helped me pick up my basket and some of the things that had fallen out. I noticed and admired the dimple in his chin and he smelled like jasmine. I love the smell of jasmine. I didn't want to seem flirtatious, so I thanked him and scurried away, heading home. It took everything I had not to look back. I was too embarrassed to see if he was watching me. I wished that I had worn one of my pretty outfits, not the plain one. I felt that his eyes were following me as I walked away, or maybe I was wishing it to be so. After that incident, I made sure to be selective about the clothes for my trips into town.

Six months later, when I was sitting under the tree by the river, eating bread, goat cheese, and honey with my friends, the discussion changed from shopping, learning, and trips back to boys. Since a number of them had already been matched, they were getting ready for the rituals. I was happy for them, although I was still bearing up under my parents' threats to make my selection soon. My father, a priest of On, had to set an example and I was part of that example. A match would be made and that was that.

I wasn't going to share any thoughts about any boys during gossip time. I listened, giggled, and nodded when appropriate. I'd seen them flirting with the boys. There had been no one that I wanted to pay attention to until now. This could never work for me and a slave.

The Hebrew

Two of the girls started talking about an attractive Hebrew slave. They said that he was in charge of running the household of the General of Pharaoh's Guard. I tried to pay close attention without anyone knowing it. Evidently, there was trouble in that paradise. Since the general was always at work and practically lived in the Pharaoh's palace, he trusted this slave to take care of everything at home. That was amazing...a respected slave? They were guessing that the general's wife may have resented this switch in power and felt it should be her responsibility to take care of things. Also, she seemed to have a romantic interest in the slave.

Sada whispered, "He is so handsome. She is going to show him off today in the market. That's why I came today. She wants everyone to see how beautiful he is and be jealous of her."

Abihail followed with, "I bet Potiphar doesn't know about this."

They all agreed. I just listened.

Eli, who worked in the kitchen at the general's home, sometimes said, "That's true. That wife has tried to lure him into her bedroom more than a few times, but he always finds a way to refuse her advances. The whole household knows what's going on but nobody's going to tell. I even tried to turn his head, but I guess I am not the one, either. He has dodged her so far, but something is going to happen. It has to. I mean, after all, she's one of the most beautiful women in the city and her husband is never home. I bet a lot of men would like that opportunity!"

Sada said, "I guess the poor woman is frustrated. My mother said that her husband is away most of the time. He must trust the slave to put him in charge of his household. It must be nice to have a handsome slave living right there in the house!"

Everyone giggled.

Although I was bothered by the conversation, I giggled. That was my cue to leave. All I needed was for my father to hear that I was a rumormonger. A priestess does not gossip. My parents were very strict. I hated to leave but I had to get home for prayer. I hoped that I would see him again at the market. Little did I know that I was never to see him there again.

The Man

One of my father's religious duties as a priest was to go into the jails to talk to the prisoners. One night at our evening meal, he told my mother about a new prisoner.

"He is a male slave who had earned an honored place in the home of General Potiphar." My mother looked at me but didn't say anything. "He was put in prison because Potiphar's wife claimed the boy was trying to get romantic with her." My father was always careful with his words because we were always listening and sometimes the servants were, too. His version of the story contradicted what I heard under the tree, but I said nothing.

"Oh no!" My mother said, "I think she is lying. Some ladies were talking about it at our study today. Evidently, she has been after him, not the other way around. Poor boy! She even grabbed his robe and tried to use it as proof."

My father went on, "I have met this boy. His name is Joseph and I had a chance to talk with him when I went to pray with the prisoners. He confessed that he would never do anything like that. He said, 'Potiphar has been good to me. Yes, she is a beautiful woman, but the general's trust was more important. He trusted me. She wouldn't give up and I couldn't tell him. That is his wife. He couldn't take a slave's word over his wife's. I think he believed me but what could he do?'"

My father believed him. "I think he is right. Potiphar could have had him put to death. Joseph seems to be a good young man. Since he has been in prison, he has earned so much respect. The warden put him in charge of some of the duties of managing the place. A prisoner with a paying job in the prison has never happened before. Now, he is an official in the palace of Pharaoh."

My mother gasped. We were all listening intently, but I hung on every word.

My mother asked, "How did that happen? From a slave to being a leader is pretty amazing."

"It seems he can interpret dreams. The pharaoh had some puzzling dreams that bothered him. He asked his wise men and the magicians for help. They couldn't. Then he heard about a Hebrew slave who might be able to help him. Joseph had gotten a reputation in prison for being a counselor and an interpreter of dreams. Pharaoh's baker had done something wrong and was in a cell with Joseph for a short time. When he went back to the palace, he told Pharaoh about the young man who said that his God helped him to find meaning in dreams."

"Really?" I accidentally said. Usually it was my brother who interrupted.

Everyone turned to look at me. That was my signal to stay in a child's place. This was confusing. On one hand, they wanted me to be a child, and on the other, a wife to someone.

My father went on as if I hadn't spoken, "That young man has saved us. It seems that Pharaoh's dreams meant that there would be seven years of abundance and then seven years of famine. Joseph suggested that Pharaoh store food and water so his people would not starve. Egypt stockpiled food. Pharaoh was so impressed that he put Joseph in charge of gathering the food.

"It has come to pass. The world around us is starving but we are doing fine. Pharaoh honored Joseph with an Egyptian name, Zaphnath-Paaneah, which means 'For God Speaks.' Joseph was honored as second ruler in all of Egypt and was told to pick a wife from any woman in Pharaoh's kingdom. Pharaoh even put his ring of power on Joseph's finger. Now when you see Joseph, he is dressed in kingly robes with servants of his own."

I remembered how dirty and tired he was, dressed in ragged clothes, when I first saw him tied together with other slaves. What a change.

Even during the training for my duties as a priestess, I couldn't stop thinking about my father's words. "...gave him a chance to pick a wife." I pushed that into the back of my mind.

As time went about, I noticed men staring and greeting me in the marketplace. I wasn't interested in any of them. Then shopping began to lose its allure. I was told that it was below my station anyway. However, it had given me the opportunity to gather with friends before visiting the sacred place of worship.

Then, one day, I spotted Joseph while I was chatting with my friends under our tree. He was so beautiful. I thought of getting up gradually, walking casually in his direction, and accidentally bumping into him again. Surely he would know that I was doing it on purpose. I didn't have enough nerve to do that. He was with a group of men who looked like they had come in from the dry area. They were dusty and two were helping an old man to walk. There was a young boy with them whose hand Joseph was holding. As they walked past, talking and laughing, he looked up and saw us sitting under the tree. He tipped his head, smiled, and moved on without saying a word. I smiled back. My girlfriends giggled and looked at me with astounded faces.

Sada was the first to speak. "What have you been keeping from us, Asinath?"

I rose, shook my head, and said, "There is nothing to keep!" I started walking home, humming. I could feel their eyes following me.

Eli yelled out, "I don't believe you!"

They all giggled as I floated down the path.

My parents noticed my happy mood and asked what had happened. I simply said that it was just a beautiful day.

The Visit

The next day during dinner, we heard what sounded like men marching nearby. Then there was a knock at the door. Father looked surprised. One of the servants headed to the door. Father waved her away and got up to see who it was. When he opened the door, men dressed in battle gear filled the doorway. We were in shock and frightened. I wondered what my father had done that would bring these men to our house.

The first man bowed and said, "Is this the home of the priest of On?

My father said, "It is!"

My mother stood up and my sisters and I trembled.

The man requested, "May we enter? We are looking for Asinath. Are these your daughters?

"Oh my God," I thought. "Me? Why do they want me? I haven't done anything wrong."

With fear in his eyes, my father shook his head and shuddered as about ten men entered our home.

I stood, bowed my head, and said, "I am Asinath."

A voice from way in the back of the crowd said, "Greetings to the priest of On. I am Joseph!" The once-scared boy from the auction block stepped from behind the men. "I hope you remember me."

My parents were speechless for the first time. My father recognized him and said, "You are the prisoner that I prayed with. Is there a problem, sir?"

Joseph continued, "No, there is definitely not a problem." He turned to face me and said, "Asinath, I have admired you for some time in the marketplace. I have spoken to those who know you and your family. I want to let all of you know that my intentions are honorable and true."

He turned back to my father. "Priest of On, my plan for your daughter is marriage. Pharaoh has given her to me as I requested. However, I will not act on this should you disapprove. I refuse to live a life with division in a family. I have had enough of that. There is no need for a dowry and I will only have one wife. There will never be any concubines. She will come to live with me in the palace and I will prove to be the husband that she deserves."

I felt my feet slip away as I was caught by one of the men, who helped me to sit.

Joseph turned to me. He walked over, took my hand, and said, "This is our first real meeting, Asinath. I will return tomorrow and we will talk. This will not happen if you are against it! Do you understand?"

I shook my head in agreement. He turned and walked away with the men following him through the door. Our servant closed the door. We were all too stunned to move.

The six of us sat down in amazement. My parents took deep breaths, smiled at each other, and then stared at me. I pinched myself to make sure that this was not a dream. My parents smiled as we listened to the sounds of men marching away. It seemed that they did not have to make a match for me after all. It had already been made.

Aunty's Flowers (1862)

There's a lady living up the road in our small town who is filled with stories about history. Everyone knows and respects her. She sits on her porch, rocking in her favorite chair and smoking her old corn cob pipe. Even the Indians come by to smoke a pipe with her once in a while. Everybody calls her Aunty Sue.

You can't miss her 'cause you pass her house going in or out of Cherokee Town. Everyone greets her and she calls out each and everyone's name as they head for school or work and when they return.

On Saturday afternoons, when all of the household chores are done, townspeople take turns sitting on her porch, listening to stories and drinking homemade lemonade. They bring her the lemons and sugar, and somebody usually goes to the well to get some nice fresh water. I don't know what else she puts in that lemonade, but it is something special. Everybody wonders what it is. She told me the secret.

"That's my secret, childrens! Can't tell a secret 'cause den it won't be no secret no mo."

She uses a special kind of honey that one of the Indians brings her and she uses it sparingly. They say it is the best lemonade ever. The men come for the lemonade, especially on a hot day. The owner of the town store makes sure she has plenty of glasses and pitchers just for the lemonade. She sends him down a pitcher every now and then.

She tells the children that it was called "bartering." She said that back in her day, few people had money, so they traded for what they wanted. She actually bought most of her things with her homemade sweet potato pies and the clothes she sewed. She is pretty good with it because she has kept a lovely home over the years.

The little children like to play in her yard. She has two

boards tied to the limbs of an old tree in her backyard. She always tells them if there is any fussing about the swinging, they will have to go home. There is never any fussing.

The young girls like to stop in for advice. I heard them talking about her one day. They said she always tells the truth. She takes their hands into her old, weathered hands, looks them dead in the eye, smiles, and kindly suggests some decisions that need to be made. They feel that her simple touch makes whatever is wrong right.

All of the women seem to like her company. That is rare. I've seen them stop by after church and then feed their families. Each woman in the town is assigned a day to take her dinner. When the women gather for a visit, it seems like a celebration of life. She just leans back casually, rocks evenly, and tells stories of days gone by. Her mind seems like a bottomless well of history that touches the hearts and souls of each of us. I learn more history from her than from school. It is amazing how she makes her lessons easy to remember.

She has to be over 100 years old and she seems to be doing very well even though she is living alone. Actually, she's not alone! She has a whole town full of people she calls family. Aunty has outlived her parents, two husbands, and four children. Now we are family too. She has grands, great grands, and great-great grands who come by and check on her periodically. Since she has made it plain that she is not leaving her home, they stopped trying to take her home with them. They don't give her any trouble about it, but most of the time they sit and listen to her stories too.

I love the stories about Kansas. She said that way back in1859, Kansas advertised for settlers. Folks started moving out west to own land. Slavery was still abounding in the states. One day her mother heard about it when she was serving dinner to guests in the big house. Her heart skipped a beat and she knew immediately she was going to leave that place. It took some doing, but with help, she, her husband, and little

Sue got away on the Underground Railroad. Instead of going north, they went west and found some land in Kansas to build a home. It wasn't much...just a lean-to that they built against a hill. Soon it became a one-room shack.

A few years later, the Civil War ended. The soldiers were sent to Fort Leavenworth to fight in the Indian Wars. Aunty said that they were known as the Buffalo Soldiers. Also, Native Americans were recruited as scouts.

Aunty said that her family made it to Kansas twenty years before the Homestead Act of 1882. It accelerated the settlement of western USA. Families were granted acres of land for a small amount of money. If they lived on it for five years, they gained ownership. Land speculators and railroad companies bought land out west and offered the land for a fee. At times, the federal government also offered the land for free in order to populate it. Promises of "bountiful" and "fertile" land drew many to the western territory.

She always spoke with joy when the name "Pap Singleton" came up. I had heard about him too. Evidently, he was interested in buying land for settlements. It wasn't possible in the south, but the west was opening up, so he thought Kansas was a potential site for black emigration and started the Tennessee Real Estate and Homestead Association with his business partner, Columbus. They bought land and started new communities of settlers. She admired the guy and said we all should respect his dream.

When Sue was only sixteen, she was enamored with the military uniforms. She would smile talking about the handsome men in their uniforms. One day she spied a handsome young officer. Her heart did a little leap and she knew this was the one. She knew it was serious because she had never felt that way before. He must have liked her too because they courted. After they "jumped the broom," the one-room shack became three rooms.

Throughout the years, they continued building so that

relatives on their way west could have a comfortable stay, plus the family was growing. Sadly, her first husband died in a battle, leaving her alone to raise their two children. She had no idea what to do to earn their keep. She didn't have to worry about the house because she owned that. However, they needed food and the growing children needed clothes.

The neighbors and the church helped out, but her pride got the best of her. She would sneak into town at night and go through the trash behind the stores. She found old scraps from the fabric store that had been tossed in the trash and used her sewing skills to make clothes for the children and herself. Others noticed and ladies started buying their own fabric and bringing it to her to make their clothes. She set up her own business. Pretty soon she was financially able to buy her own fabric.

Sue met her second husband because of a man called "Pap." In 1873, Benjamin "Pap" Singleton, a former slave, purchased 1,000 acres of public land and called it "Asylum for the freedmen of the South." She praised Pap for being what she called a brilliant and kind man.

Benjamin "Pap" Singleton, ca. 1880
(Public Domain Image, Courtesy Kansas Historical Society)

By 1874, a group of 300 Blacks established the Cherokee colony on Pap's land. She said that Singleton swore he persuaded over 7,000 folks from Kentucky and Tennessee to settle there. Since she was already a settler, they built the town around her. The way she tells these stories makes them come alive.

I love learning history at Aunty Sue's knee. Sometimes she serves us some of her yummy butter cookies with a smile. That is what she calls them *Aunty's Yummy Butter Cookies* I can tell when she has them because the smell just rolls down the streets. I don't think I have ever seen her without a smile. I never thought of her as an easy person for some reason. She always seemed like she could handle herself in a fight but there was rarely any need to.

My mother once said, "That woman is amazing! Her smile can stop a fight. You should have seen her stop what might have been a battle between two men. It was amazing to see grown men back up as this tiny little lady spoke calmly to them."

It is 1941 and her smile still produces a warm feeling in me. It has been that way all my life. What she gives us is far greater than what we give to her. I guess it is a kind of bartering.

One day, a friend and I sat on the steps of her porch, drinking lemonade and eating butter cookies. I asked Aunty if she could have anything, what would it be? What she said made sense because it is pretty dusty in this Kansas town. Her answer was sweet and poetic. She said:

"I can't smell no flowers when I'm gone.
So, if you want me to have some,
I'll just take 'em right now.
I sho will!

After I pass dis here life,
I won't be able to enjoy no company.
Oh, don't feel bad later.
Just come on over and let's sit and talk.

Pass me that ivory pipe I love.
Not the corn cob one.
Let me rock on the porch in my chair
And sing my favorite old hymns.

Ask me about the days when I could kick up my heels.
You won't be able to hear my good old stories soon;
I'm taking 'em all with me.
Had me a good life, I has!

Wants me a big ole funeral,
That's what I wants
To celebrate my dying, 'cause
Lord knows I celebrates my living.

Put on my best nighty and slippers
And comb my hair real pretty-like.
Then lay me out on a nice soft pad with a fancy pillow.
I'll be ready...ready for the Glory Land.

So, come on over to see me now
And remember I can't smell no flowers when I'm gone.
But I likes to smell 'em right now.
I sho does."

So, spoke Susan Mabel Cottman, our Aunty Sue, the heart of our town. I have to do what she said. The next time I go over, I WILL have her flowers!

The Voyages (1620)

I will always remember the first time my mother said, "Martha, we are Puritan!" I wasn't sure what that meant or why she said it, but it seemed important. She explained that Puritans separated from the Church of England, the Protestant Church, and the Catholic Church to start our own church. Some folks agreed but they tried to practice our trends within the Protestant Church. She explained that the churches in England had unnecessary ceremonies and practices that were not rooted in the Bible, and we followed the Bible. Then she asked a question that answered itself.

"Who wants to belong to a religion designed by Henry VIII so he could divorce his first wife so he could marry another? It's ungodly and it sets a bad example."

My father shook his head in agreement. "The church is too corrupt to be saved. I won't belong to it and I am certainly not raising my family in anything that is not of God."

I had heard all my life that the persecution for separating was awful and that is why we had to leave England. Even in our village of Yorkshire, it was unsafe. So, we left for Leiden, Holland, when I was only four.

Mr. Brewster and Rev. Robins led us to Amsterdam in 1608 to escape religious persecution. Our secret church services were not sanctioned by the Church of England and were against the law, so a trip to Leyden was planned.

Leyden seemed to be a good choice for a settlement. It was an active seafaring area and tolerant in allowing residents opportunities to worship as they wished. I liked living there. Since it was peaceful, we lived there for twelve years. Our men were not hired for high-paying jobs, but they were able to make a living in the garment area. My father said it was better than the jobs they had in England.

The Meeting

Once settled, church meetings and Sunday services were weekly high points. The meetings were exciting, especially when I watched my father take a leadership role. I was so proud of him standing up at meetings and stating his opinions. Rev. Robins always opened the meetings with a prayer.

I remember him saying, "I like living here. I am grateful that we have found a place to live peacefully." He paused as the people clapped. Then he continued, "But I am worried that our children are losing our culture." There were some moans from the people. "We are Englishmen, not Dutch. We need to find a place of our own where we can continue our culture, worship the way we like, and be in control of our earnings. I hope I am not the only one who sees this!" Every hand went up in agreement.

Then Mr. Clayburn said, "A few of us have looked into moving again. We need more information but we are looking into that new land, the Americas. It might be the perfect place to go. I have heard that it is an untrodden land. We could create a new society for freedom there. The problem is how to pay for the voyage."

Mr. Bradford chimed in. "You're right. It will be costly. Let's not fool ourselves. We do not have money for a trip, especially for the whole group. So, we will not all be able to go at the same time."

Rev. Robins held up his hand and said, "I have read that there is empty land in spite of the natives. Homes could be built from the wood from the great forests there. We could take some seeds and I bet the soil is rich."

Father said, "I agree with Clayburn. It sounds right to me." There were sounds of approval from the congregation. "Who is willing to go?" All I heard was applause. "What say you, Rev. Robinson, sir? We will need some spiritual guidance in the new world. Are you willing to go?" Cheers filled the room.

Rev. Robins spoke. I sensed a sadness in his voice. "All praises to our Lord! I think this will work, but I cannot go. I want to, mind you, but I have to stay at this church. I can't just let God's church fall down here. It took too much hard work for us to build it up. I have to wait until I am sure that someone can take my place here." Some people sighed. My father sat down quietly.

Mr. Winthrop took it from there. "But we will need your spiritual guidance in the new world. You have to go!"

I saw my mother touch my father secretly with her elbow to quiet him. I had seen her do that many times. It always worked because it gave him a moment to think before acting. Mother said that sometimes he just needed to calm down before he said something that he hadn't quite thought through! He frowned in her direction and smiled at Mr. Winthrop.

Rev. Robins responded, "You're right, sir. With that I do not disagree. I will make sure that one of our senior ministers will be on board. He will take my place and it will be fine. He's a good man and knows the Bible. Remember God will be with you. Once there is someone here who will be able to take my place, I will surely be on my way."

It was then that I saw Malachi for the first time. There was something special about him. He was among a group of strangers who opened the church doors. Everyone but Rev. Robins seemed startled. We all turned to see who was entering.

The man in front of the group stepped forward. "My name is Andrew Coddington, sir. We are sorry to interrupt but we're grateful to be here. It was a long trip and we are glad to get here."

Although we knew that Puritans were still being mistreated in England, it was usually during the day that they joined us. The numbers were growing so much that I heard the women talk about it the next day while they were cooking.

As my mother was making bread, she said, "It is getting

too crowded. Pretty soon there won't be enough jobs here for all the men."

Mrs. Walton agreed. "We are going to have to figure something out. The Dutch people don't seem bothered about it, but you never know how folks will adjust. As for me, I am ready to go!"

"Usually it was announced when new people are coming so we could welcome them," my mother said. "I wonder why we didn't know about this group. They look so weary and scared. I guess we looked that way when we first arrived, too. Remember the men had to sneak away so they wouldn't go to prison?"

"I remember," said Mrs. Walton. "I was sure that the wives were going to have to go to prison too. It is strange that they let the families go. I guess they were glad to get rid of us. It was a bit fun, going on the boat ride with all of the women, even if a lot of us did get seasick. That was awful. Poor Mary. She almost had that baby on the ship!"

"I was praying for her. Seems so long ago," my mother said as she put the bread above the fire to bake.

New People

Rev. Robins welcomed the new families and explained that they could stay in the building next to the church. It was built for newcomers until they could find a home of their own among us. Two men guided them to benches at the back of the room.

The tall boy towered over the men; it was apparent that he was not yet a man. His face was that of a boy. It was his face that really drew my attention. He was so handsome. His clothing was according to the law, modest and covering everything but hands and face. We learned as children that dressing fancy is a sin.

Malachi's long, dark hair was tied at the back of the neck just like some of the men. It wasn't his clothing that made him stand out, nor his hair. He was wearing a gray suit and a white shirt with a big collar, just like all of the men.

Mother said that back in England, only wealthy people wore fancy clothes. It is the law! I am used to our way of dressing. I like colors. The white aprons are necessary because we are always working. We wear them every day to protect our clothing. I cover my hair with a cap.

Our men's hats distinguish us as Puritans. We wear a lot of black or blue clothing. Blue is the color that servants wear in England. Sometimes I wear brown for modesty. I made a pretty green wool dress to wear on the trip to the new land and a yellow linen skirt for my first day there. I wanted to make something with orange material but I didn't have that color. Orange is my favorite color. Mother said those colors mean renewal.

The Decision

The meeting continued when Ruth Abbot's grandfather shouted from the front bench. "I think we should go back to England. Maybe things are getting better. I miss being home."

John Winthrop replied quickly, "This is your home. Why do you think these people keep coming? You know that we are treated better here. That is why! We are free to praise God the way we want, when we want. No one is holding you here. Anyone who wants to can go back. There seems to be no rush on that. As for me, I shall not!"

Rev. Robins said, "You have our blessings and may God keep you safe, if you choose to go! We are here tonight to work on setting up a life of freedom, in a place of our own, a place where we can prosper and raise our children, where we don't have to worry about getting punished for how we worship."

Mr. Hutchings, who is usually quiet in the meetings, stood. "We cannot return to a place where our worship has to be dictated by the Pope or a King or Queen. It is to be of God and God alone."

Ruth's grandfather didn't give up. "I am old and I don't think I could make that voyage. It might be best if I went back home. No one will bother an old man. My family will not be going to that strange land with you. I hope it all works out well, but I want to be buried in England. I can't take that chance right now. If I were younger, I just might!"

When I glanced at Ruth, I noticed that she seemed to sigh with relief. I wasn't sure if that was because she agreed or disagreed. Her mother reached out for Ruth's grandfather's hand and Ruth's father patted the old man on his back. I wonder if Ruth would go alone and leave her family behind. Since she was sixteen now, Ruth would be allowed to go on her own.

People began to talk among themselves until Mr. Hutchings said, "Each man has to make the choice. You have to do what is best for your family. What about you, Mr. Allerton?"

My father stood. "We will go." He looked at my mother and she nodded in agreement. He took her hand and pulled her to her feet. "Speak, Mrs. Allerton."

"My husband knows what is best for us. So yes, we will go! I am looking forward to it!" she said. "I don't fool myself. This is going to be hard work. We don't really know what is out there, but if my husband says it's time, then it is time for me and mine."

My father continued, "Here is the good news. A request was made and I am happy to say that we are once again blessed. Since we can't afford the trip for such a large group, we have been looking for financial assistance. Luckily, the Plymouth Company is willing to take a chance on us. They have about seventy investors that will loan us about 1,500 pounds. All we have to do is pay them back with our profits from harvesting when we get there, and send them things native to that land like timber, fur, and fish. I'm sure there is much more. We would have to salt the fish to make it last the journey. That should pay off our debt. What say ye, ladies?"

A number of the women clapped.

Rev. Robins stood. "I hate to tell you this, but the King has sent word to Holland that he is still the ruler of any Englishman, no matter where they live." The congregation grumbled. "The Dutch people have accepted that. We have got to leave this place!"

Rev. Robins asked each man to offer his decision. After a few stood to talk, leaving was approved. However, Ruth's family was the only family not going to the new land. Our next step was to prepare.

The congregation purchased maps and the works of Captain John Smith, one of the original founders of Jamestown. Father said that he was one of the most knowledgeable men in England about North America. Mr. Hutchins and Rev. Robins met with Captain Smith to request that he be our guide and military advisor. However, they felt that his personality was not what they wanted. He would dominate the group and he was too expensive. Their second choice was a man with experience but a different temperament, Miles Standish. He accepted.

Through all this serious talk, I couldn't stop thinking about the new boy. I wanted to turn around to get a better look and smile, but young ladies were trained not to act in a way to make the adults take notice. So, I sat there, hoping and looking straight ahead. I could make some kind of connection later. I hoped to get a chance to greet him and introduce myself at the end of the meeting, but the new emigrants were requested to leave first so that they could get settled. The rest of us stayed to create and approve the plans for the trip.

My parents met the new people the next day when we went to the holding building. I tried not to make it obvious that I was more than happy to make that visit. Finally, there he was. I met Malachi, his sister, and two active little brothers. His parents, George and Jane White, seemed like nice people. They were so happy to be in Leiden and they weren't sure if they wanted to go on to the new land. While they were talking, Malachi and I were able to have a chat. I liked that he spoke to me first. He was not just good to look at, but also had a kind spirit. Suddenly, the tulips seemed more colorful. The wood larks' songs sounded more melodic and the windmills seemed not so large. I didn't know what was going on in my mind, but it was nice.

A New Friend

Malachi and I saw each other often in the crowded town while doing chores. Every now and then we got a chance to talk. His conversation was mostly about his life in England and how happy he was that they left that "Godforsaken place." He was relieved to not have to worry about getting into trouble simply because he was a Puritan. Puritan clothing made them easily identifiable. We became friends a month before it was time to leave for the new land. Things were moving fast. However, I looked forward to seeing him on the ship. In the new land, there would be plenty of time.

On the morning of the trip, I awoke to the smell of the sea air mixed with the aroma of mutton stew. I love that smell and wondered if it would be the same in the new land. I wanted to hold on to that smell. It would always be a memory of this home. I would miss Leyden. It was all I knew. I had mixed feelings about leaving. I didn't remember too much of England because I was so young when we left.

I felt relieved that we were already packed and ready. As I opened my eyes, I heard the laughter of new people in our home. I knew that they must be moving in as soon as we left. Mother was showing them the things that we would leave behind, hoping that they would be put to good use. It would be impossible to take everything with us and I could tell that she was hopeful that all would be replaced once we were settled. She said, "We can make what we need when we get there. Other ships will bring people with supplies."

The people interested in living in our house seemed grateful, and their joy dominated the conversation. My mother slipped in, "I wish you well here. This house has served us. I do hope to see you in the new land one day." We lived in a two-room cottage. We were lucky because most of the cottages only had one room.

I slept on a pallet on the floor in my parents' bedroom. My big brother's pallet was on the other side of the room. They let me sleep later than usual that day because we were leaving and my chores were done. Normally, they would wake us up with the sun. Mother had even filled the pitcher with water so that I could bathe. Thank goodness! I didn't have to do that. I poured the cold water into my basin and washed up hurriedly. It was important to not miss a spot, so as not to offend someone on the trip to England. I put on my green shift with the big white collar. It was important to me to look my best on the journey.

An Old Friend

Surprisingly, my friend Ruth came into the room. She whispered, "Martha, I am not leaving Leyden. My family is going on the boats today to England and they are going to stay there." Tears ran down her cheeks.

"What are you saying? You are not going to the new land?"

"No, I am not! They aren't either. They will go back to England. It's a long story and I don't have time to tell it all. I'm in love with Peter."

"Peter. You mean Peter Jansen."

"Yes. We are going to marry and live with his parents. It's all set."

I was shocked. "You never told me anything about this and we are supposed to be best friends. At least I thought we were." Although she was teary, I didn't like it, but I was happy for her. "Are you sure about this?" I asked.

"I am very sure! I haven't told my parents yet but Peter's parents said it was fine with them."

"Well, I hope everything works out for you." I admired her bravery in staying. I would have a difficult time separating from my family. Selfishly, I was a little sad because I had plans for the two of us to learn the new land together. That wasn't going to happen. I would have to get another best friend. There would be lots of people going, so maybe that might work.

"I've got to go. I am meeting Peter by the old barn down the lane. I wish you well." We hugged and said goodbye. She ran out the door.

Charles's pallet was in the kitchen near the fire. My little brother was usually out of the house before everyone else, looking for trouble to get into. He cracked the door and peeked in with a funny look on his face. I guessed the excitement of new people coming to move into our house caused him to stay around, getting into people's business.

By his expression, I knew he had been listening. His look was discomforting, and I had to do something quickly.

"Come in here," I said, pulling him in by his head. "Are you going to tell Mother?"

"Tell Mother what?" He grinned slyly.

"About Ruth?"

"What about Ruth?"

"You know!"

"No, I don't! Oh, do you mean about her staying here and getting married?" He knew that I knew he was listening. "If you don't tell, I will!" he said, looking like he'd just caught the biggest fish ever.

"And if you do…when we get to the new world, I will not go exploring with you."

"That's not fair! You promised!"

"Don't you dare get angry. Now YOU have to promise. Promise not to say anything about what Ruth told me."

"That is not fair!" He stomped his feet.

"If you want me to go exploring with you, then you have to keep this secret. I know that is hard for you, but this is important. You can do it if you want to."

"I might find other people who will go with me."

"You might, but you might not. Anyway, I am your sister and I won't let anything bad happen to you. You can't say that about anyone else."

"Oh, I won't tell," he said as if forced.

"Good, I am taking you at your word and offering it up to God. God will be watching you."

He stomped out of the room.

Port 1: Canals

When we arrived at the port, the seagulls greeted us with squawks of hunger. Their bold approaches proved that they were used to people feeding them. I was surprised to see so many travelers. I thought it would be just our group. The small port was busy, filled with people saying farewell. Travelers began loading their belongings as they boarded boats for the trip back to England. From there we were to travel to the new world.

We boarded several boats on the Rapenburg Canal. It was the perfect day for a sail. Father said that there was no way a ship could navigate the narrow canals. This one fed into the larger Vliet Canal, which flowed from Leyden toward the busy port in Delfshaven.

Quite a few people stayed to watch as we drifted away. Rev.

Robins and his family were among the shouting crowd on the platform. Rev. Robins opened his Bible and began to preach a sermon. My father held my mother's hand as we waved good-bye. Malachi and his family were there too. I wondered if I would ever see him again. He was sure that his family would come to the new land and we would meet again.

I tried not to think about Malachi even though there was something special about the short time we had known each other. Although his family had not been in Leyden very long, Malachi believed that they would come to the new world later. We did not say goodbye. The plan was that I would see him again in the new world.

He had said, "Once plans are made, we will be on our way to our new home. They are trying to find financing for the next group."

There he stood with his family on the dock, waving. We smiled at each other as the boats pulled away. Some boats were filled with our belongings and some with people. A tear formed in my right eye as I waved goodbye to him and to the only home I knew.

The trip was rocky because the water was a wee bit trou-bled. Father had taken us on fishing boats before, so this wasn't that much different. Finally, we floated so far that we could no longer see the dock.

Port 2: Holland

When we finally reached Delfshaven, the *Speedwell* was waiting for us. Compared to our boats, this ship was huge. I was glad to embark because the seating was cramped in the boats. It felt so good to get out, stretch, and walk a bit before heading to the waiting ship to England.

There seemed to be more seagulls at this port and they were definitely larger than the ones that greeted us at the canal. As they circled the pier, squawking with excitement and alarm, they scattered their droppings here and there. Some women were cooking Poffertjes for sale and keeping an eye on the birds. I loved sugared butter cakes and was glad that I learned how to make them. A boy was walking about with tulips for sale and I wondered what flowers grew in the new land.

The sailors were calling out directions to make sure that the ship was ready to sail. People from different towns were lined up with us to get checked in with our bags. The captain, Christopher Jones, stood on a high deck looking down, directing all activity. The salty air was so strong I could almost taste it. I guessed that the ocean was so vast that it would be unfair to compare the smell of an ocean to a canal. The air was brisk and Father said it was perfect for the sails of the ship.

I tried to remember our voyage to Holland so I could make comparisons, but I couldn't remember much. All I could remember was holding onto my mother.

Father greeted Mr. and Mrs. Standish as they boarded the *Speedwell* in Delfshaven. Once I was on the deck, I felt the movement of the ship and that, I remembered. The pressure of the water against the ship made the vessel move a bit from side to side. The memory came back to me and we hadn't left port yet. I looked out at the land, the water, the dock, and the people. That is when I spotted Ruth's family. Her grandfather, mother, and father were first, her youngest brothers next. Then came...I was shocked...Ruth. The eldest brother, close behind her, seemed to be talking to her back. I could see his face clearly. It was not a pleasant look. Ruth's head was down so I couldn't see her face.

A large crowd covered the pier. Among the crowd stood Peter, almost hidden behind a number of people. His left eye looked strange. The skin around it was dark and his hat looked crushed.

Suddenly, my little brother came up behind me and grabbed

my hand. "I guess Ruth's plans have changed!" He laughed, "Glad I didn't tell!" and ran off.

I had been so excited about this trip that I never thought about how others felt. There had to be a fear among the excitement of going to an unknown world. I realized that I had mixed emotions. This was a dangerous church mission but I knew that God would get us there safely. I had never thought of that before, even when I prayed. I was just praying because everyone else was. I wanted to assure myself of how wonderful it was going to be. It was sad to leave our church and some great friends, but we would finally have a place of our own and we would all be together again.

I wondered if the people who decided to stay felt deserted and if they would really come later. Those who chose to go back to England couldn't be sure of how they would be received by the separatists who had stayed there or if the English treatment of them would get better. Yet we couldn't be sure that everything would turn out the way we wanted it to.

Port 3: Southampton

The *Speedwell* sailed for Southampton, England, to rendezvous with the *Mayflower*, another ship, in England. Thank God because the *Speedwell* started to take on water. My parents were worried. My father said he was glad that it happened before we left to cross an ocean.

Once we pulled into the dock, we said our goodbyes to some families that chose to stay in England, thinking that we would soon be on our way. Ruth's family was one of them. The activity of people leaving the ship and getting their baggage kept me from getting near her. However, I was close enough to see that Ruth's face was different from the usual pink cheeks that framed her constant smile. She looked pale. I could tell she had been crying. Since I wasn't able to hug her because her brothers swiftly guided her through the crowd and down the plank, we waved from a distance. I was sad because I thought that I would probably never see her again.

After we were all off of the ship, some men went to work on fixing the leaks. Instead of leaving the next day, we had to stay in England for two weeks until the ship was ready. We stayed with family in England waiting for the repairs to the *Speedwell*. That was fun. I met cousins that I had heard about but never seen and they shared family stories.

Finally, the approval was given that the *Speedwell* was safe. Our Puritan group was divided. Some were assigned to the *Speedwell* with us and others to the *Mayflower*. Then grumblings started because some of the passengers for the *Mayflower* were not separatists, or even religious, but had booked passage seeking economic opportunities in northern Virginia, their intended destination. I don't think my father liked that idea of splitting us up. However, there would be enough room for everyone because two ships would be enough space.

Port 4: Dartmouth

On August 5, 1620, both ships were ready, and the passengers were more than ready. We left Southampton's Plymouth Harbor, leaving the sounds of seagulls flitting about overhead. What a spectacular sight it was. With sails flapping, passengers waving from the deck, and sailors busy with tasks, we had finally set sail. The talking on deck was loud but cheerful. The seagulls flew above us, squawking as if they were going on the trip with us.

However, right after the captain shouted that we had just cleared the English Channel, he announced that the *Speedwell* had begun to leak again. He must have relayed the information because both ships turned around and headed back to England. The cheerful chatter turned to sobs and angry tones.

Once again we had to wait. It was important to fix that ship once and for all.

Father was concerned and said to Mother, "If we go back, we have no place to stay. I have a feeling that this is going to take a long time to fix."

The captain diverted the ships to Dartmouth, the closest port. Before we disembarked, a man from the shipping company boarded with a message to the travelers. "Fear not!" he shouted from above. "The shipping company will pay for your overnight stay in the two local boarding houses and some in the homes of local families."

After repairs were completed once again, we left on August 24. Then, three hundred miles out at sea, the captain announced, "I am sorry to tell you that we will have to turn around. The *Speedwell* is leaking again."

Sounds of anger, disappointment, and praying filled the air.

He continued and there was a hush. "We think the problem started when the ship left the military. It had been refitted with a larger mainmast post to carry an oversized sail. That weight has caused the hull to separate, creating the leaks. She may not be able to make this trip."

I asked Father, "What is the hull?"

He held onto my hand and said, "It is the body of the ship...everything but the masts, rigging, and the engine." I noticed that my father looked tired and sad and tried to smile. "Don't worry, little one, all will be well."

Both the Mayflower and the Speedwell returned to Plymouth Harbor. The Speedwell was deemed unseaworthy. We all fell down on our knees to thank God for saving our lives.

By this time, some of the passengers were upset and left. There was no place on the Mayflower for all of the Puritans who had been on both ships. Only eleven people from the Speedwell could board the Mayflower, leaving twenty people to return to London. A combined company of 102, including three pregnant women, were able to continue the voyage to the new land. The *Mayflower* set off alone, leaving us behind. My mother wept silently, wiping tears as soon as they appeared.

This was the third try. The *Mayflower* headed to the New World. Led by lawyer John Winthrop, some of our friends from Holland departed from Plymouth on the *Mayflower* on September 6, 1620. As I watched the ship pull away, I didn't know if I was happy or sad.

My mother was upset but my father was angry. They had heard a rumor that the *Speedwell* had been sabotaged. There was no money to purchase tickets back to Holland. We didn't want to stay with relatives any longer. It was important to not wear out our welcome. My parents wanted to leave England.

My father went to the ticket clerk to request a way to get us back to Holland. Luckily, Father was able to barter our fare that had been paid to go to the Americas to pay for our tickets on a ship back to Leyden. I was happy it was not on the *Speedwell*. He promised that we would take the trip to the new land on the next ship headed that way. I wasn't so sure if he meant to do that or promised so that Mother would be calm as we went back to Holland.

We were filled with mixed emotions as we boarded a ship two days later and headed for Holland. No plans to try again were discussed. We were weary and a bit dismayed but also a little happy that we had a place to return to and that we had not taken that voyage on that broken vessel.

* * *

What really happened to the Speedwell?

Rumor 1: Members of the crew later confessed that the *Speedwell* had been sabotaged by order of its own captain. In refitting the ship before leaving Holland, they had supplied her intentionally with masts that were too large in order to get out of his contract. Reynolds and his crew had been hired by Thomas

Weston, the merchant adventurer who orchestrated financing for the expedition, to remain with the colony for a year so they could use the ship. Captain Reynolds sabotaged the trip so that he could keep his pay, claiming it was no fault of his that the ship leaked, and then have it repaired and sold for his own profit.

Rumor 2: It was reported that the "cunning and deceit" was because the captain desired to get out of his commitment. Seeing that the ship was poorly provisioned and fearing that the "victuals" would run out before his contract did, the captain ordered every inch of sail unfurled, with the result that he soon had the excuse for turning back. Years later, a different rumor said that the Dutch wished to undermine English efforts to settle near the Hudson River, and "fraudulently hired" the captain to effect "delays while they were in England.

"**Conclusion:** The *Speedwell* was, in fact, seaworthy and could make a transatlantic crossing was well established in 1635 when Captain John Thomas Chappell brought it across from England to supply the Virginia colonies above Jamestown. This would be its last voyage, however, as the ship was now over 50 years old, and, afterwards, it was refitted, sold, and lost to history; becoming only a footnote to the *Mayflower* voyage for 400 years now."

***

The Speedwell is not completely lost to history. The dramatic scene before her departure from Amsterdam is depicted in "The Embarkation of the Pilgrims" in the Capitol Rotunda in Washington, D.C., and the same scene is reprinted on the back of the rare U.S. $10,000 bill.

Protestant pilgrims are shown on the deck of the ship *Speedwell* before their departure for the New World from Delfshaven, Holland, on July 22, 1620. William Brewster, holding the Bible, and pastor John Robinson led Governor Carver,

William Bradford, Miles Standish, and their families in prayer. The prominence of women and children suggests the importance of the family in the community. At the left side of the painting is a rainbow, which symbolizes hope and divine protection. Weir (1803–1890) had studied art in Italy and taught art at the military academy at West Point. The dimensions of this oil painting on canvas are 548 cm x 365 cm (216 inches x 144 inches; 18 feet x 12 feet).

https://www.worldhistory.org/article/1637/the-loss-of-the-speedwell--foundation-of-democracy/

Embarkation of the Pilgrims. Robert R. Weir (Public Domain)
US Capitol Rotunda…Created: 1844 date QS:P571, +1844-00-00T00:00:

Chapter 2
Theatrically Speaking

– Viola Davis

Telephone Face Off (Spam Calls)

Scenario 1

Me: Hello?

Telemarketer: Hello, my name is John Smith and I am calling for the Alzheimer's Association. How are you today? We are so happy that you donated to us last year and since we are collecting donations to wipe out this horrible disease, I am calling to see if you would like to contribute again this year. Can you...

Me: What did you say? My hearing is not the best. Getting a bit old.

Telemarketer: I am calling for a donation for Alzheimer's. It looks like you gave to our organization last year and we were wondering if you would like to participate again. You will win a nice gift if you donate at least fifty dollars.

Me: Huh? My hearing is going. Did you say Alzheimer's? My father has Alzheimer's, and I don't have any money right now. It's taking all of my life savings. He is such a good man. Everybody likes him.

You called at the perfect time. Are there any applications where I can get some financial help? Thank God you called. Can you help me? You see, I am alone in this world and I need some help.

Telemarketer: (Click!)

***

Scenario 2

Telemarketer: Hello, can you hear me?

Me: (Nothing)

Telemarketer: Hello, can you hear me?

Me: No!

Telemarketer: Hello, this is Jim.

Me: Hello Jim.

Telemarketer: I am calling because you are having a problem with your computer and we can help you.

Me: I don't have a computer.

Telemarketer: (Quiet) Come on, lady. Everyone has a compu...

Me: (Click)

***

Scenario 3

Telemarketer: Congratulations, is this Sally Wells? Sally, this is your lucky day! You just won a free trip to the beautiful Bahamas. (Clapping)

Me: Wow, a free trip? I don't have to pay anything? Is this that publisher's thing? I always wondered if that was real. I didn't hear a knock on the door. Are you coming to my house today? I have never won anything. I am excited! My husband died, though. He would have loved this. I could use a trip. Is it for two?

Telemarketer: Yes, it is. You can take a friend. All you have to do is...

Me: I don't see you. When are you coming? I'm not dressed up. I guess I'd better get off the phone and get ready. Oh my goodness! My husband would love this but he can't go, though. He's dead. Do you know a nice man that would go with me? Maybe you! You sound kinda nice. You could be my friend. I have his ashes. Maybe together we could take them on the trip and spread them over the Caribbean. He would love that...adventurer, you know! Have you ever been with a seventy-five-year -old woman?

Telemarketer: (Click)

***

Scenario 4
(This message was left on the phone.)

Telemarketer: Hello! This is Susan. I haven't seen you in a long time. How are you and your family? Give me a call back so we can catch up. My new number is 202-354-----.

(Most people know someone named Susan. It doesn't sound strange.)

Me: Hello! (That's when you find out that you have called a pornography site. So you hang up quickly and report it to the telephone company.)

Telephone Company: We are so sorry that happened to you, but we can't do anything about it because you called them back.

Me: But here is the number they left for me to call. Can you do something about it?

Telephone Company: 'Fraid not. They pay for their phone so they can call anyone. When you called back, it became your problem. Sorry!

Me: Okay! Lesson learned! (Click)

Please Don't Cut Down All of the Trees! 2020 (A Monologue)

Why were people hoarding toilet paper? Mr. Scott and Ms. Charmin probably laughed all the way to the bank. Why didn't I invest in paper goods, Clorox, and Lysol when I had the chance? But no...it didn't sound lucrative. I missed those financial opportunities and that will haunt me for the rest of my days. It is almost as bad as my father-in-law not investing in contact lenses when he was approached long ago.

The supermarket shelves that housed toilet paper were bare! As soon as the news shouted "COVID!" people acted as if they had lost their minds.

Whenever there had been a fear of a natural disaster, like a hurricane, a flood, or a tornado, the bread and milk would disappear from the stores. With the blast of Covid, it was toilet paper that was the prey.

People raced to the supermarket, the bulk stores, the dollar stores, and online in search of this paper treasure. Stockpiling seemed to be a major tactic in readiness for this new virus. It was scary! Grocery carts, steered by racetrack-inspired wannabes, raced to pile up counters with packages of paper goods. Dashing around corners as if in the Grand Prix, consumers eagerly crossed the cashiered finish line and then ran to their cars, onto their next quest for more of the valuable commodity. Those who usually selected high quality paper with 4-ply, long lasting, even color-coordinated sheets of paper became less picky about their selections. The soft and hard, long lasting, not so long lasting, thick, and thin tissue vanished as if never having existed. The spoils went to the fastest and the most devious. Buyers didn't care if the rolls were with or without the cardboard center. The hostile, untrusting environment was not an issue in the expeditions. The goal was to be the victor at all costs.

Law enforcement had to be called in some stores to protect the people from toilet paper battles. Names are not listed here to protect the innocent and the guilty. Arguments over parking spaces ensued because time was of the essence. It was important to get to those shelves while there was still stock. Thank God for the organized management of these outbursts that prevented a Toilet Paper War. There were lines outside of the store, allowing only a few in to shop for a specific time period.

Folks didn't realize that there was enough toilet paper for everyone before the mad dashes began. It seemed the whole world had one mindset: "Get that precious commodity so that your family would be safe."

One lady had a large thirty-eight-roll pack stolen from her unlocked car. That was her fault. She should have covered up the package with a blanket and locked the doors before she went back into the store. Her goal was to pretend that she had not been there before and get another package. I bet her plan was to head for a different cashier to avoid being recognized as someone who had already purchased. She knew that one person was allowed one package. How could you feel badly for someone like that? She was cheating!

One lady performed as if she was an award-winning running back. She snatched the last package from the basket of an unsuspecting woman and ran for the door like she was heading for the goal post. Unfortunately for her, she was stopped short of the goal by a lineman in the form of the store manager. No touchdown for her. She had the nerve to argue with management and left empty-handed.

My guess is that a clean "bottom" is a universal desire. I guess no one wants to return to a time of long ago when using nice clean rags, newspaper, Sears catalog pages, or leaves from the trees was the norm. Hell might be like that! I am sure there are places where other procedures are necessary and toilet paper is not treasured. I can't imagine what that might be like.

The lack of that precious tissue must cause nightmares about a trip to a public bathroom to quell a natural disaster by not checking ahead of time. I understand that fear. I face it and it is terrifying. The fear of a toilet paper shortage became as contagious as the danger of the virus itself.

In my prayers I beg, 'People, please don't cut down all of the trees for toilet paper! I need the air. We can live without toilet paper but not without oxygen. Leave the trees alone. I already receive too much unnecessary mail using up those essential plants.'

It took a week after the word "Coronavirus" was first mentioned for terror to grip the hearts of man and wo-man. I know it did mine. However, fear does not deter me from doing what is right. I bought one large package of toilet paper at each store I visited. After about a week of refusing to hoard supplies, I changed my mind and went shopping for toilet paper at more stores. After all, I didn't want to be the only one without it. I am almost ashamed to confess this—I joined in on the Toilet Paper Bandwagon. After I secured my two large

packages of eighteen rolls each, I wanted to use a megaphone to shout, "Stop it, people. There is enough for us all!" Hypocrite!

Just in case, should you ever hear a familiar voice from behind a lone stall in a public bathroom shout, "Somebody hand me a nice fresh leaf...please!" that would probably be me! Do not feel sorry for me, and do not laugh. I will probably have a private roll of extra soft toilet paper without the cardboard center hidden in my big pocketbook! If you don't hear a snickering from the stall, it may not be me but someone in dire need. Go outside and get a leaf or maybe carry some leaves or pages from the many catalogs you receive in the mail in a plastic bag in your pocket...just in case!

Mary The Great (Skit)

Based on the life of Mary Fields (1832 – 19140)

*Wikipedia - Public Domain: https://www.lwvin.org/content.aspx?page_
id=5&club_id=42001&item_id=57635*

***

Characters

Interviewer
Camera woman
Mary Fields
Butch (dog)

Setting

Two bright lights are directed center stage. One straight-
backed chair and one rocking chair face each other. Two
microphones are on the stage. One is handheld and is placed

on the straight-backed chair. The other is on a post beside the rocking chair. A recording device sits on a table facing each chair. On an easel facing the audience to the left of the setting is a framed picture of a black woman on a horse-drawn carriage. To the right of the setting is another easel with a portrait of a woman holding a rifle. A woman stands behind the straight-backed chair, positioning a camera to record any occupant of the rocking chair.

Scene 1

A female dressed in a business suit enters stage left, carrying some papers in a folder. She sits in the straight-backed chair, opens the folder, finds a pencil in her purse, and begins to look through the papers. She places the papers neatly on the table, picks up the microphone, blows into it, and begins to speak.

*****

Interviewer: Welcome to the first broadcast of "Herstory: Interviews to Remember!" We will also be recording this evening's program. Our task is to combine our interviews with outstanding women to create a meaningful historical documentary. This broadcast is designed to be informative and entertaining. Hopefully it will prove to be a valuable learning experience. We will bring to you women who we feel have contributed to society but have not been in the limelight.

Sifting through time to find a character to interview is like shopping on the menu of a respected restaurant. There are numerous interesting and delicious choices that no one has ever tried. Since time is filled with alluring possibilities, we are having fun finding some undiscovered treasures. We reach out for those special folks for "Herstories" that are often eliminated or falsely told. It is fascinating to see how their lives transfigure the lives of women today.

Today's program looks at the 1880s with a visit from a unique woman by the name of Mary Fields.

***

Scene 2

(A door can be heard opening and shutting. A tall black woman carrying a rifle and chewing a cigar stub walks into the room. She is wearing a black skull cap and a long, dark dress that touches the ground. A black apron hugs the front of her attire. Her boots are sturdy and worn. She grunts and takes a place in an empty rocking chair. A black and white cocker spaniel mixed breed trots in with her and rests beside her chair. She places the rifle across her lap with the barrel pointing outward toward an imaginary audience. She looks around, then settles back into the rocking chair and starts slowly rocking. The dog looks up. She smiles at the dog, pats his head, and continues to rock.)

Interviewer: Thank you for meeting with us today, Miss Fields. It is an honor! You are one of my "sheroes." Please have a seat and get comfortable.

Mary: (She stops rocking and concentrates on the interviewer.) Is that so? Sheroe, that is an interesting word! I never heard say of that word befo'—"sheroes." First, just call me Mary. What can I do for you?

Interviewer: I have so many questions that I don't know where to start... Okay. I guess we should start at the beginning. Where were you born?

Mary: Slavery. That's where I's from. I bet you knew that. It was a hard life. Don't quite know the day, though. There's no record of it. Some folks says I's had an interesting life. Interesting is not the word I would use, though. I guess it is if'n you wasn't no slave. I was born somewhere in Tennessee. At least that's what de told me. I never really knew. Don't talk much about it.

I tried to hide sometimes when I was a young'un. It worked when I was real little but could never hide after that. I was always a big gal. You can see that! Folks used to think I was older den what I really was. Neber was thought of as a beauty, so I learnt to use my hands. Dem pretty girls had a tough time of it. Thank da Lord I ain't neber had to go through what de did.

Grew to be 'bout six feet tall and got to be about 200 pounds when I was a youngster. I guess you can see dat now. Good thing, too, "cause when the break come, you know, da freedom time...I could do men's work. Did a bit of everything but never in da big house.

Made me some friends along the way. My best friend was a little girl who was a'kin of master. We was childhood playmates. She was kind. Didn't meet too many of 'em back den. We was playmates. When she grew up, she became a sister in the Catholic Church. I was proud o' her. Then she became Mother Superior Amedeus at a convent up in Ohio.

It was her who gave me a job housekeeping at the convent...good work. Pay wasn't great but it was better den nothing. I got a place to sleep and pretty good food. After a few years, her boss sent her out to Montana to another convent to start a school for Indian childrens. I missed dat gal. Den I heard tell she got sick. Dat's when she send for me to come and take care of her.

Interviewer: Did you go?

Mary: Sure 'nough I went. Wasn't nothing hold me dere.

Interviewer: What kind of work did you do and did you like it?

Mary: Like it? Never thought 'bout liking it or not. It was work, but I guess I did like it! I raised chickens, cleaned everything, grew vegetables, and fixed things! Oh, I was good at fixing. Even built one of the convent buildings with my own hands.

The nuns was nice enough. I liked 'em, for sure, but I could neber be no nun, though! No, ma'am. It wasn't in my spirit.

I like to hang out with the mens. Not in the dirty way. I could play cards, cuss, and drink most of them under the table. I was the "onlyest" woman that the law let into the saloon. No, ma'am, women were not allowed in the saloons. Just me.

My reputation for drinking in the saloons and pulling a gun on a few men lost me my job, though. I couldn't let them men treat me po-ly. Folks said I had the temperament of a grizzly bear. That is what I wanted them to think. They liked me, though, but the bishop didn't! He kicked me out of the very convent that I had built with my own hands. Ain't that sumpthin'? That's how mad he was! Strict man, he was!

Interviewer: Oh no! What did you do then?

Mary: Moved on, I did! That's what I did. Had no choice...moved on! Opened up some eateries. I was a good cook so it was natural for me to do that. Folks liked my sweets most of all. Some of the Indians would bring me some of dere honey. Made stuff taste real good. Da eatery didn't last for long 'cause I gave free meals to po folks, plus my bookkeeping was real bad. It wasn't working out!

Then I heard tell about the U.S. Postal Service. Got me a contract with 'em in 1895, to carry the mail. Yep! At sixty, I beat folks out by hitching a team of six horses faster than anybody. Loved dat job! Never missed me a day. They gave me some snowshoes. If'n the snow was deep, I'd walked dem sacks of mail to wherever they had to go. Humph, I wasn't no young'un then, either! I was the first black woman to do that job. It was dangerous but I was sure good at it. Had to fight off wolves and bad weather. I guess that's why dey have the saying that "neither rain, sleet, and the dark" can stop mail. Didn't stop Mary! No, sir!

I got some nicknames. They called me Stagecoach Mary. Some names I liked and did bother me a bit. For a while I was the only Black person in town, so some called me Black Mary. Dem Indians called me "White Crow" 'cause they said I acted like a white lady but I was black. I didn't mind that one. Got along real good with them Indians. Stagecoach Mary was the one I liked most. Worked that job for eighty years until I was seventy years old. My body was slowing down so I couldn't do it no mo!

I started "laundrin'" and "babysittin'." I could do that work right at home. Some of those folks I gave free meals to supported me. I loved the chilluns and they loved me. See, you never know what's gonna happen down the line. Folks just tended to like me, in spite of my gruffness. I may come off as a badass but I got a good heart. Dey even used to call off school and the whole town would celebrate my birthday. Ain't dat something?

Interviewer: I guess helping others means one day they may help you. My mother always said that you should treat people right as you climb up the ladder... you may see those same people as you go back down.

Mary: Yep! Dat's true. Dat sho' is da truth. I met me some nice folks in my life. Some I had to knock out, though! Gary Cooper, you know him. He's an actor. Well, I knew him when he was a little bitty thing. You can read all about it in a 1958 *Ebony* magazine. He said 'bout me, said, "She was born a slave but lived to become one of the freest souls ever to draw breath... or a .38." Yep! (She looks down at the dog at her feet.) That sho' is true! Right, Butch? Well, come on, dog. We done spent 'nough time jabbering. We got things to do, people to see, and places to go. (As she rises from her chair, the dog rises at her feet, looking intently at her face. Mary turns to leave.)

Interviewer: Miss Fields, thank you so much for spending this time with us today. I enjoyed talking with you. What an amazing and meaningful life.

Mary: Child, just call me Mary. My momma gave me dat name. Don' need no "Miss" in front of my name. Stagecoach Mary is good enough, too! Come on, Butch! (She walks away with the dog trotting along behind her. A door closes and one light goes out.)

***

Scene 3

Interviewer: We have just had the pleasure of meeting Stagecoach Mary, an unbelievable woman. She is a unique and interesting person. So glad we got a chance to meet her.

In 1959 famous actor Gary Cooper wrote an article for Ebony magazine in which he wrote, "Born a slave somewhere in Tennessee, Mary lived to become one of the freest soles ever to draw a breath or a .38." After meeting her, I totally agree.

Hopefully you are as enlightened as I am from spending some time with her. It is nice to read about someone but actually meeting them and hearing them speak creates a different perspective. That is why we do this show. We have learned so much and I am honored.

Thank you for tuning in. We know hope that you have been enriched by this bit of history. Hopefully share the information you learned and invite others to join in next time for "Herstory: Interviews to Remember."

Next week, another fascinating personality from history will be here. Every third Wednesday evening at 6:00 p.m. I will be here waiting for you. Each guest will be a treasure. Good night and make some "herstories" and histories of your own.

A Box Story (Skit)

Every night, thousands of Americans are putting their life at risk by sleeping on the street. Being homeless can be traumatic if it happens.

Characters

Jennifer
Mac Daddy
Man
Woman 1
Woman 2

Setting

Any urban area in the United States where homeless people reside. Tentative sheltering constructions abound on hidden paths and near thoroughfares. A thirty-five-year-old woman is sleeping in a large box. The crowing of a rooster is heard in her mind but also on stage. A forty-year-old unkempt man wearing an old top hat walks with dignity from off stage to a large box resting on its side toward the opposite side of the stage. He stretches and yawns.

Time: Just before dawn.

Man: (A man comes out of a tent and lumbers away.) Mornin'.

Mac Daddy: (Man standing beside a large box.) Top of the mornin' to ya! (He flips his hat at the man walking away mumbling. He peeks into the box.) Wake up, my love. (He takes a deep breath of air.) Sweet Lady, the sun has beaten you in welcoming another glorious day once again. (He taps on the box three times.) The cock has crowed thrice. It is time to go forth. You don't want to miss the world as it goes by. Had we lain in each other's arms of late, you would be happy to greet the morning sun with such a beautiful smile. Keep not that smile from me tonight, love of my life.

Woman: (Walks by pushing a grocery cart. The man tips his hat.) You sure are a persistent one! Anybody in their right mind would have given up by now. I ain't mad attcha. (The woman walks off to the right.)

Jennifer: (She speaks from inside of the box.) Get away from my house, Mac Daddy. Why do you keep on bothering me? How many times have I told you that my name is Jennifer Irene Brown, not Sweet Lady, and I am certainly not your love.

Mac Daddy: Evermore, this be not a house, my love... but a box...a mere refrigerator box. (He opens the flap and offers her a hand to help her out.) Tonight, I pray thouest will remove all of those covers and conjoin with my flesh. Oh, what a time t'will be!

Jennifer: (There is tussling in the box. A smack is heard when she hits his hand and out she crawls, an overly dressed woman in different outfits and covered by an old blanket. He steps back and tips his hat.) I am going to knock you into next week if you put your hands on me, you lunatic. I am Jennifer Irene Brown and don't you ever forget it. I graduated first in my class and I remember everything. (She looks at the man with remorse and raises her hands to the sky.) I certainly don't need any help from you. Nobody touches all of this unless I say so. (She brings her hands down the sides of her body from her head to her hips.)

Mac Daddy: (He reaches out his hand once again.) Come, my sweet, let us to toilet. Just look at ye. It is hard to secret such loveliness under all that dirt and grime. (He sighs.) Forsooth, I do love thee.

Jennifer: (She recoils.) What is the matter with you, man? Get away from me. I don't know why you come around here talking like that. I have a husband. (She goes back into the box grumbling. The box moves about). Filthy old man...got the nerve to call me dirty. I wash every day! He's the one that always smells awful and he thinks I am going to have sex with him. Just the thought of it makes me sick. Yuck! On second thought, he doesn't smell bad today. I think he must have some cologne too. I guess he found some place to wash up, thank God! (She sticks her head out of the box to see if he has gone. She spies him standing right by the box. She holds up a balled fist in a raggedy glove and yells.) I've got things to do, places to go, and people to see. (He sits down beside her box, whistling a tune, and waits patiently. She hums the same tune.)

Mac Daddy: Husband, you say? Where be he now? Take me to thy husband. (He laughs.) Maybe he will give thee to me. Evidently, he is not present! Did you run him off, dear lady? Far be it for me to say, but it looks like you are alone in this world. So, since you are alone and I am alone and we are both alone, why not we be alone together? No one should be alone.

Jennifer: (She comes out of the box and walks with her arms loaded. She walks behind the box and rolls out with a cart filled with miscellaneous things. He stands up to face her. She puts her hands on her hips and addresses him.) That makes no sense! I keep telling you...every single day...that I am Jennifer Irene Brown. I have a college education. See, I remember everything! I grew up on a farm. We had chickens and cows and pigs, too. I met my man in college. My husband "w-w-w-was" a good and handsome man. He was an English professor and not some piece of a man living in squalor. We have two beautiful little boys. (She scratches her head in thought and repeats.) We have two little boys. There! See, I have a good memory. I don't need you hanging around trying to make fun of me. I came from a good home. My mother and father raised me right. I am not some floozy that you can flop around with. I have a family. My husband loves me and I love him. You probably don't know anything about that kind of life. Just look at you. You're nothing but a bum!

<u>Mac Daddy</u>: (Rises and puts his hands behind his back.) Dearest, I dare not hurt thee with my humor. I speak of love for I am your husband. (He turns sadly from her and walks back the way he had come, shaking his head and mumbling of love.) Fear not, fair maiden, for I shall return.

<u>Jennifer</u>: (She yells after him.) Thank you kindly for leaving! (She takes the clothes out of her cart and folds each piece neatly and puts each back in the cart. She sings "Summertime...and the livin' is easy" as she works. She goes back into the cart and drags out a small container of cans and puts them in the cart. Then she takes off her blanket, shakes it out, and covers up the cans. She speaks joyfully.) I am going to make some money today...yes "indeedy." Once I turn in these cans, I'll have enough for some breakfast. No eating out of the garbage for me this morning. No, sir. They don't clean out those nasty garbage cans. I'm not doing that! I am Jennifer Irene Jones... No, was it Jones... It's Brown. I'm Jennifer Irene Brown. My daddy is a minister, Rev. Joseph Jones at the Holy Crown Church, and he is so proud of me. (She takes a little pencil and a small notepad out of her coat pocket, wets the tip of the pen in her mouth, and begins to write.)

Let me see, Number 1... (She puts the tip of the pencil in her mouth before writing the first sentence and then looks up from the paper.) Go down to 10th Street and make sure the boys get to school on time. (As an afterthought she continues.) I'd better make sure they don't see me this time. Last week I scared them a little. They're so cute. That little one looks just like my husband. I just want to reach out and hold them but I know I can't do that. I can't afford to get into lock up. That woman that calls herself their mother will have me thrown into jail if it happens again. She thinks I'm nuts! I heard her. (She walks around.) One day I am just going to tell her who I really am. I am not ready for that battle yet but it is coming. She can deny it all she wants. Those are my boys. I'd better use that tree across the street today and hide behind it this time. I was too close before but I just wanted to be near them. I am not going to follow them this time. One day they are going to find out that I am their real mommy and they'll love me and not her. She reminds me of a Rottweiler.

Woman 2: (A woman sticks her head out of a tent.) Will you shut up all that noise? (She goes back into the tent.) People are trying to get some sleep around here. I got to wake up to this noise every morning.

Jennifer: Let's see...Number 2. (She starts writing again.) Sorry, Miss Betty! Just trying to take care of my business.

Woman 2: What business? Getting on my nerves?

Jennifer: If I find some cookies today, I'll bring you some.

Woman 2: That would be nice. Go ahead and take care of your business then.

Jennifer: I'd better get over to the gas station and wash before Jake wakes up. I am so glad he is lazy. It makes it easy to slip that key and open the bathroom and then put it back again. If his boss finds out all he does is eat the honey graham crackers, drinks milk, and sleeps, he might fire him and I can't have that. He is a lazy cuss, but he is my lazy cuss. I bet if he knew what I was up to, he'd probably let me do it anyway. He may even know what I am doing and let me go. It is the best when his girlfriend comes around at night, I can even get a hot dog or a sandwich and no one's the wiser. Actually, I would be better at his job than he is. It beats a blank. At least I don't have to go all the way down to the bus station to wash up. That wouldn't give me enough time to see my boys.

Number 3. (She writes.) I'll take the cans, get the money, and go to Skeet's Shop. They'll give me my breakfast for a quarter. Maybe I'll get a bagel and a coffee to go. Eating light keeps me thin and trim. I guess that is what drives Mac Daddy wild. I have got to maintain my girlish figure. Okay, that's Number 3. (She looks all around to see if anyone is watching. When she is satisfied, she goes into the cart and digs down deep, bringing up a jar of money.) With today's money, I'll have about a hundred dollars. Pretty soon I will be able to get a nice room and maybe a red outfit from the Salvation Army or the Good Will. Maybe I should get black instead of red. Yeah, black. It goes with everything. Then I will be ready for a job interview.

That's Number 4. (She writes again.) I'll get yesterday's paper from the trash near Reading Terminal. There are always loads of papers there. I'll look to see about job openings. I certainly am qualified. That college degree must be good for something. Just have to remember where I put my degree. Oh well, I am sure there is a record of it at the college if I need it.

Dinner... What am I going to do about dinner? Number 5. Let me see. What day is it? (She rummages in her cart and pulls out a TV guide. She flips through it.) Yesterday was Sunday. Last Sunday was the twelfth, so today is the nineteenth. No, it's Monday, so it's the twentieth. Good Lord, Christmas is around the corner and I am no way ready. My mother would be ashamed.

That boy was here yesterday with blankets and food. So he probably won't be back until next week. I can have dinner at the Halfway House tonight, but I am not sleeping there. I don't care how cold it gets. Those people look sneaky and somebody stole my shoes the last time. They aren't getting any more of my stuff. People need to understand I have my own house. They need to get their own house. My house has a nice warm fireplace and everything. I think I'll cook a ham and a turkey this year.

Okay...Number 6 ... Last and not least I will treat myself to some dessert today. I'll stop by Burton's Bakery for some day-old pastry. They sell the best and I haven't been there for a while, so they'll give me something. (She puts the list and the pencil back in her pocket, walks over to her cart, and starts to go on her way. She is stopped by Mac Daddy calling her name.)

Mac Daddy: Sweetness, where are you off to?

Jennifer: (She rolls her eyes at him and sighs.) I don't have to tell you my business.

Mac Daddy: Low and behold, my love, I just thought you should know that it's going to snow tonight. We are going to have a Winter Wonderland. It is going to be beautiful! You would fare best at the YMCA Shelter on South Street. I just booked us a space. I will meet you there at 6 p.m. Let us synchronize our clocks.

Jennifer: (She looks up to the sky.) Who is this man? There is something familiar about you, Mac Daddy! I don't know what it is, though.

Mac Daddy: (He points to the sky.) The answer does not lie in the stars, my dear lady, but here in my heart. (He places both hands over his chest.) For the bells toll for thee. (He points to her.) Tonight, my fair lady, there will be more than a chill in the air. Already the snow begins. (He holds his ragged gloved hand out to catch a snowflake.) Take me to thy bosom to bask in your warmth...lest I perish in the crystal beauty of this whiteness. But, seriously, we must sleep inside tonight.

Jennifer: Look, I have things to do. None of which is sleeping in a shelter. What do I care about the weather, I am Jennifer Irene...

Mac Daddy: I know...Jennifer Irene Brown. That name will not keep you warm tonight. Now look, I have tried to tell you that I am your husband. I still have to take care of you...you know what we vowed "in death do we part" I took those vows seriously! Hell, I can't keep you warm tonight. I wish I could. We will sleep inside! There will be no arguing about this, Jennifer Irene Brown; I have the last say on this.

Man: (The man returns eating an apple. He looks at the two and shakes his head. He goes into a tent. Jennifer and Mac Daddy watch him, then continue their conversation.)

Jennifer: What are you going to do, drag me somewhere?

Mac Daddy: If I have to. So be it!

Jennifer: Then you'll have to do it. I've got my own home. It's big and beautiful. My husband and my children live with me there and...

Mac Daddy: (He walks over to her and slaps her face.) Think, woman. We are in the streets. (She falls down and begins to sob. He bends down and hugs her. He speaks softly.) Look at me! (She doesn't. He speaks in a louder voice.) Look at me, Jenny! Who am I?

Jennifer: (She looks up. Her body looks weak.) Michael?

Mac Daddy: (He smiles at her.) Michael who?

Jennifer: Michael Aaron Brown.

Mac Daddy: Thank God! I thought I had lost you completely this time. I am Michael, your husband. Only you can call me Mac Daddy. It's a love thang. Do you remember now? (He holds her and begins to rock her.) It's too cold to be out here. Come on. Let's go find some help. Remember I told you when I lost my job that we have got to take each day one day at a time. I am not ready for us to give up and die. We've got those two children out there somewhere in a foster home. I am tired of life's crap. (He rises and pulls her up. The snow falls.) Come, my sweet lady. Let me take you away from all of this. (She sobs as they walk away, holding hands.) At least we'll not freeze tonight. I just found out that the YMCA needs someone to teach English to some of the immigrants. They are looking for a new cook and you are good at that. I just had an interview this morning and it worked out. They know that I am in financial trouble but are willing to give me a chance. Put your list aside and kiss this box goodbye. It is going to melt in this snow anyway. No need for your cart. Let it be a blessing for someone else. I think we are going to make it, sweetheart. Just stay with me. Can you do that?

Jennifer: But what about the babies? I see them at the school each day.

Mac Daddy: Those are not our children. I know where they are. They are in a good place. Once we get these jobs and a place of our own, we can go to the agency and get them back. They are fostered, not adopted, but with a good family. I have been watching. But you have to work with me on this thing. If you lose yourself, we will never get those boys. Can you do that?

Jennifer: I think I can, Michael Aaron Brown. (She says it with surety.) I know I can! (She looks lovingly at the box, picks up a can from the ground, and puts it in the cart. She rolls the cart over to the tent where Betty is sleeping. Michael and Jennifer walk away holding hands. They both look straight ahead.) After all, I AM Jennifer Irene Brown.

Woman 2: Now don't forget my cookies!

Jennifer: I won't! (She turns and waves.)

Did History Ignore? (Skit)

(Remembering Olympians, Tidye Pickett and Louise Stokes)

Characters

Host: Doris Darnell
Tina Pinkett
Lisa Stone
Camera woman

Setting

Lights directed center stage. There are microphones on each chair. A recording device sits on a table in front of the single chair. On the wall facing the audience is a framed picture of a group of women posing. They are dressed in dark blazers, white skirts, and white shoes. Some are wearing white hats. (They represent women on a United States Olympic Team.)

Time: Imaginary Time is a mathematical representation of time that appears in some approaches to special relativity.

Scene

(A woman adjusting a camera stands in the back, facing the chairs, positioning her camera to be able to move from side to side for recording.

A female interviewer rushes in carrying papers in a folder. She sits in the single chair, facing the other chairs. On the table are 3 bottles of water. She opens a folder and begins to look through the papers rapidly. She places the papers neatly on each side of the table, picks up the microphone, blows into it, and begins to speak at the camera. "One-Two!" She glances at her watch, gives a nod toward the camera, and begins. The camera woman begins recording.)

Act 1

Interviewer: This is "Herstory: Interviews to Remember!" Our broadcasts are designed to be informative and entertaining. Each show is will offer a memorable experience, and information that you may not know about. It is our goal every week to make the world aware of little-known women who have faced extraordinary challenges. I am your host for the evening. My name is Doris Darnell .

Finding just the right people for this show is a challenge, because, surprisingly, there are so many choices and it is hard to pick just one story to tell. It's like trying to select a favorite pair of shoes. If you are like me, a shoe fanatic, that is quite a task. There are so many interesting styles, shapes, and colors that it is hard to choose just one. However, a woman must do what a woman must do!

History is filled with alluring people of different styles, shapes, sizes, and colors. Although it is quite a task making a choice for "Herstories," somehow we do it. We find women who are often not in books, may not make the news, or their stories are "miss-told."

Remember the movie *Thelma and Louise*? They were quite a pair, but that was fiction. Today you are going to meet two trailblazers, the real deal! I had never heard about these two United States female athletes who were sent to the 1936 Olympics to represent the United States. Let's meet Tina Pinkett and Lisa Stone.

So, Welcome to Herstory!

Act 2

(A door opens. A honey-colored woman carrying a briefcase enters. She is wearing a tailored pinstripe suit. A matching hat, kid gloves, and black mules complement the outfit. She says hello to the interviewer. The interviewer rises from her seat, shakes her hand, and points to a chair. Gracefully she approaches an empty chair, picks up the mic, and takes a seat. She takes off her gloves and sits.

Right behind her, a chocolate-colored woman enters. She is wearing a beige pants suit and brown penny loafers. Her crossbody bag compliments the outfit. The two women greet each other with hugs, smiles, and laughter. She shakes hands with the interviewer, approaches the other chair, then faces the interviewer with mic in hand.)

Interviewer: Well, hello, ladies. My name is Doris Darnell and I am honored to be the host for the evening. Please make yourselves comfortable. Feel free to take a drink of water when you need it. After all of the questions I will be asking, you may need to take a drink.

Welcome to Herstory, a program that allows our viewers to get to know women who have made positive contributions to society. Thanks so much for being with us today. It is an honor to meet you two "sheroes."

Ladies and Gentelmen, I have great pleasure in introducing you to Tina Pinkett and Lisa Stone. Your stories are intriguing and important. I can't wait until the world hears you. Ladies and gentlemen, these two women were selected to compete in the Olympic games in Berlin. I don't want to give out all of the information. It is more important for you to hear it from the women themselves.

So, ladies, I have some questions for you. Feel free to answer them any way that you would like and add anything that you think is important or wrong.

That year got a lot of attention. Hitler had come into power in Germany and part of his theme was to promote what he called a "superior people." Those Olympic Games did highlight superiority.

I read that there were eighteen African American athletes that were on the American Olympic Team that year. I didn't know that until former President Obama honored them and presented the families with recognitions. Shame it took eighty years for that to happen. Wow!

Lisa: I know.

Interviewer: I had only heard of one black person associated with that 1936 Olympics and that was...

Lisa & Tina: (They both answer at the same time.) Jesse Owens!

Tina: He is a legend. One of his records lasted for forty-eight years.

Interviewer: Really? I didn't know that. My father used to talk about him with pride.

Lisa: Most people haven't heard about the others that were there. Poor Jesse, he was only twenty-three. We were all young. He got all of the recognition but it came with some disrespect, too. Jesse was a great athlete and a nice guy. One of the German athletes became his close friend. He put his towel down at the spot where Jesse needed to start his jump for one of the qualifying events and that was a big help. They remained friends until World War II when his friend was killed.

I read that Jesse said he wasn't snubbed by Adolf Hitler or the German people. Jessie said that Hitler did not congratulate any of the winners. However, he did give Jesse a congratulatory wave. It was our own people that upset him. Jesse would tell anybody, "Our own president never even congratulated me or any of the black athletes...not even with a telegram and I won four gold medals!" Only the white Olympians were invited to the White House.

Interviewer: Wow, I didn't know that. That was so unfair.

Lisa: To be honest...the Germans who took care of us in the Olympic City were nicer than the people back home.

Tina: True! There were eighteen of us and fourteen medals were won. That is one-fourth of the medals won by the Americans that year. I remember every one of us. Don't you, Lisa? Let me see...there was Dave Albritton, John Brooks, James Clark, Cornelius Johnson. We decided it was easier to remember them in alphabetical order. It's easier that way because somebody is always asking me who they were and I don't want to miss anyone.

Lisa: Okay... Let's see, then there was Willis Johnson, Howell King, and James LuValle. I remember Art Oliver and Fritz Pollard, Jr. They were such gentlemen and they looked out for us.

Tina: Don't forget Mack Robinson, Jackie Robinson's big brother. I think he came in second in one of the races. He was fast.

Interviewer: I read somewhere that when Mack came home, he had trouble getting a job and became a street sweeper. It said that he wore his Olympic jacket while he was sweeping the streets. Sad! Ralph Metcalfe became well-known, though.

Tina: That is true about Mack. Ralph went into politics. He became a Senator or a Representative...something like that.

Lisa: He was a United States Representative. That's a big deal! So proud of him.

Tina: Ralph won a silver and a gold medal in the 100 and 200 Relay. The guy was like lightning! The folks in his town knew about his wins and celebrated him. I don't think it ever made the papers in other places.

Lisa: Let's see, there was also John Terry, then the "Ws"...Archie Williams, Jack Wilson, and John Woodruff. They were all great athletes.

Interviewer: Amazing! That team set the pace for Olympic teams to come. So what was going on before that Olympics?

Tina: Well, let's start at the beginning. We were selected because we were considered the best in our events. There were probably others that didn't get picked who were good too, but I was so happy we got picked. At first I felt lucky but then we had to work through the rough times.

Interviewer: Did you know each other before the Olympics?

Tina: Lisa is from Massachusetts and I was raised in Illinois. We met at competitions, leading up to the 1932 Olympic Games in Los Angeles. We would see each other at competitive meets.

We were subjected to abuse when we were only seventeen and eighteen years old. For instance, when we got on the train in Denver going to Los Angeles, we were given a separate room near a service area. We ate our meals in our room rather than the banquet hall with the rest of the delegation.

Lisa: We were fine with it but that doesn't make it right. In other words, it wasn't surprising. One night when we were sleeping in the bunking compartment, something happened. I was in the top bunk. Tina was on the bottom. All of a sudden ice water was thrown on us. We screamed because we didn't know what was happening and it was so cold. A highly recognized female athlete had thrown a whole pitcher of ice water on us. She was not alone. We both screamed and all we could hear was laughter as they walked away. There was no punishment issued. I bet if we had done that to them, the outcome would have been different.

Interviewer: Unbelievable! What did you do?

Lisa: We didn't know what to do! We hadn't been around her to cause any trouble and had no idea that anyone was thinking about us. We were surprised that we got any attention at all. So this was a shocker. We had to change our clothes and the bed sheets. The next day, Tina confronted her and they got into it, pretty good. Tina was not about to let it go. I stood beside her for support. As brave as that thrower had been the night before, she was surprised to be confronted.

Interviewer: Did she tell you why or apologize? (Both women laugh.)

Lisa: Tina? Did we get an apology for it? (Tina shakes her head.) No, there was never an apology. That would have been a surprise.

Tina: Apologize! That reminds me of one of my aunt's saying, "Do chickens have lips?" No! She never apologized. I didn't expect one. I had to get it off my chest, though. Actually, I awaited her punishment but it never came. You always know that down the line something is going to happen. You just don't know when or where.

Interviewer: Was that before '36?

Tina: It was in 1932! In '36 we were the first black women to qualify for the U.S. team but were later replaced. Somehow we were put back on the team.

We traveled to Germany by ship in '36. It was the first time for us to ride on a boat. I mean a ship. Some folks got seasick. The colored athletes were housed separately from the white athletes in our American section. The reason offered was that we probably would be more comfortable that way.

<u>Lisa</u>: Well, just speaking for myself, I was. At least I didn't have to worry about ice water in the middle of the night.

<u>Tina</u>: I know, but why do nasty, mean things? It still bothers me. During the day we were all up on the deck playing games and just having fun, but when it came time to eat, they separated us. I could never understand it. Most of the time we got along fine. It didn't kill our joy, though. We were excited to finally compete and represent our country.

<u>Interviewer</u>: I read that a deal was made that two Jewish runners, Marty Glickman and Sam Stoller, were benched at the last minute. Part of the deal of the U.S. participation was that Hitler agreed to allow Jewish athletes to participate. He even ordered a German Jewish woman who had fled to England to come home and participate for Germany. Then he must have changed his mind. She didn't get a chance to participate, did she?

<u>Tina</u>: No, she didn't. We met Gretel. Remember her, Lisa?

<u>Lisa</u>: Sure do. Gretel Bergmann was amazing. That was Germany's loss. She would have won them some gold medals. I think we made a good impression on her.

<u>Interviewer</u>: (She flips through some papers.) Gretel Bergmann. It says in a magazine from England that she was a German track and field athlete, who became the British high jump champion in 1934 after she left Germany because of the Aryan laws.

<u>Tina</u>: I liked her and was glad that I didn't have to compete with her. The U.S. team was prepared to come away with most of the medals. We talked about putting aside the racial and social struggles, to be able to represent our country.

Lisa: We were so excited to compete in the XI Olympiad. This was the biggest competition in the world. My hometown raised money so that I could go.

Interviewer: I read that you both were supposed to run the 4x100 meter relay but were replaced by two women who performed slower than you. How did that turn out?

Lisa: The U.S. team won a gold without us, so we didn't get any glory or medals for that.

Interviewer: Okay. (She looks at her iPad.) Looks like some viewers are sending in some questions. Here is one. "I read that there were 331 women competing that year. Is that true?"

Tina: I am not sure of the number but there were quite a few women in the Olympic Village. I qualified for the relay and the 80-meter hurdles. That would have made me their first African American woman to compete in the Olympics. On the day we arrived I was told that someone else would take my place in the relay. However, hurdling was a singles sport so there was no legal way to prevent me from competing. Unfortunately, I hit my foot on a hurdle and broke it. That knocked me out of a medal. In the U.S., the hurdles would fall down if hit, but in Germany, they were secured to stay upright, so my foot broke instead of the hurdle falling. I think my heart hurt more than my foot.

Lisa: We were intent on stomping out that "Master Race" business by winning for our country, but I didn't have the chance. It was like being robbed when I was replaced. The coach knew I would win. She knew it, but I guess that didn't matter.

Interviewer: (She glances at her iPad.) Although your names are not in the record book, you are sports groundbreakers. Here is another question from a viewer. What has life been like since then?

Lisa: It turned out okay for us. I— (She looks at Tina, who shakes her head positively.) I was accepted to compete at the 1940 Olympics but it was canceled due to World War II. So I found another sport, bowling, and I was good at it. I started the Colored Women's Bowling League and won many awards. I got married to a Caribbean cricket player and we had a son. We raised my stepdaughter also. My job as a clerk for the state Department of Corporations and Taxation was just right for me. I was even honored by naming a building in Roosevelt Park after me. There is even a statue of me standing proudly in a park area. I am so proud of that.

Interviewer: That is absolutely wonderful. What about you, Tina?

Tina: I went to college and became a teacher in Chicago. My parents were so proud of me. Then I became the principal. I worked at an elementary school for twenty-three years. When I retired in 1980, the school was renamed the "Tina Pinkett Elementary School" in my honor. That was pretty wonderful.

Interviewer: Looks like our time together has come to an end. It has been such a pleasure talking with you two history makers today. Thank you both so much for being on the program.

Lisa: I enjoyed it. This was so nice.

Tina: This was nice. So glad we could be here.

Interviewer: I am in awe of your courage and the important steps that you've made.

Tina: You're welcome.

Lisa: Thank you for inviting us.

Act 3

Interviewer: Well, folks, hopefully you have learned something new today. I know I have. While Tina and Lisa may be little known to some sports fans, their bravery and determination in the face of overwhelming adversity paved a way for female athletes to come. That is why we wanted you to meet these "sheroes." Thank you for being faithful listeners. We hope that you have been enriched by this experience. Go out and share the information.

Be sure to join us once again next week on "Herstory: Interviews to Remember." We will have another fascinating interview. Tune in on each third Wednesday evening at 7:00 p.m. and be pleasantly surprised. Good night and make some herstories and histories of your own.

FGM: Female Genital Mutilation (Skit)

Characters

Host: Cynthia Goode
Lady #1: Ebrima
Lady #2: Caissho

Lady #3: Farhana
Lady #4: Layla
Doctor: Dr. Tomo

Scene

A woman dressed in a black suit and white shirt sits at the head of a circular table. Five more women are seated at the table. The audience surrounds the table. There is a glass of water on the table in front of each woman. Another woman is placing printed programs, pencils, and pads on the table at each seat. A spotlight centers in on one of the seated women and a sign with FGM framed is in front of her on the table. The camera points to each speaker when it is their turn to begin.

***

Host: Good evening, ladies and gentlemen. Welcome! I am Cynthia Goode, your host for this evening. An article that I wrote drew some attention from a number of people and from it, this presentation was created. We are going to get into that, but first, thank you for taking the time out of your busy day to be with us for this program. We are virtual and live tonight. We have a studio audience as well as those viewing from their homes. Cameras and microphones are in place so that you will be able to see and hear each presentation. Everything seems to be in working order so, so let's get started.

This is the first program on topics under the title "Unspoken Crisis." All of our guest speakers are here and ready. Tonight's fascinating topic is FGM. (She picks up the sign with the letters on it and then sets it back on the table.)

Most people may not have heard of FGM. We are all learners tonight because I have not talked with any of our guest speakers until a half-hour ago. I am very interested to hear their stories.

First, let me tell you what these letters mean, just in case you have never heard of this before. It stands for Female Genital Mutilation. (Sighs can be heard.) FGM has been happening for many years. It is an old traditional procedure in dealing with sexuality. However, it still takes place today in a number of countries, and secretly in some parts of the United States, Canada, England, and France, although it is against the law.

Today we are hosting women who have actually experienced the procedure. They will tell you about it so that you know this is not hearsay. I was impressed and grateful for their willingness to share their life stories. Hopefully their information will save lives. What you will hear tonight is for sharing...no more keeping secrets. We want the word to get out so we can educate others.

So, let's start. While you are listening, you can write down any questions you might have on the pads you were given and those of you watching at home can write them in the chat. Someone will pick them up from the audience and someone is monitoring the chat. After all of the guests have spoken, I will ask the questions. We may not be able to get to all of them, but I will try. I am going to combine the ones that are similar. (She turns to the women at the table.)

Ladies, we will just go around the table. You can tell your story and introduce yourself. Just say what is on your heart. The topic is Female Genital Mutilation. (She nods to the first woman.) Let's begin.

<u>Lady #1:</u> Good evening, everyone. First, let me say that I am not ashamed of what happened to me. It makes me sad. I am twenty-two years old. It happened to me when I was a baby, so I don't remember it. I found out that my clitoris was cut when I was just a week old. This was a practice where I was born and still is in some parts of the country. Just like a boy is circumcised, girls are so-called circumcised also, but it is different. When I was told about it, I used to think that it was a religious rule but I found out that it predates all religions. I didn't realize what had actually happened to me until I googled it.

When I was eight years old, I was promised "in marriage" to a male that lived in California. Arranged marriages are not unusual to me. From my experiences, most of them last. When I was older and went to meet my husband, his family and mine were ready for me. There were loads of people celebrating. That was a happy time. A woman came to tell me about positions to make sex more comfortable. She rubbed me with lotions and seemed very kind.

Some women took me to his house and left until my husband came in. I cried from the pain of intercourse. It was definitely not what I expected, at least not for me. They said it would hurt and they were right about that. I went to a doctor the next day. Due to my pain and the tearing, the doctor said that I needed to be cut open. He said once that happened, I had to have sex right away to keep it from closing back up. My husband was so understanding, but I felt like I was on fire. When I listened to friends talk about the pleasure they experienced, I realized that I wasn't experiencing that, so I did some research. It was then I found that my condition was permanent. At that moment, I decided to do something to try to stop this from happening to other girls. That is why I am here. My name is Ebrima and that is my story.

Host: (She nods to Lady #2.)

Lady #2: I will go next! In school, the girls teased me and called me the girl with three legs. When I asked my mother about it, she said it was time for me to get my gift. She said, "It is time to become a woman." I was excited because I was told that every girl participated in a special ceremony, even my mother. I remember her saying, "People will respect you now."

The next day, she took me to a strange building. There was something about it that I didn't like. There was a smell that made my stomach sick. When I tried to run, I was grabbed and taken to a room with a long table. People were touching me in my private parts. I fought back but they made me drink something. When I came to, I was in great pain down in my woman area. It was finished.

The cutter said, "Now, girl, a man will marry you! You are clean!" Everyone cheered. I knew she was the cutter because everyone looked to her to answer questions and she was cleaning a sharp knife.

When we got home, family and friends were there for a party. My legs were tied together for fourteen days. Using the bathroom was the worst. I got an infection and the doctor said it was touch-and-go for a while. I thought I was going to die. My mother and grandmothers sat with me, saying it was going to be all right. I couldn't understand why they let those people hurt me.

It was explained in this way: "The clitoris is looked at as a man's penis. They don't want women to get the urge for sex and run after men, so they cut the clitoris." I asked, "Why don't they cut off the man's penis?

It is okay for him to get urges but not for women?"

I learned that if you don't take your child for this operation, you are labeled as a bad mother. I don't care if they call me a bad mother. I am not allowing my child to be slaughtered like that. Childbirth is another story. I hope other mothers are paying attention.

My name is Caissho.

Host: (She nods to Lady #3.)

Lady #3: Excuse me if I take my time. I have difficulty talking about this. I almost feel like I am degrading the customs of my people, but I totally disagree with it. (She sighs.) Okay, I can go on now.

About a year ago, I went to our family friend, who is a midwife. She has been doing the procedure for many years. She said that when a woman does not have the procedure, she itches. She is unclean. This procedure keeps you from scratching all of the time. That is when I realized that she is also a victim. She said that one of her friends does it because she has ten children and needs the money. Since somebody has to do it, why not her? At least she was honest.

I remember when I was about eight, we were told that we were going to be made clean and it was wonderful. My girlfriends and I were happy because everyone made it sound great. I remember hearing the women talk about some girls proudly saying, "That one is clean now. A man will marry her." Of course, I wanted to get married one day. I didn't understand what that meant.

Then my time came. There were three of us giggling and so happy when it was our time to become clean. When they took the first girl in, we waved happily. Then we heard her screaming. It was an awful sound. When they came for me, my mother walked with me into a room of women. I was blindfolded. They laid me down on a piece of material. The women held my arms and legs and the pain began. It was indescribable. I fought with all of my strength but I lost the battle. I was shocked. I thought I was going to die. I could feel the blood dripping out of me. I didn't know the impact as a child. I had been excited because everyone else was. People respected me after the circumcision and I felt relieved. That pain is long lasting and when you have to urinate it is horrible. (She begins to cry softly. Someone approaches with tissues. She wipes her eyes.)

My name is Farhana.

Host: (She nods to Lady #4.)

Lady #4: It happened to me when I was older...sixteen years old. I learned that my mother had been putting it off. She was told that I would never get married if I had not gone through this womanhood thing. My parents said it was a gift from my grandmother, who was leaving to go back home to her country. She wanted to make sure I was taken care of before she left.

I talked with my girlfriends at school, but they had no idea what it was about. When the day came, all of the women in the family were there. I was told that my aunts were in the room waiting to help. It was a happy time, at first. There was hugging and talk of how proud everyone was. Then they took off my clothes and held me down. They wouldn't let my mother intrude. If struggle is part of the practice, I obliged them. When I saw that razor blade, I screamed. I was blindfolded. I wished that I could have fainted. The hurt was enough to stop my heart. I wish it had. Once the blindfold came off, I saw that there was blood everywhere.

As they sang, unknown women washed me and

put strings around my legs to tie them together. A few days later, my skin began to blister from the heat. It was an awful time. I was told that my chances for getting married were high now and that was true. At this point I wasn't sure I would live long enough.

After I got married, the sex was good for him, not so much for me. When I was twenty-one and pregnant, I went to the doctor. He asked questions about the cutting. He referred me to a specialized midwife who explained what had happened to me.

"Since you are mutilated, we have to do some cutting to help your baby out. One way or the other, we will have to operate. Don't worry about pain. We will give you something for that. If you get any infection, we can will treat them." My husband did not understand because he was not from my country. He just thought I was small.

Maternity was horrific. I was told that it was dangerous for me and my child to deliver vaginally. I was in labor for four days. The medical people didn't know how to help at first. They were shocked. I thought I was going to die. Due to the circumcision, they would have to cut me for the baby to come out. Together we chose a cesarean birth. That was eleven years ago. I had a boy and thank God I didn't have to worry about going through that with my child. I have gotten used to painful intercourse. I think my body has widened on its own. I decided that my son would be an only child.

After all that I have been through, I swear that if I have daughters I will protect them from this business. Yes, I am pregnant again.

My name is Layla.

Host: I can tell by the quiet in this room that you are all as stunned as I am that there is such a practice still going on today. I know that you are filled with questions. We have a specialist with us, Dr. Lisa Tomo. She is going to give you more important information on this topic. Just write down your questions. Doctor? (Two women are stationed about the room. They begin to collect the questions and bring them to the host.)

Doctor: Hello, everyone, I can see the shock on your faces. I want to start with an explanation. Female Genitalia Mutilation is when a female's private parts are cut. It usually happens before puberty. There are four types.

Type 1, clitoridectomy, is removing part or all of the clitoris; Type 2, excision, is removing part or all of the clitoris and the inner labia—the lips that surround the vagina—with or without removal of the labia majora—the larger outer lips; Type 3, infibulation,—is narrowing the vaginal opening by creating a seal formed by cutting and repositioning the labia; and Type 4 are other harmful procedures to the female genitals, including pricking, piercing, cutting, scraping, or burning the area.

Host: (Sighs.) Whew! That is scary. (She picks up one of the papers with a question.) Let's take a look at some of the questions. When women come to you, what do you tell them? Can it be fixed?

Doctor Tomo: They come to us for clarity and help. They know they have a problem, that is why they come. First we try to build trust. Since this is done to them with the approval of their own family, it is difficult to build that trust. As professionals we need to listen to clients and not judge.

Some of them have grandmothers encouraging their own children to get their grandchildren home so they can get the procedure. These are human rights violations, but it has been passed down through the generations as doing something that is right and healthy.

We as professionals must ask questions. As you heard, many women do not realize that they have been through FGM because it happened when they were babies. Their bodies have healed and they have gotten used to how their body works.

The procedures increase during the summer when girls think they are being taken on a holiday or going to the home country for something special that is happening for women.

Cynthia: No, that is too much! I can't imagine my grandmother doing that. (She reads from the question paper.) There have to be some problems once this is done. What are they?

Doctor Tomo: Because it is not our practice here, we think it is barbaric. There are problems that women have with infections, passing urine, and pregnancy. Sometimes the vaginal opening is too narrow to give birth. Then there is psychological damage. There is no sensation in the vagina. That is intentional. A midwife told me that the reason why it is done is to keep women from seeking sex.

Maternity can be a challenge. As you have heard, some women can get pregnant. The cutter leaves a small opening so that the semen can get in. Giving birth is extra dangerous for both mother and child. Labor can last for days. Most medical people don't know how to help but we are learning.

Cynthia: (She holds up a paper and reads the question.) Do girls die from this?

Doctor Tomo: Some short-term complications include fatal bleeding, anemia, urinary infection, septicemia, tetanus, gangrene, necrotizing fasciitis, which is a flesh-eating disease, and endometritis. It is not known how many girls and women die as a result of the practice, because complications may not be recognized or reported.

Cynthia: I'm really going to send up some prayers on this one. Who does the actual cutting on the girls?

Doctor Tomo: FGM is often performed by traditional circumcisers or cutters who do not have any medical training. Anesthesia and antiseptics are not generally used. It is often carried out using sharpened knives, scissors, scalpels, pieces of glass, or razor blades. Too many times the tools are not sterilized. But in some countries it may be done by a medical professional. That is how entrenched it is in the culture.

FGM often happens against a girl's will and/or without her consent, and like you have heard today, girls may be forcibly restrained. If you are born into communities where this is practiced, then you may become a victim.

Cynthia: Well, this was really informative. I hate to stop now but unfortunately, our time is up. This has certainly been enlightening. I know I have learned something from this discussion. Thank you ladies for coming here to tell your story. You are very courageous. We appreciate your information. (The women acknowledge the appreciation.)

Layla: Thank you for allowing us to have our say.

Cynthia: Thank you Dr. Tomo for being with us today. The information you have given us is so valuable.

Doctor Tomo: I am glad to be able to offer this information. It is important. Thank you for inviting us.

<u>**Cynthia**</u>: To our audience, here and at home, I know that you are leaving with an abundance and so am I. Although I have read about this topic, tonight has opened my eyes even more. This is Cynthia Goode signing off! Thank you for joining us. We will be coming to you next month with another intriguing program. Don't miss it! See you next time. Good night!

The Continuous Nightmare (Skit)

(Dedicated to Science Fiction Writers Octavia Butler, Stephen King & Rod Serling)

> *Don't stop dreaming just because you had a nightmare.*

– Jill Scott

Characters

Woman
Girl
Mother

Scene

7:00 a.m. in a bedroom. A small hand reaches from the bed and pushes a button. A woman smiles as she opens the door and peeks in. Three walls in the room are painted hot pink. A fourth wall is covered in cork and filled with drawings, family pictures, graded schoolwork, and report cards. The sheets and pillowcases match the wall in color. White flowers punctuate a quilt that almost hides the form of a small body. The window above a white desk and chair is covered with sheer white curtains enhanced with pink polka dots. A white lamp sits behind a clock radio that suddenly begins to shriek. A small hand reaches from the bed and clamps down on the clock radio. The noise halts.

***

Scene 1

<u>Woman:</u> Time to get up, Lazy Bones.

<u>Girl:</u> (A little girl rises from the bed.) Okay, Mommy. I am glad you woke me up. I was having another bad dream.

<u>Woman:</u> Oh, I am so sorry, sweetheart. Nightmares can be scary. You're okay, though. Home, safe and sound. Get yourself washed up and ready for school. Your clothes are on the chair. Make up your bed and I will see you in the kitchen.

<u>Girl:</u> (The little girl stretches and gets started. The woman heads back to the kitchen.) Okay, Mommy.

Scene 2 (8:00 a.m. in a kitchen)

(The woman is working between the stove and the sink and the girl enters. The woman's back is to her girl as she glances over her shoulder.)

<u>Woman</u>: I love that outfit on you. Pink is your color. Are you ready for Miss Johnson today? I know you think she is mean but you are doing so well, so don't worry about that. Just keep on doing what you do. So, what was your dream about this time?

<u>Girl</u>: MMMM! It smells so good in here. Pancakes and bacon?

<u>Woman</u>: Yes!

<u>Girl</u>: I thought you were only going to fix that on the weekends. Cereal is okay with me.

<u>Woman</u>: I just feel like treating you today. You are such a sweet little person. So, tell me about that dream.

<u>Girl</u>: I dreamed the same old thing. Some lady was pretending to be you, again. Momma, she looks just like you. She smiles like you and her voice is exactly like yours. I know it's not you because she has black bump on her cheek. She keeps trying to get me to go with her. She has candy and toys. I almost went one time but I ran, but this time I went!

<u>Woman</u>: That black bump is called a mole. Some people call them beauty spots. Maybe I would be prettier if I had one. I am surprised that you went with her this time. Why did you do that?

<u>Girl</u>: Because it always stops when I say no and get away from her. I always wake up! I just wanted to see what would happen. I hoped that if I went, I could get it to stop.

<u>Woman</u>: So, what happened?

<u>Girl</u>: She said we could go to a fun place. I could eat whatever I wanted and play all kinds of games. She even had my favorite books. Then while we were riding in the car, I saw something strange. We passed a big sign that said "Welcome to Kinder-Garten Town. We like children. They taste good." My real mother would have known that I started reading last year. I jumped out of the car when she came to a stop sign and ran as fast as I could. That's when you woke me up.

Woman: Good! Perfect timing. (She places a plate of food on the table in front of the girl.) Here is your favorite breakfast, just the way you like! I put the butter and syrup on them for you.

Girl: (The girl looks down at the food as her mother leans in for a kiss. She takes a deep smell of the food.) Yum! (As she closes her eyes and puts her cheek up for her mother's daily kiss, she realizes that her mother would know that she likes jelly on her pancakes, not syrup. When she opens her eyes, she sees a cheek with a small mole beside the smile coming toward her. She screams.) You're not my mother. (She jumps out of her seat and runs.)

Scene 3 (7:00 a.m. same day)

(A clock alarm goes off. A small hand reaches from the bed and pushes a button. A woman smiles as she opens the door to a bedroom and peeks in. Three walls in the room are painted hot pink. A fourth wall is covered in cork and filled with drawings, family pictures, graded schoolwork, and report cards. The sheets and pillowcases match the wall in color. White flowers punctuate a quilt that almost hides the form of a small body. The window above a white desk and chair is covered with sheer white curtains enhanced with pink polka dots. A white lamp sits behind a clock radio that suddenly begins to shriek.

A small hand reaches from the bed and clamps down on the clock radio. The noise halts.)

Mother: Time to get up, Lazy Bones.

Daughter: (A little girl sits up in the bed, wipes her eyes, glares at the woman suspiciously and then smiles.) Okay, Mommy! I am glad it's really you! I keep having this dream. The places change but someone pretending to be you is always there. I think I know what to do now when that happens.

Mother: How do you know when it is really me?

Daughter: That is my secret. Maybe someday I will tell you!

Chapter 3
Personally Speaking

– Madeleine Albright

My Quadrangle:
A Place to Remember (1962 -)

Carnegie Library (1909), Cheyney University, Pennsylvania, November 10, 2009. Public domain image. From Wikimedia Commons, the free media repository. Original file (1,582 × 1,143 pixels, file size: 335 KB, MIME type: image/jpeg). https://www.blackpast.org/african-american-history/cheyney-university-pennsylvania-1837/

Leaving the safely of home and parents is a big deal. Some parents talk about the freedom of becoming an empty nester. Some go through a kind of mourning and others celebrate the success of their child moving into another phase of life.

I didn't know if I was happy or sad that day when my parents drove me to college. It was only an hour away from home but it seemed far away. Strangely, I felt abandoned when I waved to my parents as they drove away. My father had protested leaving me because boys were eyeing the new girls arriving. My mother calmed him down and gave the order.

"She is going to stay right here."

My parents did not look back. Tears streamed down my face. I had never thought that I was actually leaving home when I went to college, not leaving home forever.

Packing had been exciting. We took our time picking out the right outfits, the linen, the supplies, and the school tools. It was fun.

Leaving me there was different. I couldn't feel the fun that was to come. At that moment, I was pretty sad. This was scary, especially for a child who had never been away from home except to spend the night with family. I was not emotionally ready for this.

Although folks were coming and going, I felt alone. I headed back to my new dorm room. I closed the door and sat on the windowsill to watch the activity below and wait for my roommates to arrive. I hoped that they would like me and that I would like them!

There was laughter, hugging, and shaking of hands as I looked down from the window. Joyful spirits floated about the huge lawn, the quadrangle. I could almost imagine college students of days gone by going through these same motions, only dressed according to their day. The school was established way back in 1937. This was 1962.

My mother had left me some fried chicken and slices of her famous pound cake to share. Although it smelled delicious,

I was not hungry. I put it in the window to stay cool so that it would be fine when those hunger pangs would slip up on me. I looked forward to sharing with my new roomies.

Suddenly, I heard singing and stomping as six young men dressed in purple and gold marched in unison. They chanted the words "Lincoln University" and something in a foreign language. About eight other men seemed to hover around them, giving directions. It was fascinating. The only thing I had seen similar to that was the drill team I had been a part of at home.

Three beautiful girls wearing crowns seemed to be dressed for a special occasion. They had large ribbons with letters on them draped across their dresses. They walked about the yard welcoming people.

My roommates finally came and we had a wonderful time getting to know each other. "So, this is what college is like," I thought.

That window became my sight on a new world as well as my refrigerator in winter. In those days, all you brought to college were clothes and linens. All meals were in the cafeteria. Once a month we treated ourselves to a steak sandwich or hoagie. One of the boys who had a car would drive to the nearest town to fill out our orders.

I could see so much from my perch. People holding hands, stopping for the forbidden kiss at the designated corner, birds preparing for seasons, squirrels on a mission, a lone fox streaking about at night, professors swinging briefcases heading to classes, and folks talking while sitting on the benches. There was so much to see.

Whenever I wanted to think, I sat in my window and gazed into the quadrangle. It was a massive yard outlined by strong stone historical buildings populated with happy people. I liked it. The boys' and girls' dorms were at each end of the quad like bookends to a grassy knoll. The sides were filled with classroom buildings, a library, an administration building, and an auditorium with a stage large enough to use as a gym.

This was my new home. We were told to keep it sacred, no trash-tossing, holding hands, or walking across the grass. We tried to follow the rules. Room Mothers were watching to make sure.

Each season offered a new essence. The fall awed us with leaves of many colors. In the winter, we could no longer jump rope on the sidewalks because the ice pieces smiled through the snow to produce a greeting card picture. It was perfect for snowmen, snow angels, and snowball fights. Then spring would bring fresh smells of flowers punctuating the renewal of the quadrangle. There was no picking of the flowers. They were ours already. When summers pulled me away, I couldn't wait to get back in the fall.

New buildings began to surrounded the old. A cafeteria was behind the girls' dorm serving three meals a day. Then new dorms were built on a new quad and I had a new window. The first real gymnasium with the Olympic-size pool emitted a smell of chlorine beaconing swimmers. Just thinking about how the school had grown from 1873 until now was rewarding. This was my world and then it was not.

Graduation on the quad was as it should be: solemn, important, prideful, and rewarding. It was what I had worked for.

I sat in my window talking to my roommates in the new dorm about staying in touch. After packing my things, I was ready, but not really ready, to leave. I took my last look at the new quadrangle and headed up to the old one for one more look. Then I waved goodbye as my parents and I drove away. Tears streamed down my face. I did not look back. This time I knew that I was off to the next step in my life. I had enjoyed the last one and hoped that what was ahead would be just as good.

It's been over fifty years and I still miss the college. Every fall, I made sure to go to Homecoming just to feel the friendships and the love of the school. Whenever I visit the campus I find a bench on the old quadrangle and sit, smiling and remembering. Sometimes tears of appreciation run down my face as I enjoy just being in the moment.

The Indigenous (1909)

I have begun to nurture an inherent need to know about my ancestors. I think that knowing my origins might help in gaining a better understanding of who I am and the world as I have come to know. Finding out about ancestry may provide a sense of place and belonging. Louis Gates' show *Finding Your Roots* is an attention getter. It makes me ashamed that I didn't pay more attention to the history of my family and ask questions while I could.

A picture of my maternal great grandparents, John and Sophie Williams, sat in a velvet mat, in a golden frame proudly on my grandmother's cocktail table. When I first saw it, I wondered about those two figures posing in wrinkled clothes. They reminded me of homeless people and I wondered if their lives had been difficult. Here I was, an educated woman and a leader in prominent associations, and these were MY ancestors?

My friends had walls filled with pictures that complimented the beauty of their families. They were so proud of the presentations and would give historical documentation about who was in the picture and where it was taken. The pride was evident. However, behind my smile, I wished I had some beautiful old family pictures to put on my walls.

Their ancestors were well dressed with perfectly coiffed tresses, lovely white dresses, and bows in their long hair. Some wore impressive hats. The men, tall and slender, donned nice suits, white starched shirts, and shined shoes as they posed for a professional photographer. Some of the people could pass for white and seemed to live in impressive homes. I am not mad at that. I understand the circumstances. Folks had to do whatever was necessary to try to have a prosperous life. However, after seeing their galleries, I could not even think of hanging my great grandparents' picture on my wall. I would be embarrassed for anyone to see it. I didn't want anyone to associate that picture with me. I felt ashamed. Strangely, I felt ashamed of feeling ashamed.

Years later, when I was moving, I came across that picture in some of my mother's things that had been stored. I started to hide it in a drawer away from the eyes of any guests that might be visiting. However, this time I stared at the two characters who were standing straight and as tall as short people could. I hadn't noticed that their faces were intriguing. I had been too busy paying attention to their clothing. I hadn't looked beyond my first impression. I wanted to find out more about them. My old critiques of what and who I thought they were seemed irrelevant.

I began asking relatives questions about them. I had been told previously bits of their story, but I hadn't paid attention. Actually, not too much had been shared. Since the older members of the family were passing away, it was difficult to put the pieces of this heredity puzzle in place.

It was evident that this interesting-looking couple were people of the soil; farmers. John Williams had told his children stories of being a slave as a child. They said that he had arrived in the United States from Jamaica. My genealogy search agreed it was the Caribbean but specified it was Bermuda, not Jamaica. That was a little bit of a conflict but not a concern. A thorough search could clear that up.

Evidently, when the Union Army marched through Virginia to make sure slaves knew they were free, he was hidden in the upper part of a barn, daring not to question. Later he realized why. He became one of those people that was not aware of his freedom until about a year after Abraham Lincoln signed the Emancipation Proclamation. That is when the story blurs until he is grown. I have some work to do to uncover those years.

I wondered if he had been married previously and had a family earlier in his life, because he was much older than my great grandmother. No one seemed to know, but it made sense. This new wife was only twelve years old when he married her. She was the daughter of his Native American housekeeper. This man had a housekeeper! She was a member of the Blackfoot Native American Tribe. They had thirteen children. I was told that large families were common for farmers. Working on the farm was a family affair. A couple of the children born to them died right after birth, so there were eleven that survived into adulthood. My grandmother was the second oldest child and the only one sent out to work in the home of a white family.

I was told that my great grandmother, the woman in the picture, raised turkeys. I found out later that she played the piano at church and taught in a one-room school. I was told that she was admired for her cooking and for her long hair, which she braided into two plaits. One of their children told their children who told their children that his great grandmother gave their children doses of honey twice a year to keep them healthy. She died when she was in her early forties. That is the breadth of my knowledge about her life.

John Williams was the short man standing proudly in the wrinkled suit. His attire did not portray success. He farmed numerous acres and did not discriminate in hiring. One of his agricultural successes was producing molasses from sugar cane and harvesting honey for his beehives. They had a mule, chickens, and a press to process the honey. However, his main crop was sorghum. I had never heard of it. I went straight to the computer to research it.

I found that sorghum is a genus of about twenty-five species of flowering plants in the grass family. Some of these species are grown as cereals for human consumption and some to feed pasture animals. Even today there is a global demand for sorghum. When I mentioned it, I was told that it is sold in health food stores today. One woman said that she had some in her pantry. It seems that China was purchasing around $1 billion worth of American sorghum a year to feed livestock as a substitute for corn until 2018, when China imposed retaliatory duties on American sorghum as part of the trade war.

My little great grandfather had his finger on a monetary pulse. His appearance in the photo did not represent his accomplishments. In my pictures, I guessed they may have been wearing their dressed up, going-to-church look. Together, they raised a family and lived well. I wonder what they would think of us if they could see how their progeny turned out.

I look at the picture periodically. I am impressed by both of them. John was a smart businessman who realized that a different attire could present as successful. Evidently that was not important to him. He lived to be 102 years old.

My mother used to laugh when she told some of the interactions between her grandfathers. John, her mother's father, had been a slave as a child. He was about 5'10" and had a dark brown complexion. Her father's father, who was the son of a slave woman and the plantation master, was about 6' tall with light skin. Mother said that they became great friends and the sight of the two of them together always made her smile.

I am glad they took the picture. It is the only one that I have ever seen of them. His suit and her dress had not been ironed. However, he had on a three-piece suit and her silk dress was probably store-bought. Although their shoes lacked shine, they were probably their "Sunday Shoes," which meant they had more than one pair. Those were not work shoes. A polished and impressive presentation might have caused a problem for their safety in Virginia at the time. Whether intentional or not, that was just fine. The picture had been professionally taken, so evidently they had the currency to pay for it.

Today when I look at that picture, I smile and think, "Well, John and Sophie Williams, you did well! I have your picture sitting on my shelf because I am so proud that you are my ancestors. I hope that wherever you are, you are proud of me, too!"

First Kiss: Sexual Abuse/Love? (1956)

Joy was always excited to celebrate holidays. Her family decorated and feasted at each one. Her birthday was her favorite. Thanksgiving was for family. Christmas was about the birth of Jesus, decorating, and getting and giving gifts. Easter was a special church day when the family dressed up and the children recited Easter pieces in front of the congregation. She especially liked Valentine's Day because it was about family love.

On Valentine's Day, her father would always give her a card and a small box of chocolates. Her mother would get flowers and candy. These are a part of wonderful childhood memories.

Every year, her mother bought her a booklet of Valentine's cards to cut out of the pages, fold, and place in the little envelopes. Joy would work seriously to create one for every child in her class and a larger one for the teacher. She placed the cards and some heart-shaped candies in little bags and put them in her book bag to take to school with a box of chocolates for the teacher. At the end of the school day, the teachers always left time to give out the cards and eat treats.

However, Joy had a disturbing experience on Valentine's

Day when she was in the fifth grade. On that morning, she ran the two blocks to school, carrying her lunch box and swinging a book bag filled with gifts. As she ran across the playground, the bell rang. She could see the children running to line up with their classes. She had plenty of time before the lines would follow the teachers to their rooms.

When she reached her class line, something surprising happened. She had to stop because a curly-haired boy grabbed her arm. She knew that he was a sixth-grader named Randy because his sister was in her class. Joy wondered what he wanted. He had never said anything to her before.

Calmly, he whispered, "I'm going to kiss you today!" He laughed and ran off to line up with his class. It bothered her but Joy thought he was probably kidding!

Each morning, class started with reading and spelling. After a short recess, they would return for handwriting. Math, social studies, and science came after lunch. The art and music teachers visited once a week and Joy was the only student in the school who worked once a week with a visiting speech therapist. She had difficulty pronouncing *sh*, *th*, and *wh* blends. Her mother called it a thick tongue, but she was progressing rapidly. It never deterred her from answering questions in class.

On special days, the teacher would make sure to have enough time for a party at the end of the day. The children were always excited and their behavior was the best. That day, the special event was to be a visit from the teacher's husband. He had a farm and harvested honey from beehives. As part of the party, he was going to do a lesson on bees, show the class the three kinds of bees in the hive, and give them a chance to taste their honey on a cracker.

Most of the children brought their lunches to school to eat in the classroom because there was no cafeteria. Joy usually went home for lunch because her mother made that decision. She wanted to stay and take the specially picked out lunch box they bought each year. At least on holidays when everyone stayed for lunch, Joy did too. This was one of those days.

When they finished eating, the children headed out to the playground. After lunch, the whole school had recess at the same time. She loved it when all of the children were outside together. Joy's plan for that day was to play Double Dutch. Since there was only one rope, the girls took turns on who got a chance to play. She loved jumping rope.

As soon as Joy came out of the school door, there stood Randy, arms folded and staring at her. She started running and he was on her heels. Joy hoped he wasn't fast enough to catch her. She could outrun almost everyone in fifth grade. Her red dress was blowing, her coat was flapping, and her braids were flopping about, but Joy didn't care. She had to get to the "Base," the place of safety for all Tag games. It would be her only safe place.

The Base was not near the building. It was not even on the blacktop. It was way out on the grass by the baseball diamond. The Base was a heavy wooden and metal box that probably covered a well. A concrete bottom sealed it to the ground. When playing Tag, it was important to get on that Base to be safe. She knew that if she got to the Base, she would be okay. Everyone knew no one could bother you there. It was so big that about five children could sit on it. She hoped that Randy would give up so she could play Double Dutch. She ran like she was in a race and she wanted to win first place.

Finally, safe on the Base, she sneered at him, hoping that he would give up and leave. Instead, he stood with folded arms and stared at her. Joy lost her recess that day. All of the children were having such a good time. Some were even playing Tag and using the Base for safety. It was not strange that the teacher on Recess Duty did not come toward them to see what was going on. Joy didn't scream out, so the teacher may have thought that they were playing a game or just talking as friends.

"Friends?" she thought. "I don't even know this boy." She was not scared of him. She was angry and thought he would get tired of waiting and missing his own recess and leave. However, she did not move off of that Base. He had placed himself strategically between the Base and the blacktop and stood daring her with his eyes. She would have to be Jesse Owens to get past him, but she was trying to figure out a plan to get around him.

In the midst of her planning, the bell rang. She was furious. She had lost her precious recess. He smiled and said, "Now what are you going to do?"

Joy acted as if she was not going to move but they both knew she had to get to the class line. She sat! He stood. She sat! He stood his ground. Just as the lines started to go into the building, Joy jumped off of the far side of the Base, sprinted around it, and darted toward the building. She assumed he was in pursuit but didn't take the time to look back to see. He didn't seem to care about getting to his class line. She had to make it to the finish line, the door. Just as she started down the incline to the blacktop, in mid-stride, a hand gripped her shoulder. It was him! She had to slow down so she wouldn't fall. He leaned in quickly as she tried to break his hold. He was stronger and she couldn't get free. All of a sudden, she felt his lips on her cheek and heard him scoff, "See, I told you I was going to kiss you today!" Then off he ran, laughing, just in time to be the last person in his class line.

Joy was furious but she got there in time to walk in with her class. She thought, "Who did he think he was? Why did he choose her? How dare he do that!" It took all of her energy to just get to the school door. She was tired.

Joy was so glad that no one saw what happened. However, she thought that maybe if someone did see it, they would report him. She just didn't know how to handle this situation. She was glad it was over. At least she thought it was over. Joy didn't tell the teacher or her mother. Randy would have gotten into a lot of trouble and she didn't want anyone to think that she encouraged him in any way.

Randy never said anything else to Joy and she certainly never spoke to him. She saw him on the playground playing basketball, baseball, or football with the boys. Joy just wanted to keep track of him. She never saw him look her way, but she kept an eye on him and made sure she stayed in a group of girls. It seemed so strange that he did that. She never mentioned it to his sister in her class. She probably didn't know about it because she never said anything.

After about a week, Joy stopped looking for Randy on the playground. She wasn't going to run if he tried it again because that didn't work and she would miss recess. She wondered, had she stayed with the other children, he might not have done it. If it happened again, she was going to tell the teacher and her mother.

After about two weeks, Joy began to enjoy recess time once again. As for Randy, he never bothered Joy again.

Over the years, Joy wondered what happened to Randy. She heard that Randy was in jail for stealing. She wasn't surprised.

Bottles & the Environment (1955)

In the 1950s, my parents began to discuss environmental issues. They decided to take steps to do what they could. I had no idea what they were talking about at first. To quell the growth of junk, my mother encouraged the reuse of glass soda bottles. Dad said it would reduce trash loaded into the dumps.

Once a month my mother chose one of us children to collect the soda bottles in her beauty shop. Now that I am older, I realize that she made sure that we all got an equal opportunity to take ownership of the bottles. Instead of seeing this as a way to help the environment or as a job, we classified it as an opportunity to get candy. When bottles were returned to the store, the soda company would collect them from the stores, sterilize them, and refill them for the next sales. Those bottles represented candy money.

Mother's customers received complimentary gifts like samples of Avon products, her favorite crackers of the week, and bottles of soda while waiting to be beautified. I often encouraged the drinking of soda with a polite "Do you care for a drink of water or soda?" They thought that I was the perfect host. Actually, I was scheming to build my fortune.

On Sundays, we were treated to sodas and a dessert as part of our dinner. We drank water, lemonade, Kool-Aid, and iced tea on the other days. Mother bought large bottles for the family meals and smaller bottles for the beauty shop. We inherited all of the empty soda bottles and kept them in crates until it was time to shop.

Always ahead of her time, Mommy introduced recycling as a way of saving the Earth. We, on the other hand, could treat ourselves by buying candy with the money we earned for bringing back the bottles to the store. I even figured out how to create a profit from the financial experience. The small bottles were worth a penny, but the big ones cashed in at three cents at Mr. Mahoney's corner store. I assumed that he was earning revenue from the soda companies on the reuse of the bottles, too, so everyone profited from the venture. My parents helped the environment, Mr. Mahoney got paid for turning in the bottles, and we, the children, bought candy.

Earning twenty-five cents might generate more than twenty-five pieces of candy. I made sure to buy some candy that had two pieces for a penny or Jaw Breakers, those big, round, hard candies. You turned colors and flavors and you could suck on one for a couple of days. At night I would let it rest on a napkin on the windowsill until morning. That much candy could hold me over until my next turn. I figured with four of us, we should get a chance once every other month because most of the time it took two weeks to accumulate enough bottles to fill the wagon. To insure getting some sweets when it was not my turn, I negotiated as if on Wall Street. I explained that by sharing two pennies worth for each of us, we all could have candy from each trip. They bought the idea.

My order from their caches was always Mary Janes. One penny bought one Mary Janes and there were two pieces in each package. In that way, I would get two pieces of candy. When it was my turn, they could also order a penny's worth of candy from my cache.

Lining up my bottles in a wagon took time and strategic planning. It was like packing a carton of eggs for the serious 3three-block trip. The large bottles were first. I placed them as guards for the smaller ones piled on, because sidewalk bumps had to be treated defensively. The bars on the sides of the wagon allowed for more room than the regular red wagon. If there were extras, I carried them gingerly in a paper bag and pulled the wagon with my other hand. I couldn't afford to lose any of them. It was imperative to avoid sidewalk bumps in making sure that my precious cargo arrived safe and sound.

The biggest challenge was not the transport. Usually two or three neighborhood school candy beggars would hover outside of the store, waiting for unsuspecting victims. They would greedily watch their bewildered prey enter, even holding the door open while smirking! They were prepared to bullet the word "Hunks" as a candy shopper exited. They were always at the front door because Mr. Mahoney didn't allow anyone to hang out at his delivery door. The children's candy law was that if they said "Hunks" as the purchaser left the store, the candy had to be shared with them. I have no idea who made that one up. The skill came with beating them by saying "No Hunks" first.

You had to outsmart them before your purchase was really your own. They got me on my very first trip, but I was ready for them after that. I figured out how to navigate a winning timing for my exits. One time I left through the rear door while Mr. Mahoney was helping other customers. He was so busy that no one saw me leave. One time, I talked my uncle into walking to the store with me, just to get some exercise. They didn't dare approach me and my candy that time. The candy pirates knew I was a challenge, so I had to make a different plan each time.

Once I had the cash for the bottles, I would meticulously shop for penny candy like Tootsie Rolls, waxed lips, candy cigarettes, root beer barrels, Jawbreakers with Bubble Gum centers, Turkish Taffies, pumpkin seeds, and, of course, Mary Janes. There were many choices. I took my time and refused to allow the impatient clerk to rush me. This was business. I wanted the most and best for my hard-earned money.

I kept my eye on the enemies lurking outside, waiting to capture my treasure. I had to time my exit to outsmart them. I intentionally took so much time that the enemy's attention drifted elsewhere. I had to get my mother a Jewish pickle from the barrel, a box of Cheese Bits, and a Pepsi. Once I had everything, I hid behind some tall boxes at the window so they couldn't see me. I tiptoed to the door when a lady was ready to leave with her purchases. When she opened the door, I was right behind her and yelled, "No Hunks!" I strolled proudly out with a bag of candy in hand and pulled my wagon with my mother's order in it. I walked with the lady to the corner. When I got around the corner, I ran all the way home.

I had won the day. I walked happily but quickly through the door, grinning. I was already planning my next escape. I didn't dare eat anything until I got home, handed out the Mary Janes, and took a deep breath.

These experiences taught me to evaluate life situations and try to negotiate valuable conclusions that work fairly for all involved while outwitting predators. Then I could enjoy the rewards of my labors.

"What Goes on In the Beauty Shop Stays In the Beauty Shop"

My mother closed her beauty shop in a rented building. She found out that some of her hired beauticians had encouraged customers to come to their houses for service at a cheaper rate. Her trust level was gone. She created a shop in the basement of our house. A construction company developed a space large enough for a sink for shampooing, spots for dyers, a place for her dressing table and display cabinet, and a powder room. The floor of black and white tiles paid homage to the barbershops of that era. There was a private entrance from the driveway, which worked perfectly for customers. That shop became a haven for women seeking beauty treatments and inspiring conversations.

People talked about everything in my mother's beauty shop. My dad said that happened in the barber shop, too. "Way back in the day, barber shops were places for medical help, also. You could get a haircut, shave, and some medicine for a sore. I bet you didn't know that! Both barber and beauty shops deal with health-related issues even today. Many psychological problems are alleviated there. Some men have escaped unforeseen terror because their women found answers when sharing problems while sitting under a dryer."

He was right! I heard all kinds of stories in the beauty shop. They talked loud so that their voices wouldn't be drowned out by the sound of the dryer. That made it easy for me to listen. I didn't have to eavesdrop, just pretended I wasn't paying attention. I even learned about politics by listening to their debates. Now I realize that the shop was an early "focus group," long before the term became popular. Due to honesty, respect, and fear of my mother, I did not become a blackmailer. The things I heard while shampooing hair were often funny and always interesting. Oh, the money I could have made from those discussions.

I could shampoo with the best of the shampooers. I was always complimented.

"Girl, you certainly make sure my hair is sparkling clean," or "Thank you so much. That massage is wonderful and my hair smells so good."

One day a woman who owned the local store came into the shop. Her hair was a mess. Everyone knew that she was rich. When I tried to comb her hair, I found that the buildup of dirt and a greasy substance was so thick on her scalp that I couldn't crack it with a comb. So I wet the hair, hoping that the water would soften whatever was impacted on her scalp. When that didn't work, I called in the professional, my mother. I didn't want to say anything to embarrass the customer, so I just pointed and said that I had to go to the bathroom.

I could tell by my mother's expression that she had never seen anything like it. She reached under the sink and grabbed a bottle of Mr. Clean, making sure that the woman couldn't see it. Mr. Clean was a new product and we used it for wiping off spills and mopping the floor. I went into the bathroom and flushed the toilet to sound like I was telling the truth. My mother poured a capful of Mr. Clean into an empty shampoo bottle and gave instructions.

"There you go. Use this, my special treatment. Apply it and let it set for two minutes then shampoo and three rinse times. Use the other shampoo once and rinse well before you condition. Make sure you rinse well and the hair is soft." She smiled at the customer and returned to her station. It worked. When my mother finished with that lady, she looked like a new woman. She became a loyal customer every two weeks.

We laughed about that event over the years. That woman had to know that she had a hair situation that was pretty awful.

What happened to me one day was a prime example of how words can get you into trouble. It was a spa environment for women, but not for me.

In the early stages of being a teenager, I made the mistake of mentioning a forbidden word. I didn't know it was taboo until I said it. It was not a cuss word or a curse word. I was trained not to use dirty words.

I was startled by a response. My mother asked me about my day and I repeated a conversation overheard on the school bus. Everyone paid attention when I said the word "pregnant!" The girls say it on the bus all the time, so I was surprised that all talking stopped suddenly. The kids were always talking about someone being pregnant. Usually they were talking about somebody's mother, but that day it was one of the girls who was absent from school for about a week. I felt sorry for the girl and couldn't imagine what that must be like. When one of the girls said that a wedding was about to happen, everyone seemed happy about it.

So I said the word "pregnant" loud and clear. No one had ever told me that the word was a "No-no!" I clearly remember the reaction to it. I was shampooing a lady and the world seemed to stop. That moment reminded me of one of my aunt's colloquial sayings, "Loose lips sink ships!" My ship sank that day and I didn't want to drown. There was no warning noise. Suddenly a quiet that seemed louder than a foghorn engulfed my soul! Evidently it was a generational word not meant for my generation. It was Grown Folks Talk!

That is when a conversation took place that I would have preferred to happen with my mother in private. I was so glad I didn't say who was pregnant. I bet some of the ladies wanted to ask me who it was, but the wrath of my mother might come down on us all. The fear that resided in my heart that day was new and scary.

The chill in the room made me repent. It was evident that I had crossed a line. If I had been Catholic, I would have grabbed some beads and spouted out a "Hail Mary, full of grace!" to protect me. My mother, who stood only 4'11", gave me that glare that often made the dog stop in his tracks. Even my big strong father would back up at that look.

She softly said, "Define that word!" When she said it, I swear it echoed in my mind like I was in the Grand Canyon; "pregnant, pregnant, pregnant!" The stillness was troubling. All conversations with the three customers in the shop had stopped and all eyes were upon me. I think the lady under the dryer turned it off so that she could bear witness to what lay ahead. Having a witness might have been a good thing, though. It was embarrassing.

I figured that I handled myself in debates at school—however, this was not the time to win. So, I gave what I thought she wanted. "Pregnant means that somebody is having a baby." I didn't know all of the ramifications of the how and why, but I thought I did a pretty good job of explaining it. It seemed simple enough to me. At that time, my confused mind believed that a girl could get pregnant by kissing a boy.

That misconception was my parents' fault. I was sheltered from life situations. The fifth-grade lesson on menstruation had not been particularly clear, either. Now I was only in the seventh grade at the time, but I knew my definition was right. The eye piercings that stabbed my soul meant for me to stop right there and not use that word ever again, especially in front of adults. It was the word that caught their attention, not the definition or the idea that somebody was pregnant.

I didn't even know who was pregnant. I knew it wasn't me. I can't imagine what would have happened if it was me but it couldn't have been me and I was going to make sure that it wasn't going to be me. This was entirely too much investigation.

My mother looked me in the eyes and said, "That is a private word. I will explain something to you later. Now go upstairs and take the chicken out of the refrigerator and pick out any feathers left on it."

I knew how to do that and I also knew that I better never, ever let that word have anything to do with me. There would be no babies...ever! I took a silent oath. I thought that this had been the perfect time to talk about the word, but the opportunity passed. Evidently my mother did not. So much learning has been abandoned because specific conversations are awkward. This might have been the perfect time to bring out some truths. However, this *was* a lesson in what not to say in the company of adults.

Later we had The Talk. My father said, "You have to think! You could be gossiping...and that is not a good thing." I couldn't figure that out at first, because gossiping was going on every day in that shop. Women would share all kinds of information, but I was a child and "children were to be seen and not heard."

My mother explained, "Some things are private. You could have caused a problem for a young girl, especially if what you had heard was not true. It was not your business to talk about, especially in a group of people. The women in the shop could have caused a young girl some serious problems. Come to me if you are unsure about something." I didn't think I was unsure. Since I was confused, I decided to not talk about anything in the shop. My grandmother always said, "Speak when spoken to."

Lesson learned! I would do as my mother ordered. "Watch your mouth!" she said. She had made it seem as if the word was the problem and it was. However, the greater issue was that it could have been a personal situation that need not be discussed by strangers.

The beauty shop was an interesting little world of its own. Ladies came in the door chatting with each other and sometimes to themselves. Strangely, I never heard a woman curse or cuss. They considered themselves to be ladies of quality. When serious talk began, I was dismissed. I was not the kind of child that would hide somewhere and try to listen. Actually, I was not interested in their conversations. Maybe it was because I obeyed my parents—then again, I always felt that my mother had secret powers and would find out if I messed up. Nothing was worth that.

It was impossible to not hear their talks. They rarely spoke quietly. While becoming beautiful, the ladies cried about sad things and laughed about happy things. They encouraged each other and shared information. I loved being there even if I couldn't be in the conversations unless spoken to. New and interesting things happened every day, but I knew that what was said in the beauty shop stayed in the beauty shop. At least my lips were sealed.

Lessons on the First Job (1960)

My mother called me into the dining room, where she sat at a table covered with papers. She pointed to a chair. I knew what that meant: a mother-daughter chat. I prayed silently, "Dear Lord, help me!"

"Have a seat. I want to talk to you."

I assumed this was going to be one of those talks that I usually tried unsuccessfully to avoid. I sat.

"It is time for you to fill out these papers to get a summer job. Your sixteenth birthday is coming up."

"But Mommy, I am working for you in the beauty shop." She never looked up.

"You need to have the experience of working outside of the house. It'll be good for you." She handed me an ink pen and a paper that said "Certification for Employment."

"Sign right there."

"Where do you think I should work?"

"Your cousins work every summer at the hospital. Why not try that? Your aunt thinks it is a nice little job! Let's try it!"

I thought "Let's" means "Let us." I was sure that she didn't mean she was going to work there, too, but I didn't say that. I wasn't able to handle what that might bring.

I filled out the form and said, "I think I would like to be a Candy Striper. Some of the girls in my class are Candy Stripers. Their uniforms are cute."

"That's a volunteer job. You are not there to look cute. You need a job that pays. You are going to need some spending change when you go to college. We'll put it in your bank account. No, they will probably put you right in the kitchen with your cousins or serving food to the patients."

I was not excited about those choices, but I filled in the information on the paper. She put it in an envelope, stamped it, and told me to take it to the mailbox down the corner.

About two weeks later, my approved papers came in the mail. My mother called the hospital and made an appointment for my interview for 9 a.m. the next day. The dietician seemed nice and she hired me during the interview. I received an unattractive uniform and a hair net and was assigned a locker. My job title was "Caller." I had no idea what that meant.

She said, "Each day, upon arrival, all workers must sign in at the office and check the assignment list. You will keep the same job all summer." My mother was writing everything in a notebook. "It pays minimum wages, eighty-five cents an hour. Of course taxes will be taken out of that. Are you able to start tomorrow?"

My mother replied, "Yes. What are her hours?"

"She will work the dinner shift. So she should be here by 3:00 p.m. and will work until 8:00 p.m. from Monday to Thursday. Come with me so I can show you her station."

We followed her to the huge kitchen. It was evening, so no one was there. She went over to a long metal appliance that I had never seen before.

"This is the steam table. It is a conveyor belt. You will stand here at the beginning of the steam table on this box. There will be a pile of menu papers that each patient has completed on this table beside you. You will call out the names of the people and what they have selected for their dinner. I will be here to help you on the first day. Don't worry, you will catch on."

I figured the job wouldn't be that difficult and I could master the task.

"When you stand at the head of the steam, the conveyor belt will begin and so will you. Place a plate, napkin, glass, straw, and silverware on a tray like this." She demonstrated. "Trays will be here to your right. Before putting the tray on the conveyor belt, call off the ordered items from each menu selection paper. Put that menu paper under the plate and place the tray on the conveyor belt. As the tray moves slowly down the conveyor belt, the selected food items will be placed on the plates by employees who are good at what they do." My mother was listening intently. "The trays will be complete by the time they end their journey. Someone will gather the trays according to assigned rooms, place them onto a cart, and deliver them to the patients. After the last plate leaves the kitchen and the steam table is emptied and cleaned, it will be breaktime for dinner in the cafeteria."

My mother asked, "Is that the end of her workday?"

"No. There is a clean-up mode. When the trays return, the kitchen crew washes the dishes in the large dishwashing machines over there. They must be sure they are dry and place them in the container next to the steam table to be ready for the next meal. The cooks clean the food preparation area. It is your daughter's job to rack the dirty glasses in square metal baskets and push them through a glass washing machine. They will come out the other end clean and dry. Your daughter's job is to then stack the baskets of glasses like those are." She pointed to the neatly arranged piles of glasses beside the large machine. "Then she is done."

My duties were clear.

I met the dietician in her office on the first day. I checked the assignment list and met the kitchen workers. There was my name on the list, right beside my title, The Caller. When the conveyor belt started, the dietician stood on the block and began the job to show me what to do. I watched intently. After about five orders, it was my turn to begin. I did exactly what I was supposed to. Of course I stumbled a bit, but it was not so bad. Although I was nervous, all went well and the dietician left. She returned after the break to make sure I understood what to do with the glasses. All was well.

Things were working nicely. The workers seemed to like me, so I felt secure. Two days later as I headed to the office, one of the women, Angie, who worked over the steam table, greeted me as she was heading to the kitchen. I checked in and looked at the list of assignments. Something had changed. Angie's name was there. My name was written over another erasure. The chart showed that I was assigned to work over the steam table.

I thought, "That can't be right!" I tried to find the dietitian for clarity but she had gone home. So, I had no choice.

Marva and Angie were full-time masters of the steam table. Angie stood on the block and I had her hot and grueling responsibility of dipping up the food. She stood cool and calm and did my job. The steam table was lined with pans of food nestled in boiling water to keep the food warm. The job entailed dipping food choices from the pans and putting it on the plates once the menu selections were presented by the new Caller. Each order listed a number of selections and I was moving as fast as I could. I had to make sure that the cooks were notified when the pans were empty so they could replace the empty pans with freshly cooked food. It was surprising how much I had learned just by watching. I hated this job. At the end of the day, I was tired from only working part-time and knew that there was no way I could do this job full-time.

It took speed, eye-hand coordination, and attentive listening skills to get each order correct. I was trying so hard to keep up and the sweat was pouring off of me. I hated it. Someone handed me a towel to wipe my forehead. I was sure that this job paid more than $0.85 an hour. After the break, I still had to rack the dirty glasses. My exhaustion was overwhelming.

I thought about this situation all night and hoped that the dietician who hired me would be there the next day. She wasn't. It just didn't seem right.

The following day, I signed in and checked the job assignment list as usual. Once again, my name had been erased from The Caller and written in for the Steam Table. I was not going to do that job again.

Then I had an idea. Since the names were written in pencil, I borrowed a pencil with a good eraser from the dietician's desk. I erased Angie's name beside my position as Caller and wrote my name in that spot. Then I erased my name on the line for the steam table and wrote in Angie's name. Smiling, I headed out to the floor, took my position as The Caller of the Conveyor Belt before it was time to start. Then I began the job for which I was hired.

Not a word was spoken to me about my actions, but I noticed that suddenly, the kitchen workers were friendlier. My cousins told me that they were proud of me. I didn't like it, but I assumed it was some kind of ritual to see what a new employee would do. I guess I passed the test. The dietician had to see the erasures and she never said anything to me about it. I accepted Angie's friendship, but, like my mother says, "Don't trust her as far as you could throw her."

By the end of the summer, I decided this was not to be my life's work. I had to find something that I liked and that paid more than $0.85 an hour. Little did I know then that my mother's foresight was to keep me busy and out of trouble and to begin to insert the idea that college would offer me different opportunities.

Each summer job was filled with lessons. My hospital job allowed for experiences that reached further than the kitchen duties. I was introduced to a work ethic. I learned to pay attention, to solve problems on my own, and to appreciate the work that goes into making the function. I learned to depend on myself and look for what is right and what is true. Most of all, that summer, I learned to take care of my own business and respect the hard work of others.

The Skirt War
(Mother vs. Daughter) (1962)

I can't remember how or when I got THE skirt. I must have bought it with some of my summer earnings. My mother surely did not buy it. I couldn't figure out why she hated it. It was just a plain black pencil skirt with a hem that fell just below my knees...nothing special.

Our war over the skirt began the night of the first Recreation Department's Summer Dance for Teens. During the day there was a day camp for the elementary school children and every Monday night from 6:00 – 8:00, teens gathered on the playground of the elementary school for a dance. Although my friends were allowed to go when they turned thirteen, I was not. Finally, when I was sixteen, permission was granted. I would see the kids coming home from the dance as we sat out on the porch in the evenings, enjoying cool breezes. My joy was overflowing but I contained myself. I didn't want to seem too excited, even if I was.

It was known throughout the community that my parents were strict, so no one was surprised about my predicament that night.

My cousin and one of my friends planned to walk the three blocks to the school playground with me for my first time going to the dance. My cousin had gone before with her sisters but this time she was going to walk with me. My girl-friend lived in a neighboring town, so this was her first time also. Her father dropped her off at my house at 5:30. We had decided to leave my house by 5:55 so that we could get the full experience. I was so excited to be going. I loved to dance and tried to pretend to be calm.

Since my mother was particular about what I wore and just to be on the safe side, I asked her, "What do you think I should wear?"

Her answer was, "Oh, just wear anything you want."

I foolishly thought that was fantastic. I had a new black skirt that I liked and picked out some other pieces to compliment what I thought was a nice outfit. A pretty purple blouse with a ruffled collar, my new black spaghetti sandals, and the black skirt. I put on a little lipstick and some earrings.

At 5:50, the girls were seated in the living room waiting. It was five minutes earlier than planned, but I was ready. They figured that a ten-minute walk would be perfect to get there by 6:00. I modeled my outfit for the girls, who were sitting in the living room ready to go. They loved it.

My cousin said, "Girl, you are going to get lots of dances in that outfit."

I went downstairs to my mother's beauty shop to get her

approval. She had a customer in the chair getting her hair curled. Another customer was sitting under the dryer. This is how the conversation went.

Customer 1: OWWW! Don't you look pretty!

Customer 2: I love that outfit. You are going to dance the night away.

Mother: Oh, no. I know you don't think you are going in that?

(Everyone was suddenly quiet.)

Me: But Mom...what is wrong with this?

Mother: You can't go out of here looking like that!

Me: Looking like what?

Mother: Like something off of South Street!

Me: What? What's on South Street?

Mother: Just take it off and put THAT skirt on my bed.

Me: Well, what do you want me to wear?

Mother: Just try something else.

Up the stairs I ran. By 6:00, my friends were wiggling in the chairs. After two more changes, Mother finally gave her approval. By then it was 6:30 on the dot. We were a half-hour late. I wore exactly what she ordered and looked as if I was going to church. By that time, I didn't care what I had on. I just didn't want to miss any more time at the dance.

It was apparent that no one was going to want to go with me to the dance after this. They grumbled all the way to the dance.

"I knew your mother was strict but this didn't make any sense."

"That first outfit was sharp!"

"I am sure glad my mother isn't like that. Good grief!"

"We missed a lot of the dance."

"Next week I am going with my sisters. I am sure uncle will drive you there."

We arrived at about 6:45. I didn't say a word, but I felt horrible about it. Even though we were later than we would have liked, it was so much fun. We forgot for the moment about my outfit situation and danced the night away. At 7:55, I felt a tap on my shoulder.

My father whispered, "Your mother sent me to pick you up."

This was a surprise. I was looking forward to walking home with everyone from the dance. My friend's father was going to pick her up at my house at 8:30. He figured that would give us time to walk back to my house. He could have picked her up at 8:00 because that is what time we got home. I knew she had no choice but to come back next week and walk with me. Her parents were not allowing her to go to the dance alone, plus they respected my parents. I think they liked me, too. She was grateful to go to the dance but not particularly happy about the amount of time we were allowed to be there. We had no choice. I knew my cousin was not going to plan to go to the dance with me next week. If she wasn't spending the night, she would have gone home then.

The three of us, with heads down, followed him to the car. We listened to the last of the music as we drove away and fumed about missing out on the fun of the last five minutes and walking home with the crowd.

Later I realized that my mother had already planned how much time I could spend at the dance. She sent my dad to pick us up so that we might not get into any boy interactions on the way home. She was always way ahead of me.

However, I didn't figure out the problem with the skirt... until my first week in college. I packed it with my things and took it with me. Whenever my mother came to visit, she secretly searched through my things, found it, and took it home. Whenever I got home, I would find it and bring it back. This went on for four years. I found out that when she mentioned South Street, she was talking about hookers. I didn't know what they were. I couldn't understand it. The skirt was not tight and it wasn't short.

It was strange that she never threw it away. I think once she got home, the skirt was the last thing on her agenda. This was like an ongoing battle.

Then one day I figured out why she did not want me to wear that skirt. On the first day of college classes, I put on my black skirt, a nice blouse, and some baby doll shoes. In the 60s, the students were not allowed to wear pants on the campus. The girls wore dresses and skirts and the boys wore suits and ties or a jacket or sweater with a shirt.

On the day of discovery, while ascending the stairs in the Science Building, a boy behind me said, "How are you today?"

I smiled and replied shyly, "I am fine, thank you."

To my surprise he came back with "Yes, you are."

One of my new girlfriends leaned in and said, "Girl, your body is banging. You are really wearing that black skirt."

When I turned around to see who had spoken, I saw a set of beautiful teeth and a handsome face. That is when I knew that my black skirt was special and I intended to wear it at least once a week! I was ready to go shopping to buy them in different colors. Sorry, Mom!

Honeymooning (Fun, Fear & Fish)

Finally, after five years of marriage, we were financially able to go on a honeymoon. Salaries for teachers were not the basis for becoming wealthy. It took a while because our main goal was to purchase a house and then to take a trip.

After leaving our three-year-old son in the safe arms of his grandparents, we were off to Mexico. Cancun was becoming a sought-after resort spot and was under construction. We thought it would be perfect for adventures and the cost fit our budget.

My husband was excited to go scuba diving, especially for what he called a "real dive." He was looking forward to using the underwater camera I gave him when he earned his scuba diving license. I had no desire for scuba but was willing to try snorkeling. I had always enjoyed swimming and floating on my back, so snorkeling seemed a perfect fit for my first water adventure.

As soon as we arrived, he reserved his dive and I scheduled our snorkeling adventure. When he returned from the dive, he talked relentlessly about what he saw and how happy he was with the camera. I must admit, it sounded interesting, but not so alluring that I would want to go on a dive.

The next day, we took a boat tour to Isla Mujeres, The Isle of Women, which included a boat ride, lunch, dinner, and a snorkeling experience. I wanted to see saltwater fish and plants in their natural habitat. Jacques Cousteau's television show nurtured my desire to see the wonders of saltwater life.

I knew it would be different from the fish in my classroom aquarium. I anticipated rainbows of colors and different species. I was never brave enough to set up a saltwater aquarium because the responsibility was more than I wanted to handle. Just thinking about it was thrilling. I probably was just as excited to go snorkeling as my husband was to scuba dive.

The plan for the day was to have lunch on the island, snorkel off a reef, and then enjoy a romantic evening of dinner on a catamaran. We boarded the boat to the island and enjoyed the freshness of the cool breeze. A guide was waiting for us and herded our group to the snorkel location.

After changing into bathing suits, getting our equipment and instructions, we headed to the welcoming, beautifully clear water. One of the rules stressed by the instructor was "Do not feed the fish." That would not be a problem for me because it had not been in my plans. I just wanted to relax in the water and take in the scenery.

With flippers, goggles, and snorkels fitted, we jumped off of a reef into the calm, inviting Caribbean. The temperature was just right. It felt terrific, like being hugged. We swam around together and then John motioned that he was going away from me to take pictures. I nodded my approval because I knew he wanted to experience more than he could if he stayed with me. I wasn't as daring in the water as on land. Since quite a few people were swimming nearby, I felt comfortable.

As soon as he swam off, I noticed small, lively, eye-catching fish swarming around two sets of dangling legs. The fish were colorful, different from freshwater fish. I was fascinated by them at first but then began to be alarmed. There were too many of them swarming in one spot. Then I realized that those two people were breaking the rule. They were feeding the fish. I tried to swim away from them quickly but my non-Olympic skills kicked in. In my flight, I became aware of a bigger fish staring at me. Feeling a bit nervous about being watched, I began to tread the water a little faster and took deep breaths through the snorkel.

The scales on that fish seemed fluorescent. If it was in a picture in a magazine, I would have been in awe of its beauty. The blues, yellows, and greens would make a color wheel seem bland. However, that didn't matter then. I did not want this attention. We were in our own private trance for what seemed a long time and then, like a submarine in a movie, he darted toward me. I could swear I heard the music from the movie *Jaws*. He came straight to my face and slammed into my goggles with his nose. While I was flailing about, he moved backward as quickly as Nemo and seemed to be evaluating the circumstances.

I assumed his choices were "Shall I eat her or just kill her and be done with it? She doesn't look delicious, but who knows!"

Before I could get myself together, the monster fish employed another attack. This time, he darted around to my right with lightning speed and slammed into my right leg. By this time, I was frantic but not stupid. I looked for floating blood in the water and thought, "All I need is to have a blood trail that attracts more sharks." I could see the headlines.

"Tourist killed by sharks while snorkeling in Mexico. She was a mother, a wife, and a great teacher. She will be missed. The President of the United States will be visiting her family and attending the funeral."

Thank God there was no blood. As I watched the whale of a fish scurry off toward the criminal feeders, my frantic swimming strokes must have caught John's attention. Thank God, there he was to protect me from the shark.

John grabbed my hand and guided me to the ladder for safety. He must have read my mind. I wanted to get out. I followed him at the speed of someone participating in swimming trials. My skills had evidently improved due to fear.

When I finally got myself together on a lounge chair, he headed back into the water, camera in hand. I saw him trying to keep a smile off of his face and I did not appreciate that attitude, but I was grateful. He was my hero.

The rest of the trip was filled with exciting, positive adventures. We had such a good time in Cancun. When we arrived home, we invited friends over to share pictures of the trip and talk about the fun we had. Our recommendation was for them to definitely take a trip there. The hotel, the food, the people, and the sales were great. Of course, we had to talk about John's dive and my barracuda attack. John's version of my confrontation was different from mine. That's okay because I know that I survived a dangerous fish attack on our honeymoon.

That is my story and I am sticking to it. I forgot that John had taken pictures of my attacker with his underwater camera. I could only base my case of truth on my photographic memory. When he shared the picture, which he had not shown me previously, I evoked the fifth amendment. I refuse to testify for fear that I might incriminate myself. The protagonist was so small, I could have swatted him away.

I had to join as laughter resounded throughout my living room. My imaginary monster fish thought I had food, not that I was food.

Anniversary Dinner

Pam wanted to be sure that the first wedding anniversary in her family's new home would be memorable. She developed a plan to prepare Surf and Turf for a spectacular dinner for her husband. This was a chance to have a romantic evening. She decided to make a carrot cake too because it was her husband's favorite dessert. Since her parents would be taking the children overnight, they would have some needed private time.

After purchasing groceries, Pam headed home. She spotted a liquor store and decided that a glass of wine would go perfectly with dinner. Since she only had a few dollars left, it had to be something affordable. She and her husband had just settled on the new mortgage and were trying to get used to a new financial stability.

While browsing the abundance of choices, she tried to act as if she was knowledgeable. However, she knew nothing about spirits.

Since she liked sweet drinks, she thought, "Why not get a sweet wine?" Although she had already made her requested strawberry lemonade, wine would be more romantic. She had read that white wine goes with fish and red wine goes with meat. So red it was going to be. Since she wanted to cook the best anniversary dinner her husband had ever had, she thought that a glass of wine served in the new fluted glasses gifted at their open house would help make a beautiful table presentation. Pam didn't want to spend too much time picking out wine because she needed to get started with the cooking. It was then she spied a plain but attractive bottle of wine that was neither white nor red but pinkish. It was peach and the perfect price.

She inquired of the man at the counter, "Excuse me, sir, is this a sweet wine?"

He smiled and said, "Yes, it is!"

"Perfect!" she said and hummed, walking back to her car, carrying her purchase.

Once the meal was ready, she placed the carrot cake with cream cheese icing in the middle of the table and set out their gold-trimmed white china, the gold-plated silverware, linen napkins, candles, water goblets, and long stem glasses. It was beautiful. The steaks were medium well and topped with onions and mushrooms. The lobster tails had been cooked just right, split and ready for seasoned butter dipping. The asparagus was roasted in the oven and smothered with a cheese sauce. Scallions and shredded cheese with a dab of garlic graced the baked potatoes. The wine was chilling in the refrigerator. She was glad that there was no need for a corkscrew to open it.

She ran upstairs, showered and donned her red negligee, whitened her teeth, brushed her hair, popped in a breath mint, and dotted her neck with perfume from Gay Paree. It was a gift from one of her friends. When Robert pulled into the driveway, Pam lit the candles, filled the tall glasses with the fluorescent pink and turned down the lights. She didn't have an ice bucket, so she placed the bottle back in the refrigerator to stay cold.

Robert walked through the door with a large bouquet of flowers and a box of chocolates. He sighed at the sight of her and sniffed her neck right after a luscious kiss. He put the flowers, which were already in a vase, on the table beside the cake. Pam filled the water goblets with cold water while he went to the powder room to wash his hands. She placed the platters of food on the table with serving utensils. She turned on soft jazz to create a mood. Everything was perfect.

Robert pulled the chair out so that Pam could be seated first and then he sat down, smiling. After saying grace, they both started sighing with delight as they ate.

Robert was the first to speak. "This is delicious, and you made my cake, too?"

"I sure did. I wanted to make our fifteenth year special." Pam's joy was all over her face. She was proud and happy.

He picked up his glass. They toasted.

"To the most beautiful and wonderful woman I have ever known. Thank you for being my wife."

Pam blushed as they sipped from the beautiful stemware. Before she could say anything, suddenly Robert's' expression seemed strange.

He looked at Pam and said, "Pam, what kind of wine is this?"

"It's peach wine. Do you like it?"

Robert continued, "No, I mean what is the name of the wine?"

"I don't know. I liked the bottle. Since we both like peach tea, I thought I would get it. Plus the price was right!"

"Let me see the bottle."

Pam got the bottle and handed it to him. She said, "Here, it says AC on the bottle."

"Pam, this is Angry Clown."

"Okay! That is a strange name for a wine."

"Do you know what this is?" The atmosphere seemed to change a bit.

"Peach wine!" she responded, just a little bit annoyed.

"Sweetheart, Angry Cow is what you see winos on the street drinking wrapped in paper bags. It is inexpensive. It's like that wine that Fred Sanford drank on *Sanford and Son*." Pam could tell he was about to laugh. It was funny. "The next time you want wine, let me get it!"

At first she didn't know what to say and then they laughed hysterically.

After wiping away her tears of laughter, Pam dumped the wine glasses and refilled them with the strawberry lemonade that she had made, just in case she didn't have enough money to buy a nice wine. Dinner was even better with the lemonade.

When she told her mother about what happened, she added that she had kept the Angry Cow wine. It turned out to be great for cooking roast beef in the crock pot. Robert didn't realize that the roast beef dinner that he raved about a few nights later was another night of him enjoying their special wine. Pam never told him. However, Pam accomplished her goal. She had created a memorable anniversary, in more ways than one!

The Hospital Room

A trip to a hospital was not on my bucket list. I wanted to travel the world, see the sights, stay in beautiful hotels, and cruise on magnificent waterways. However, things don't always work out the way you want them to. Getting sick can put a damper on plans. However, when you're sick, the hospital is the place to go so that maybe later you can dip into that bucket.

I often drove by a growing medical complex on my many daily travels to work, rarely glancing in that direction. I was born there, had given birth there, and visited sick friends in that very building. I had never been ill enough for a stay, nor had I imagined that I would ever be that sick. Then one day, a pain stabbed me in the side and off I went straight to the Emergency Ward.

The waiting room, like an international airport, was filled with people waiting to be seen or waiting for those being seen. I worried that I would be sitting suffering for quite a while and I dreaded that thought. However, once my information was exchanged, I was sent to a room. That sent a mixed message. I was grateful but couldn't help thinking that my situation must be serious and my insurance must be top of the line.

Cheerful nurses made sure I was prepped. They checked my vitals with such care and positivity that I thought the pain was going to go away on its own. After probing and pondering, the prognosis was I was not going home.

I said, "Can't you give me a pill or a shot?"

The doctor looked serious when he said, "No, we want to find out what is causing that pain and then maybe you can get a shot or a pill. We'll find out what it is! You have to be patient, patient."

Although I was scared, I knew I was in the right place. Through the pain, I liked the doctor's quick wit.

I was pushed in a wheelchair through the halls, looking scared. People moved out of the way so that we could pass. I could read the "so sad for you" look on their faces. White-clad health saviors moved busily about the halls. A Lysol smell was prominent as we approached my assigned room. I was glad my bed was near the door.

The woman in the first bed on the left side of the room, next to the door, said, "Hello new person. Welcome to Room 408."

I was a bit confused by her cheerful voice. After all, this was the place for sick people. Machine clicks, moans, and sounds of curtains being pulled rang out like a bad choir. However, I attempted to smile back.

Two beds sat on each side of the room. I struggled to find a restful position in one of them as the nurses busily hooked me up to some equipment, praying silently for a mind-altering drug to nullify the pain and put me to sleep immediately. When I awoke, my glance across the room settled on the smiling, welcoming being across from me. She leaned forward in her bed.

"My name is Joyce. What's yours?"

I was hesitant because I am a suspicious person—plus, I wasn't in the friend-making mood. However, it took too much energy to avoid the question.

"I'm Sandy!" I said and went to sleep to escape a discussion. I wondered why she was there. She looked like the picture of health, but my perspective may have been skewed.

Whatever was going on with her, it did not hinder her mysterious daily routine.

The nurses and doctors moved among the other three patients. I rested and awoke to a man's voice. Hoping it was my doctor with some answers, I forced my eyes open. Unfortunately, it was not my doctor.

A man entered, walked over to Joyce's bed, and kissed her. He stayed all afternoon. I assumed it was her husband and went back to sleep. Surprisingly, that evening a different man came to see her. He greeted her in the same fashion. It couldn't have been her father. Fathers don't kiss daughters like that.

She seemed to be in good spirits until it was night. I could hear her trying to muffle sobbing. Maybe her illness was serious or the triangle situation was stressful.

Since I was feeling a bit better, I decided to give each patient in the room a title. That gave me something to think about other than wondering about my own problem or what Joyce was up to. Her love life was none of business.

Her title became "Playa, Playa!" A Player is someone who makes a person feel special when really they are just one in many. They flirt one day and ignore the person another day.

Next to Playa, Playa in the second bed was "Mrs. Agony," a hip replacement patient. I felt sorry for her in the midst of my own agony. Her days were spent seeking ease. Each rustle of her sheets was accompanied by wailings and pleas for medication. Pushing a button was not sufficient. The answer was always "We are so sorry, but you can only have a certain amount of morphine. We don't want you to get hooked on it." Although begging didn't work, she was relentless. Trips to therapeutic exercises and visitors filled her days. Finally, after much rehabilitation and a solid diet, her pleading stopped. Her bed was next to a wall of windows that ran along the back of the room.

Next, on the right side of the room by the windows and across from Mrs. Agony was Bed #3. That was where "Happy Tourist" nested.

She seemed like a happy soul who related to the staff as friends. She was so familiar that I thought she worked in the hospital. They seemed to know her, too. She even greeted the custodians and the television renewal fee collector as if they were movie stars. She hummed while shopping through the hospital menus as if ordering at a five-star restaurant. One would think she was on vacation.

I laid suffering between Happy Tourist and the door in Bed #4. Pains in my side felt like I was being stabbed with a ragged knife. For what seemed an eternity, I tried to find a comfortable lying position. My gallbladder was infected. Mrs. Agony and I periodically performed groaning duets.

My husband said that I was being observed in case they would have to remove my gallbladder. They wanted to wait to see if the medicine would kill the infection first. I was ready to get it out. Three days later, the medicine worked. I had time to relax, talk with my roommates, and watch TV.

Playa Playa and I laughed and talked about life, soap operas, the latest movies, and anything else we could think of. Although I was curious about her situation, I never commented on it. I figured that if she wanted me to know, she would tell me. Our discussions took my mind off of why I was there.

Then one day, she said, "My life is a mess! I know you wonder what is going on. My husband doesn't know about my boyfriend. I don't know what to do about this whole thing. I sure didn't think I'd have to be in the hospital. It drives me crazy trying to make sure that they are not here at the same time. I was planning to leave my husband and I got sick."

I didn't feel sorry for her and I gave no advice. She didn't ask me for any, thank goodness. If she had, I don't know what I would have said. I had enough of a struggle trying to maintain a positive relationship with one man. This was complicated but I had learned the hard way to keep out of grown folks' business. I hated to see her leave but was glad she was well enough to go. It had been interesting watching how she handled each man each day and I wondered what she would do when she left. It took everything I had to refuse to be a busybody. We exchanged phone numbers before her husband came to pick her up. I liked her in spite of the deceit.

That afternoon, Happy Tourist was informed that she would be going home the next day. I expected squeals of joy. That was the day her giggling stopped. She moped all day. That night I saw her stick her finger down her throat, causing herself to vomit. Then she rang the emergency buzzer. When the nurses arrived, she said, "I can't go home. I am still sick! See?" She tearfully showed them something that I didn't want to look at.

I wondered why she wanted to stay in the hospital so badly that she pretended to be sick. In this case I felt I had to step into someone else's business. I just thought it awful that she was taking up a bed that a really sick person might need. I am not sure if that was my train of thought or if it was that this lady might be a bit "nuts." When the curtains were drawn around my bed for my morning bath, like a kindergartener who found out a secret, I told. I became something that I hated—a Tattletale. To my surprise, the nurse already knew.

She whispered, "Yes, we know. She needs attention. Her sons don't visit her. This is her way of being with people who care. She harms herself. This time she got into a bathtub of scalding hot water. Her doctor is getting her psychiatric help."

"Oh, my goodness," I thought. "She really is sick!"

Happy Tourist was not so happy, after all. It was a learning experience for me! This woman needed love and attention, just like everyone else. My feelings for her changed once I heard about her predicament. I felt sorry for her and hoped that things would change. However, I wasn't sorry that I tattled. It was then that I thought maybe what each of us needed was a mind-altering treatment to get us through pain.

When I was released the next day with my gallbladder intact and uninfected, I waved goodbye to Mrs. Agony, who was sitting up in bed, smiling, and Happy Tourist, who seemed no longer happy. As I was rolled out of the door, two young men entered and headed to Bed #3. I heard sounds of joy as Happy Tourist screamed out their names. I left Room 408 feeling a sense of joy. All four of us seemed to be healing.

As my chair was guided through the corridors, dotted with staff waving goodbyes, I felt special and vowed to send a tray of sandwiches and cookies to the staff to say thank you. As we drove away, I thought each of us in Room 408 were needy in different ways. Hopefully each will feel healed, physically and/or mentally, at least for a time. Drugs may not always do the trick. Sometimes minds have to change on their own. Lily Tomlin once said, *"The best mind-altering drug is the truth."* Sometimes the truth is hard to deal with, but has to be faced.

By the way, Joyce and I stayed in touch. Her smile is real now. Playa Playa got a divorce and also dropped the boyfriend.

The Only One Upstairs

Getting Alzheimer's must be the pits. I saw a picture of what happens to the brain. It begins to look like scrambled eggs. In the beginning stages, some folks seem to know that there may be a problem and others seem unaware. It is scary watching someone going through it. Scientists have worked for years to find a cure. They have found ways to slow the progress but not a cure. Each day progress on dealing with this disease seems to be moving ahead. I imagine that not knowing you have it might be a saving grace.

A few of my friends had an early onset. They had both had caring husbands as caretakers and did not have to go into a nursing facility for quite a while. Unfortunately, they both passed away in their fifties from a world that I hope never to visit. Alzheimer's is a sneaky illness. First there is a little memory loss, which seems characteristic of aging. I can attest to that. Then it seems to explode like a bomb. Trying to understand the disease is complicated for caretakers. Being forgetful does not necessarily mean that Alzheimer's is around the corner. The best explanation I heard was "If you go upstairs and forget why you are there, you do not have Alzheimer's. It is when you go upstairs and you don't know that you are upstairs that there is a real problem." That is a different story.

When I was a child, if an elderly person acted strangely, someone would say, "Oh, Miss Anne is just senile." Senility was explained to children as memory loss at old age. It was accepted as a normal stage of life. No one seemed surprised by it. Usually, the older people remained in the family setting and there were a number of people there to be caretakers. Those times have changed.

Even as an adult, I never thought that diseases like cancer or memory loss would touch my life. I never really thought about it. All hell broke loose. About a week after burying my mother, my father acted strangely. A day after the funeral, he had a car accident. I thought it might be a response to losing his wife. As if it wasn't enough to lose one parent, then the other one started having challenges. I had never seen him act strangely before. I think my mother was dealing with it and didn't talk about it. I first noticed it when my father was trying to put his socks on over his shoes. I realized that this could be serious when he was accepting that as the right behavior.

When I questioned him, he replied sternly, "I know what I am doing. I was in the military." Evidently, my mother had been compensating for his retention problem. She must have been frightened. It sure scared me when his care became my responsibility.

He was able to live alone with my constant daily visits for a while because it was mild. Then one night some devilish teens ordered pizzas to be delivered to his home. Once the pizza's deliverer arrived, the teens robbed the man of the pizzas and ran. They didn't take any money, just the food. The police knocked on my father's door because the order was directed to his home. The neighbors across the street saw and explained what had happened. This seemed to be the catalyst that set off my awareness even more. Later that night my father walked into his neighbor's house in his pajamas, saying that he was lost. I got the news the following day from a relative who was a friend of the mother of the neighbor. Now the community was aware of his condition. I didn't want that information to seep out just in case deviant minds might cause more issues.

It was devastating to this man who had been my protector, who loved me and was so full of joy.

Where was my dad? I wanted him back.

He was slow in his responses but able to tell me what he remembered about the incident. He explained that he had a dream of being lost in the nearby town. He was trying to find his way home and a nice lady walked him to his gate. I didn't know what to do. I needed time to think. Then the next week, my cousin, who was on his way to work, saw Dad walking in his underwear about three blocks from the house, carrying his shoes. He brought him home and called me.

It was time to take him home with me. I knew that it was going to be difficult. I had to be cunning in how to approach the idea. I offered him a little vacation at my house. He accepted. We went to the movies and out to dinner. One day we even cooked together. After two days he insisted on going home. That meant I had to stay at his home at night because he refused to move into my house. I tried to negotiate a deal with him to have a friend stay with him periodically. He refused. Some men who knew began to ask him to borrow money. I had to put on my evil scary aura and stop that business.

God works in mysterious ways. An old girlfriend of his got hit by a car and was in the hospital. I went to see her and took my father with me. After she returned home from the hospital, she began to visit him. Then she began to spend the night periodically. She was a blessing. It gave me an opportunity to breathe.

As the disease progressed, he began to stuff things down the toilet, move the furnace controls, break the keys to the garage, and pull the piping under the hood of the car. That one worked well because he was unable to drive.

She began to stay almost every night for about two years until she got sick. It was back to my drawing board. He would not allow a caretaker in the house. That meant that I was the source of his care once again.

Although this was a serious time, some things were funny. For instance, one day after visiting his friend in the hospital, he asked where she was when we got home. We explained a few times that we had just visited her in the hospital. Then he went upstairs to change into his pajamas. My brother and I waited for him to come down for dinner. I could hear water running in the bathroom and assumed he was washing up. It seemed to be running too long. I went to the bottom of the steps to call him. He turned off the water and calmly came to the top of the stairs, donning two undershirts, one on his chest, as it should be, and the other one somehow fitted as underpants. It was quite the sight to see his two slimmer-than-usual legs protruding from the arm holes of the shirt.

"How is this?" he asked seriously. "How do I look?" My father was always a well-dressed man. He had been the star of church fashion shows. The women swooned over him. He had always been selective about his attire. This was a far cry from his usual behavior. What a shock!

"Dad, you have your undershirt on as underpants. Don't you want to put on a pair of the new ones we just bought?"

"I know what I am doing. I was in the military!"

As he came downstairs, I ran into the kitchen laughing and said to my brother, "Get ready!"

My brother's eyes widened. "What? He's not naked, is he?"

I assured him it wasn't that bad, and then my dad strolled into the kitchen in his two undershirts. He stood proudly in the kitchen and said, "How is this?" With his arms out-stretched, he continued, "How do I look?"

My brother looked like a deer in headlights. "Dad, you have your undershirt on like they are underpants."

"I know what I am doing. I was in the military," he repeated. He sat at the table as if he was dressed properly. I did not look at my brother. We had a delicious dinner and a wonderful conversation as if everything was fine. Then Dad announced that he was going to bed. He headed upstairs. Strangely, the undershirt on his bottom did its job. Thank you, God! Finally, when I looked at my brother, we tried to smother it but we laughed hysterically.

However, most times were not funny. It started with Sundowners Syndrome. Every night, Dad had an urgent need to go somewhere, but couldn't explain why. He would flip on my light and ask, "Who are you?" This happened off and on, all night, every night. I explained more times than I could count.

"I want to go home," he'd say.

I tried a calming approach by responding, "You are home. This is your home, Dad."

"No, it isn't."

I began to understand and decided to come up with a better response because of our history.

He and my mother had moved back into my grandparents' house twenty years earlier to take care of her. Since he felt this wasn't home, maybe he was referring to the home that I had grown up in, but he wasn't.

One night I asked him the address he wanted to go home to. He responded with the address of his childhood home. He remembered it exactly. I responded with, "Okay, we will go there as soon as the sun comes up!" He would be convinced for the moment.

Another nightly question was "Who are you?" That scared me the most because there were loaded guns in the house and I didn't know where they all were. I didn't want him to think I was a burglar; he was a crack shot.

My grandfather had been a competitive shooter. I found the rifles and unloaded them, but it was the handguns I was worried about. I had found one and gave them to the pastor to lock up in the church safe. My dad had been the Chairman of the Trustee Board and one of the guns had been purchased for him to carry when transporting money to and from the bank.

Every night I had to explain who I was. Eventually, he would understand that I was his daughter and go back upstairs, but only for a few moments.

On one particular night, he said, "Where is everyone? There is nobody upstairs." It took a while to realize that he was going back in time. When he came home from World War II, the nights upstairs were filled with six people. My teenage uncle, my grandparents, my mother, and I were up there with him. Now it was just him. They were all gone. That was a sad moment and hard to explain.

He saw me as a stranger sleeping in a downstairs bedroom that had been built onto the house years ago for my grandmother. The house must have seemed different to him. He wanted a home filled with bustling activities, listening to the radio, celebrating holidays, the smells of cooking good food...a place of love. It was all gone and he was the only one upstairs.

At first the nightly interruptions got on my nerves. Then I stopped being annoyed even though I needed rest. He couldn't help it! The darkness tapped into fears of being unsafe and insecure for both of us.

He kept saying, "I want to go home!" When I'd tell him that he was home, he didn't believe it. I asked him for his address and he gave me the address of his home when he was a little boy. The doctor said it was called "Sun Downers." I realized that I was not able to handle his care.

Strangely, about five years earlier, I was in a conference and at lunch one of the women spoke about a care facility near my home. Her mother loved being there for the independent living building. One day I stopped by to take a look. I was impressed. I knew that, should the need ever arise, this would be perfect.

I had to trick him into staying in a respected facility near my home. There was no way he would go willingly. It took a genius plan to get him to that safe place where he could get the care he needed. I pretended that the director was a friend that I was visiting. I introduced my father to him and we toured. My dad was impressed by thinking it was a place to stay if I was away for a weekend.

On our second visit, we had a game leader invite him to participate while I talked with my pretend friend, the manager. I left and returned with his clothes and things to fix up his unit. Then I was told that the managing team would take it from there. The cost was phenomenal. I took out a loan on his house to pay for his care.

I visited at different hours on different days just to be sure his care was sufficient. Finally, I was able to get some rest at my own home. On my visits, we spoke of lots of things, especially the woman he called the "love of his life," my mom. He said, "You know why she is the love of my life? She gave me you!" A tear crept into my eye. My dad was a beautiful person.

We talked of the love he had for his friend who came to stay with him during his struggle to stay sane. He was grateful. I hope she knew that.

One day he called to say that he was at the casino in Atlantic City and he was ready to come home. "Can you please come and get me?" My answer was "I'll be there in about fifteen minutes." I lied. It was a good lie. I am sure he forgot about that as soon as he got off the phone.

He loved people visiting. He was always trying to share his pureed food with guests, who surely did not want to partake. It was his nature to be a host. My parents enjoyed hosting friends and family. You could not leave their home without dining and dancing. So, I wasn't surprised when he wanted to share, even in the facility.

One night the choir that my parents and I sang in at church came to put on a concert for the patients. Everyone but my dad was seated. One of the workers came to get me. He was laying on the pool table having some stress. When I walked in, his body jerked and I jumped. All of the workers looked to me to do something. I said, "We need a doctor."

One lady responded, "Your father always says that you are a doctor. We thought you might be able to handle this."

"I am not a medical doctor, I am a Ph.D. Don't call on me if you get sick or you will die!" He started to rally and we all laughed. My father rallied finally. He went to the concert as if he was in perfect condition. We all had a wonderful evening of music.

One day while a group of family members was visiting, one of the patients opened the door to his unit, looking for Grand Central Station. Everyone looked surprised. My response was, "If you go back the way you came, go straight down that street, and turn right, it will take you straight into Grand Central Station." After his thank you, he went on his merry way. I locked the door. My father responded, "See, I told you I don't have any privacy."

However, I began to look forward to visiting him and talking with the patients. Then one day it was time for hospice care. It was indescribable to watch someone I loved fade away.

When my father was eighty-seven, he died. I hope he is back upstairs with my mother, uncle, and grandparents once again. In a place where he is with family and friends.

An Encounter on a Marble Bench

Samantha was always amazed when something surprising happened to her. She wondered if it was good luck or a blessing. She realized that she had received support, been saved from trouble, and sometimes she'd receive a smile that she interpreted as "I've got you!"

Some of her church training nurtured her optimism. Although this belief may seem naive or stupid to some folks, she didn't care what others thought. She had received benefits in circumstances over which she had no control. Whether they came from angels or good people, she felt blessed by them.

One example happened when she went to the cemetery to put flowers on the graves of her parents, an uncle, and her husband. Her parents and uncle were settled in the military section near each other, but her husband was a bit away. She was not looking forward to visiting a cemetery, but it was a family responsibility, a family tradition.

Her husband's family did not participate in these kinds of rituals. He had told her that it didn't make sense to visit people who were no longer alive. However, he couldn't reprimand her, so she planned to visit him anyway. She wondered what he might think of that if he was able to see her.

At the specified area near the military gravesites, there was a "V" formation in the road. A U-turn was necessary to park nearby where she remembered the sites to be. It was then that she noticed an elderly man sitting on a marble bench on the grassy area between the "V."

They were the only people in that section. That seemed unusual when compared to the last times she had visited. Being a little paranoid, Samantha made sure that she was aware of anyone in her environment, especially when she was alone.

There was no acknowledgment between the two. However, Samantha intentionally glanced in his direction to make sure she knew of his exact position. He was looking down as if in prayer.

She parked the car, gathered three bunches of flowers from the back seat, and headed in the direction of where she thought the graves were. Since she had been there before, she thought she knew the exact location of the graves.

Her plan was to pray and decorate the three spots, then drive around to another section to honor her husband. The last time she had visited him, a bee had chased her away. Although she knew it was a crazy thought, she told the bee, "Okay! I am leaving, James!" She thought it might be her husband's spirit and she had to laugh. Thinking about it made her smile but she hoped that the bee was long gone.

After a while of searching for the plaques, she came to the conclusion that she couldn't find the sites. That was strange. Previously, when she came with others, there was no problem finding the location. She wasn't going to give up and go to the office to check the map unless she had to. Instead, she continued to wander.

Finally, she accepted that she couldn't find them. Suddenly there was a strange wailing, punctuated by gulps. It sounded like a wild animal caught in a trap. Samantha realized that it was coming from her. She was no longer the calm person who had bravely buried people that she loved. She was a little girl missing the people she loved.

"Get yourself together, girl," she shouted above the wailing. Her shoulders, which always stood straight and firm, started twitching. It was difficult for her to stand. She tried to calmly search through her purse for tissues. Finally, after circling about again, she breathed a sigh of relief—there were the sites she had searched for. She had passed them numerous times. Her weeping continued even though she felt that she should have calmed down. If it echoed throughout the cemetery like voices in the Grand Canyon, people might pay attention, and she didn't want that. Since there was only one person in the section, she didn't care about that.

Samantha wondered who she was crying for...her loved ones or herself? She was ashamed when she realized that some of the tears were about them leaving her and that was selfish. So, she prayed, placed the flowers, and stumbled back toward the car, a sobbing mess.

As she approached her car, a soft voice called out, "Young lady, young lady, hello!" It was the man on the marble bench nestled in the green grass at the "V" formation. He beckoned to her.

Samantha walked across the road and headed toward the man. She felt compelled by his presence even though she wanted to get out of that place.

He patted the seat next to him and said, "Please come and sit with me for a moment."

She thought, "Who is this man?" Although she was suspicious of strangers, she was not distrustful of this man. Concentrating on each step, she moved, as if magnetized and sat down! Strangely, the seat was warm and comforting, as if someone had sat there before her.

He opened his hands slightly toward the sky and said, "This is a beautiful day to visit, isn't it?"

She hadn't noticed the weather. It was sunny and just cool

enough to be comfortable. The trees were changing colors and the air was fresh and brisk. Samantha appreciated the peaceful, immaculate setting. She shook her head in agreement.

Unexpectedly, she began to feel better. Then she remembered when her mother bought two plots. She had said, " This cemetery is lovely. You and James should think about getting plots there, too." That was so far from Samantha's reality that she paid no attention.

Her mother had smiled and said, "People take walks there and it's nice enough to have picnics."

Samantha had laughed, saying, "There is no way I am taking a walk in a graveyard and I am definitely not having any picnic there." They had both started laughing.

Samantha's mother had winked and said, "Think about it!"

She did, thirty years later!

Now she was on a bench with a stranger in that very graveyard and it was no longer bizarre. The two strangers, an elderly man and a young woman, never really looking at each other, began to communicate in the cemetery. It was a unique conversation that seemed so sad that Samantha wanted to explain to him that she was ashamed of herself for making such a scene.

The man reached into his coat pocket, took out a wallet, and said, "This is our bench, my wife and I." He pointed slightly ahead and to the left and continued, "She is right over there. We were married for a long time. It was love, real love. Here, look at this! Isn't she lovely?" He presented a picture of a young woman with long, dark hair. It must have been taken about fifty years prior.

In between fading sobs, Samantha smiled and said, "Yes, she is."

Then he turned to pictures of the two of them together. The joy that he exuded was contagious.

"Good looking couple," Samantha responded.

He flipped to a picture of a handsome young man in a

uniform loaded with medals. "See, that's me!" He explained that the picture was taken during World War II when he was a Commissioned Officer on a submarine trying to keep the Germans at bay.

Samantha was impressed. She had never met anyone who had been on a submarine and certainly never one who had served on one.

Proudly she said, "My dad was a soldier during that war. He was a Sergeant in the Army, stationed in France."

The man smiled and said, "Really?"

She nodded.

He continued, "You must be proud of him. Those were difficult days!" Then he turned to a photo of the submarine on which he served. He talked excitedly about his escapades during sea battles. She enjoyed seeing this man that she didn't know so animated. She felt proud of him, too.

Samantha wasn't sure how long they talked that day. It could have been ten minutes or it could have been hours. Time was not important, but she noticed that her tears had stopped. She had calmed down and that was important.

He then looked at her and said solemnly, "Just remember, you have an open invitation, my dear. Whenever you are visiting and feeling sad, just come over to our bench and sit down. You are welcome to sit here anytime. I guarantee you will feel better." At that moment, although they never once touched, Samantha felt hugged.

When she stood to leave, the man looked up and said, "It was very nice talking with you, young lady."

Samantha smiled back and said, "It was even nicer talking with you. Thank you so very much!" She waved as she walked to her car. As she pulled off, she felt refreshed, relieved, and ready to visit James, even if he didn't want her to.

Samantha accepted the encounter as a miracle. She hadn't realized that her spirit had been broken by losing her loved ones. Although Samantha had a way of making people believe that she could handle anything, she was vulnerable just like everyone else. That man was my blessing.

As she drove slowly away from him and toward her husband, she felt much better. When she looked through the rearview mirror, to her surprise, no one was sitting on the bench. No one was even near it. The two of them had just been the only people in that huge section of the cemetery. Now there seemed to be people moving about, standing over graves, placing wreaths, and filling vases with flowers, but there was no one on the bench.

Samantha was grateful for the moments shared with the man on the marble bench. It was just what she needed. She thought that she would probably never see him again, but she would remember what happened forever. She couldn't remember what he looked like. She believed that she had been blessed by an angel and she was more than fine with that!

***

> *Let mutual love continue. Do not neglect to show hospitality to strangers, for by doing that some have entertained angels without knowing it.*

– **Hebrews 13:1,2**

Chapter 4
Relatively Speaking

– Tom Clancy

Laura

It Is Time

I was only nine years old when my life drastically changed. Everything was going along just fine until 1931. My brother, George, was only six. Brother was his nickname. Everyone who knew us called him Brother.

Late one night, Mama peeked into my bedroom and whispered our secret alarm message: "Laura. It is time!" I jumped up right away as she headed next door to Brother's room. He knew what to do. We had talked about it and practiced enough to make sure there would be no mistakes. This was serious and we both thought of ourselves as secret agents in the midst of solving an important case. As if robots, we reached for the hangers that had been tagged with a red ribbon. I had told him that red meant danger, so we had to be quiet whenever we got the secret message. After washing and dressing hurriedly, we headed to the meeting place, just inside the basement door. We were silent.

Mama left some lights on in a few rooms before she met us. Brother started to say something but Mama put her finger to her lips and shook her head. She guided us through the door and then locked it. Since we had been drilled on procedures, we knew that our job for that part of the journey was to each carry a sealed mason jar of Mama's famous lemonade and one favorite thing. While balancing a basket of fried chicken and her over-sized purse, she pulled out a flashlight and a compass.

Then off we went. Mama first, my brother next, and then I followed after. We walked quietly up the four wooden steps, and I lowered the slanted door slowly, trying not to make a sound. Following Mama, like a hen with her chicks, we headed toward the rows of tall corn plants. Planning this night seemed like an adventure and I was surprised that sadness forced a tear from my eyes. I had a feeling that we might never see our home again.

My daddy was a landowner, a farmer, and an auto mechanic. It was rare in our surroundings for a black man to own land, and certainly not as much as we had. Most of his friends were sharecroppers. They were never able to pay off debts. Dad said that most workers struggled with reading and writing. They simply signed contracts with an "X" to represent their names after they were told what they thought was in the contracts. They were fooled into deals that seemed fair only to find out that they were falling deeper into debt every year.

Daddy was able to not fall into that trap and because of it he was both respected and hated. Many sought his guidance. He had inherited acres of farmland from his father but my father did not like farming. He always said that he wasn't good at it and that he had done enough farming as a child to last him a lifetime. So, he hired farmhands to work the land. This gave him a chance to concentrate on the work he wanted to do and help some of his friends.

Working on automobiles was his love. He was fascinated by how they looked, how they worked, and the thrill of driving them. His favorite was a car that he was putting together from pieces of other cars. He hid it in an old shed out back and only worked on it after the workers had gone home. There was something mysterious about his work on that car. He only let our family see it. When he showed it to us, there was a long explanation about every facet of that car. Daddy started it from the base of a 1930 Model A Ford, whatever that was. He was so proud of his experiments under the hood. He believed that his work would make a car more efficient and someday he might create a new model that astounds folks.

Daddy had a reputation as the best auto mechanic for miles around. People were at our house every day bringing and picking up cars. I heard them talking about Daddy's fine work. I was fascinated by what they said about him, but the money that I saw paid to him for his work made me think that Daddy must be rich. Periodically, some of the men even gave extra.

One man handed Daddy some money and said, "Here you go and there's two dollars extra. I appreciate how you take care of Old Betsy!" Then he rubbed his car as if petting a pet. "She stays purring like a kitten."

"I appreciate that!" Daddy responded. "Why thank you, Mr. Kelly. I am glad I get a chance to work on such an interesting old car."

Another man said, "Mr. Heins, your business is sure 'nough booming!"

He was right! People came from all over to get their cars repaired at our house even though there were other people who were also in this line of work. They had shops in town and at their homes. However, it sounded like my dad got most of the business.

His success on the farm and his auto work allowed the family to move out of our grandparent's home into a brand new one. For about four week-ends, Mamma and the neighboring women cooked food and worked on quilts while men pitched in to build us a new house. That house was a beauty. It was larger than most homes in Emporia, Virginia. I even had my own room and I loved it.

I liked living on the farm, until one night when I heard Daddy whisper to Mama that a couple of his farmhands had told him that some folks in town said, "Henry is too smart for his britches! We need to take him down a peg!"

Daddy said he had a feeling there was a problem. He had noticed that the name-calling and challenges to fight were growing whenever he went to town for supplies. It got so bad that he started getting his supplies in another town.

At dinner one night, he looked at mother and said, "Mary, it's time...before trouble comes." I could tell he was worried because he would get a kind of wrinkle across his forehead that looked like he was deep in thought.

My mother said, "Whenever you're ready, I am too." Then she turned to my brother. She said, "These words—'It is time!'—are our secret words. One day soon I will say that to you and you must do what I am about to train you to do. This is a family secret. What happens in this family is our business only. I like that idea."

That night, my parents began to cut out a path through the corn and high grass on our property. It started quite a ways from the house. Daddy told us to never tell anyone about it. Then we did a "Pinky Swear!" The path was not on the land that he had the farmhands working. It was quite a ways behind the house. You had to be a giant to be able to see where the path started.

Mama marked the direction from the house to the path by tagging specific plants and trees with tiny blue ribbons. She used her compass to place the tags. Three nights later, the task was completed. The path was about the width of a car and it ran straight through the property. It ended miles away at a rarely traveled dirt road. That road could not be seen from the main roads or from our house.

When Daddy had a number of cars in the yard to work on, I'd volunteer to be his tool handler, just so I could spend some time with him. He said, "Laura, one day we are going to live in New Jersey. I think you and Brother will like it. We have a lot of family there and it is not far from New York City. We will be leaving outta here at night, so we have to be very quiet."

I asked him why.

He said, "There are some folks who are not so nice and we may need to get away."

My answer was "Okay, Daddy!" I really didn't understand. I didn't want to leave our brand-new house, but if Daddy said so, then I knew everything was going to be okay!

He went on, "Your momma has everything ready for us to go. All you have to do is make sure that you and your brother are ready to move out when we give you the signal. The signal message is 'It is time!' Do you understand?"

"Yes, sir," I answered. I watched Daddy as he worked on his favorite car. It was beautiful, all shiny and new-looking. Suddenly, he took some tools and made dents in the car and scratched it in specific places. This was the car that he worked on more than any of the other cars. Once, I heard him tell Brother that he was putting his best stuff in that car because it was special. It just didn't make sense to me. Why would he do that? Before I could ask him why, Mama called us for lunch.

Later that evening, after the workers had gone home, Mama came out of the house with two suitcases and a shovel. I noticed that on the porch step was our money box. She picked it up and handed it to me. Although she never said a word, I knew to follow her. We marched away from the house, through the corn, following the blue ribbons, and then through the high grass.

To my surprise, we came upon Daddy's favorite car. Mama dug a hole in the ground beside the right rear tire and put the money box in it. She got some big stones and placed them over the spot where she had buried the box. Then she lifted the suitcases onto the floor of the back seat of the car. Suddenly, she looked toward the house and began to cry.

"Mama, why are you crying?" I asked.

"Don't ask so many questions, little girl. I can't answer them right now but I will someday."

I glanced toward the house to see if there was something sad going on there but I couldn't see why she was crying. Even from there we could visualize the beauty of the house, although most of what we could see was the roof. We held hands walking all the way back to the house.

The next morning, Mama got us up extra early. She drove our family car to a train station and bought two tickets. We asked about the tickets and she just said it was a surprise and to not tell anyone. I love surprises so I knew I could keep it to myself.

When we got home, she took me aside. She told me that Brother and I would be the ones taking a train ride from the big station in Richmond one night. We had never been on a train before, much less one from such a big city. I was excited.

She said, "Laura, these are the tickets. Since you are a big girl now, I am going to need you to look out for your little brother on your trip. You will be the one to hold the tickets on the train. Put these tickets in your Sunday coat pocket, now! When we leave for the trip, make sure you wear that coat with the tickets. It is going to be a great experience. You and Brother are going to ride on the train to visit Aunt Emma and Uncle Jim."

I was so excited. They were my favorite relatives.

"They will meet you at the station when you get to New Jersey. Daddy and I will be on our way in the car, but we have to make a few stops first. Once you two sit down on the train, a man called a conductor will take your tickets and see that you get to the Newark train station in New Jersey. Just sit back and enjoy the ride. I'll make you some lunch to have on the way."

"What a wonderful secret," I thought. It was safe with me.

The next day I saw a farmhand give Daddy a nod and whisper, "Mr. Heins, they's a-coming for you tonight." I noticed a change in the mood of my parents as their plans kicked into high gear. The day went as usual with the farm workers. Then Daddy took his gun and a box of bullets out of his hiding place. I always knew where it was but I never told Brother. I was afraid that he might think it was a toy.

Mama told Daddy that his gun would be useless and could definitely get the whole family killed. With legs planted firmly on the floor, Daddy looked into her eyes and quietly but firmly said, "I am going to take this gun with us, just in case." She sighed, hunched her shoulders, and stepped back from him. I had never seen such a look on Daddy's face before. It was scary.

That beautiful moonlit night, I made sure that I had on that my Sunday coat with the tickets in the pocket. Mama, Brother, and I walked down the hidden path, heading to Daddy's banged-up special car. Strangely, the walk didn't seem so far this time. I guess I'd gotten used to it. By the time we got to the car, my father was sitting behind the wheel with the motor running. I saw the money box resting on the front seat as Brother and I settled into the cushions of the back seats. Mama picked up the box, put it on her lap, and sat in the front passenger seat. Off we went. As we pulled away, I felt a lump in my throat. I looked straight ahead, although I wanted to turn around.

I thought, "This is just a little vacation and we'll be back in time for school." Brother looked at me and started to speak. Everyone was quiet. I put my finger to my mouth and shook my head just like Mama. "No!" He settled back in his seat and pulled his toy car out of his pocket.

We were off on an exciting journey and we were ready. The four of us rode slowly away, silently saying goodbye to our beautiful new home. When we were about two miles away from where the car had been parked, I saw Daddy glance in the rearview mirror. The reflection of lights rising in the night allowed for a truth that hurt my heart. I knew they were flames. Mama did not turn around. She looked straight ahead. I wondered what she was thinking. Maybe she thought of Lot's wife in the Bible. Pastor said that she turned around and looked at what happened to her. Maybe Mama knew that there was a place ahead for us where there would be no need to flee in the night. Maybe she knew that it was more important to plan for the future and not worry about the past. I knew that our beautiful house would live forever in our hearts.

I am sorry that I never asked her what she was thinking that night. We rode on in silence, heading for the Richmond train station.

Dear Diary, "As-Salaam-Alaikum"

> *I'm for truth, no matter who tells it. I'm for justice, no matter who it is for or against. I'm a human being, first and foremost, and as such I'm for whoever and whatever benefits humanity as a whole.*

– Alex Haley, *The Autobiography of Malcolm X*

June 13, 1964

Dear Diary,

I am so glad that Jamal is interested in going to Harlem to hear Minister Malcom speak about his pilgrimage to Mecca. He has some new ideas that he wishes to share. Minister Malcolm has become one of the most powerful speakers in the world. He is on television and radio, quite a bit, speaking about injustices.

Since this is my birthday, I mentioned that the trip to hear Minister could be my present, even though I had to wait. Actually I knew that was a way to get two presents for one birthday.

June 22, 1964

Dear Diary,

I was so glad that Jamal was interested in going to Harlem to hear Minister Malcom X speak about his pilgrimage to Mecca. Since his trip, there has been a clash in ideologies with the leadership. The parting of the minds is difficult to watch. It could divide what took hard work to build.

Minister Malcolm has become the most powerful speaker in all the world. We see him on television often, speaking about injustices. We even attended some of the meetings in our city before his pilgrimage to the holy city, Mecca.

My sister-in-law and her husband introduced us to the concepts of Minster Malcolm's theories. When she started working on plans to start a school in our city and her husband was honored as a minister, Jamal and I began to interact more with the members and the leaders in the temple. We became friends with some of the leaders like the Imam and his wife. We were invited to dinners with the city temple leaders.

It is nice to see both the fun and the business side of the leaders. Most of the time the discussions are about the delicious food, current politics, and playing games. There is an unspoken vow to not speak to anyone about any business discussed at dinner.

I even offered our house for a women's retreat and pool party. I look forward to these times. We have gotten to see the jovial and the business side of leadership. The unspoken rule is to respect private time. Enjoy the food and the friendship.

June 23, 1964

Dear Diary,

Minister Malcolm X has changed his name again. Mother says that Malcolm Little is his real name and when he joined the Mosque he became Brother Malcolm. I know him as Minister Malcom X and now he is El Hajj Malike El-Shabazz. His change of philosophy is all over the news.

Jamal and I are excited to get a chance to hear him in person and learn about this new Organization of Afro-American Unity (OOAU) that he is starting. We respect the minister and want to learn about his change of heart and mind. He seems excited to tell us about it.

June 24, 1964

Dear Diary,

I took care in choosing my attire for the upcoming meeting. This will be a special day and I want to present myself in a dignified manner. My parents always say that appearances are important. They constantly question my attendance at any religious events that are not of Baptist origins. They were a bit different when I said that we were going to the event. I think they were interested.

I am going to wear an ankle-length black A-line skirt, a tweed jacket with a matching head wrap, and a long-sleeve, collared white button-down blouse. It is appropriate and dignified. I am topping it off with a pearl necklace and earrings. That simple statement of elegance will make the outfit pop, just a little. It is not my aim to stand out in the crowd. My black suede low-heeled boots will be perfect in case the walk from the car is long.

June 26, 1964

Dear Diary,

I was excited this morning just thinking about going to hear the minister. He is such a powerful speaker.

We both dressed in no time. I could tell that Jamal was looking forward to going because he usually takes more time than I do to get dressed, but not today. With my keys in my jacket pocket, extra money in my bra, and my little purse in hand, I was ready for the security check at the door.

We left early so that we could get a good parking place and a seat. That was wise because there were plenty of spaces in the lot when we arrived. The two-hour drive to New York seemed much longer, but we made it.

When we finally got to the entrance of the building, people started coming from every direction. We planned to meet at a bench outside of Door 22 when the event was over because the men and women did not sit together at the meetings. Jamal headed to the left entrance. He wanted to get a seat near the front in a reserved seating area. I headed to the women's entrance on the right.

I was greeted by women at the reception desk with "Al Salam Alaikum, peace be unto you!" Since I was new to the Harlem group sponsoring the event, I did not know any of the women. I noticed that those in charge of inspections checked me out a little bit longer than those they recognized. I guessed they had to be careful of any new faces. However, once I showed my sister-in-law's card, their manner became charming. She told me to show it so that I could get a reserved seat. I was guided to a chair not far from the front and on the end. It was a perfect location.

A woman in the next seat did not look my way. I wanted to greet her, but she was not interested. That was fine with me. I knew that it was important to be quiet. I wanted to think that she was just being quiet.

Suddenly, I felt a hand on my shoulder and looked up. The wife of the Iman of the city temple gave me a hug as she was escorted to a front row seat with Minister Malcom's wife. Now, suddenly, the lady sitting next to me wanted to chat. Unfortunately, I was not interested. Instead, I glanced to the left to see if I could find Jamal among the "Oh, I'm sorry!" I felt reprimanded. However, my excitement about being there was so overpowering that this request was not troublesome.

My sister-in-law came from behind the stage. Some heads turned to follow her as she placed glasses of water on a table. We caught each other's eye and waved.

It was a large auditorium but not big enough to host the crowd that day. I supposed that some folks would be standing unless there was a fire hazard rule. Not everyone was allowed to enter. Speakers were placed strategically on the outside so people who could not get in could listen. I was glad that we had gotten there early. A man dressed in a dark suit and bow-tie went to the podium to place papers atop it. Immediately a sense of peace hovered over the room.

At first I felt alone among unknown faces, but for some reason, I felt safe. Then once comfortable in my seat, a female usher approached me and said, "My sister, please uncross your legs." Although my skirt was to my ankles and all was hidden, I guess at their meetings crossing legs was not allowed. I immediately obliged and apologized but I was annoyed. My sister-in-law came over hugged me and took her seat in the front row where seats were reserved for the women leaders. It was strange that Mohammed Ali's wife was not among the female dignitaries. I was looking forward to seeing her there. I found out later that her husband had to make a choice and this was not part of his decision.

Suddenly a calm voice spoke firmly over a microphone notifying the audience that the program was about to start! Then the voice began to identify men who were walking in a line onto the platform.

I looked for Jamal again, but this time his attention was directed forward. Everyone turned to the stage and the program began right on time. Silence filled the room.

The honorable Elijah Mohamed's son, Wallace, walked out and was presented. His presence was regal even though he was not tall in stature. However, his being there was surprising, since I had heard that Minister Malcolm and Minster Wallace's father were going in different directions. I was glad to be there so that I could hear firsthand what was going on.

Everyone rose in respect as about six men stood before the chairs on the stage. When the guest speaker was announced, the crowed showed approval by clapping and standing in respect. I stood up, waiting, and then there he was. This beautiful, tall, caramel-colored man seemed to glide to the podium. Once he spoke and signaled that everyone be seated, the quiet became filled with his strong voice of courage, seriousness, and some laughter.

There was something magical about his presence. I held my breath for a moment and then tried to concentrate. I felt like someone was massaging my soul.

He said, "As Salaam Alaikum, Mr. Moderator, our distinguished guests, brothers and sisters, our friends and our enemies, everybody who's here."

The audience responded with "Wa Alaikum Salaam." I was too dazed to speak. While staring at this amazing human being, all I could think of was his greatness. There is something about a star. An aura of respect floats around them. Thank goodness no one knew me. I must have looked strange sitting there with my mouth open.

One thing I can remember him saying was, "We want freedom by any means necessary. We want justice by any means necessary. We want equality by any means necessary." After he explained his new awareness, it was enough for me! I was ready to sign on the dotted line.

Then he finished with, "I thank you for your patience here

tonight, and we want each and every one of you to put your name on the list of the Organization of Afro-American Unity. The reason we have to rely upon you to let the public know where we are is because the press doesn't help us. They never announced in advance that we were going to have a meeting. So, you have to spread the word over the grapevine. You have to call out the people. You have to take charge in answering any questions. I depend on you. Thank you. Wa Alaikum Salaam. Peace be unto you!" And he was gone.

A roar of clapping and the crowd's response of "Wa Alaikum Salaam" echoed as the minister led the men on the dais toward the opening through which they had entered. We had sat in that room for at least two hours, yet it seemed like five minutes. I wasn't ready to go. I wanted more, but it was over.

As I headed for the door, I spotted the woman who requested that I change my sitting position. She smiled and said, "Wa Alaikum Salaam and upon you the peace!"

I smiled back at her and repeated it.

Walking through crowds is never fun. It makes me feel claustrophobic. Then I saw Jamal waiting for me near the bench. We walked slowly and quietly together to the car, deep in thought.

As we got into the car for our trek back home, I remembered some parts of the minister's speech. Jamal thought I was kidding when I told him that. He asked me to repeat them. I don't think he believed me. It's strange how certain things stay in your mind. He laughed in disbelief until I started.

"The minister said, 'We declare our rights on this earth to be a human being, to be respected as a human being, to be given the rights of a human being in this society, on this earth, on this day, which we intend to bring into existence by any means necessary.'"

Jamal looked at me, surprised. "Wow, I guess that was meaningful to you!" he said. I shocked myself by remembering those words. It was meaningful.

Jamal thinks it is time to give this thing some consideration. The man makes sense. I think we need to discuss everything and then make that decision. His teachings have swayed me into a different mindset.

June 27, 1964

Dear Diary,

Jamal and I agreed. We are joining the Organization of Afro-American Unity as soon as possible. We liked the idea of understanding an orthodox version of Sunni Islam and respect that the minister is working with civil rights leaders on improving American race relations and taking his ideas to the United Nations.

***

February 21, 1965

Dear Diary,

Thirty-nine-year-old El Hajj Malike El-Shabazz was killed today. His pregnant wife and three daughters were sitting on the front bench. My heart hurts for them, for us, and for the world. He was shot twenty-one times while speaking at the podium in the <u>Audubon Ballroom</u>, 3940 Broadway at West 165th Street in the Washington Heights neighborhood of Manhattan, New York City. It has been eight months since the speech he gave in Harlem. Now his voice is silenced by bullets.

(https://www.biography.com/news/malcolm-x-assassination)

The Innocent (1988)

(This true story is dedicated to women who had to face unexpected realities. Names have been changed to protect the innocent.)

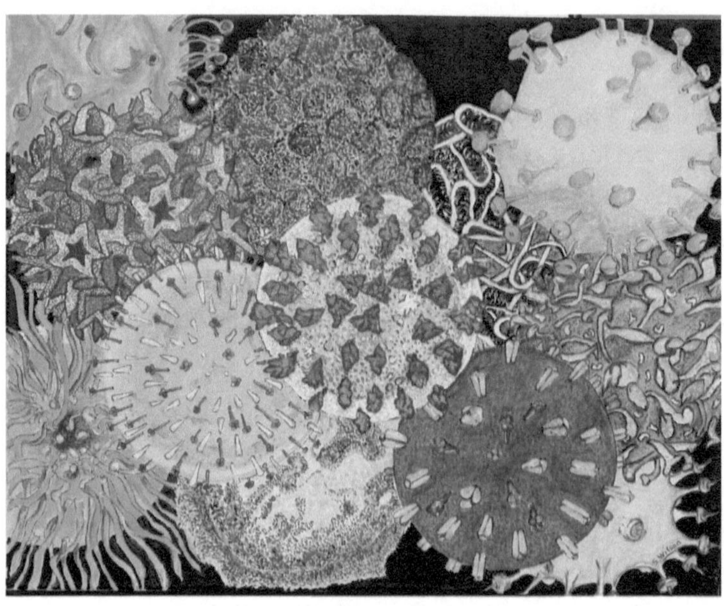

Lois awoke in a strange dark room with a salty taste in her mouth. Her unfamiliar bed was located somewhere between the beeps and hums of machines. She wondered what had happened! She remembered having severe pain before heading to her doctor. She was wheelchaired to the connecting hospital and signed admittance papers. She would have signed anything to stop the pain. Now she awoke with a tightly bandaged abdomen and a nurse checking her vitals.

"Good, you are waking up," the nurse said as she placed a thermometer in Lois's mouth. A blood pressure sleeve squeezed her arm. She slowly took in her sterile environment.

"Ouch!" she said softly. "That is tight! Am I catheterized?" She remembered, after having her first child, she did not want to have to get up from the bed to go to the bathroom, and she hated bedpans. Lois prayed she was catheterized. After receiving an affirmation, she sighed with relief and went back to sleep.

That was all that she could remember about that first day. The next morning, a glow of sunlight forced through large windows haloed a nurse hovering over her.

"Good morning, Sunshine!" the nurse said as Lois squinted and tried to cover her face with her free arm. Suddenly, agony hijacked her body. Her grimacing face invited an explanation of the morphine drip.

"I know," said the nurse. "Today may be a bit challenging. We are going to help you as much as we can with the pain, but the medication from the operation is wearing off. The doctor ordered a morphine drip and that should be a big help. Let's get you washed up and ready for your breakfast. We are going to start you off with a liquid diet. I know it doesn't sound good, but you'll progress soon. You probably don't have an appetite yet anyway."

Lois wondered what merited all of this, so she asked the nurse. She replied, "Your doctor will be in later to explain everything. Right now, let's just get you moving."

After the chore of getting washed and drinking a bit of nourishment, Lois went back to sleep. She didn't know how long she had been out when, through her grogginess, she recognized Doctor Moreno walking through the door. A food tray sat on the table over her bed. Lois's' stomach growled but she was not hungry. Breakfast was not delicious but she did try.

The doctor spoke with the nurse and they both shook their heads in approval. As the nurse left, the doctor eased into a chair beside the bed. She held Lois's hand and spoke of her successful procedure.

"Everything is looking good. I had to get my favorite patient back in working order."

"I bet you say that to all of your patients." They laughed but it hurt her stomach. Lois tried to apply a little pressure on the bandages to suppress the pain of laughing.

"I know it hurts to laugh right now but that will get better." Dr. Moreno introduced herself, offered a reason for the operation, and tried to explain the procedure taken. She added that there were no complications. To Lois, it sounded like she had been fileted like a fish, cauterized, and filled with antiseptic. She pushed the button for the morphine drip, hoping to counteract the physical and emotional agony that struck suddenly like lightning.

"The stitches inside and out will fade away but you have to be careful so you don't pull them. We are going to get you up to walk a little after lunch. It is important to get up and about after an operation! You have got to keep that body in working order."

Lois was confused. "Dr. Moreno, how did this happen? I was fine and then suddenly the pain took over my body."

The doctor looked into her eyes and said, "I hate to tell you this. Okay, here's the deal. You had chlamydia!"

"Chlamydia?" Lois sat up. She said it quietly but the words seemed to bounce off the walls, almost overshadowing approaching footsteps. She was glad that she was in a single room. "That's impossible! Isn't that a sex disease, like gonorrhea and syphilis?"

"We see a lot of cases. Yours was bad. It had been generating for years and had infected your intestines. Chlamydia is a common STD that can cause infection among both men and women. It can cause permanent damage to a woman's reproductive system. It can make it difficult or impossible to get pregnant. Chlamydia can also cause a potentially fatal ectopic pregnancy."

Lois was in shock. She thought about her first pregnancy.

The twins did not make it. There was a baby she carried for 8 months and it had died before birth. There was a quiet in the room and then Lois spoke. "Thank God I two of my children had successful births. I don't have to worry about getting pregnant at fifty years old, I hope." She settled back down in the bed.

Now that her patient had gotten what she thought was the worst part of the news, Dr. Moreno continued. "We had to remove and burn the lesions that were on your intestines and do a few other things. You are fine now!"

"Oh my God! Chlamydia? But I have only had sex with..." She sighed and didn't finish her sentence.

Hospital workers were moving about in the hall outside of her room. Her morning tray was removed and a tray filled with unappetizing liquids for lunch was placed on her table. She was too shocked to eat anyway. She couldn't cry. Anger began to seep into her soul. Suddenly a figure appeared in the door. It was impossible to see who it was because the upper body was blocked by the biggest bouquet of flowers that Lois had ever seen.

As if choreographed, the two women turned to see who was entering behind those flowers. Lois knew who it was! She would know those hands anywhere. Like a model on a runway, Lois's handsome husband strolled into the room, smiling!

"So how is my beautiful wife today?"

A Mask Is a Mask: COVID

(2020)

The battle to stay healthy is ongoing for everyone. Staying current with health care is a must. As a child it seemed to be yearly moments just for booster shots. Now that applies to adults also. Germs are everywhere. Microorganisms appear to be beautiful in photographic renderings, but what they carry is not. Being struck by any of them can be catastrophic. Caution and medicine are important in keeping them at bay. It is comforting that scientists are constantly at work trying to find cures for the ailments of the ages.

If someone had told me years ago that a small piece of material would make a difference between life or death, I would have waited for the punchline. However, in 2020 reality struck. Some folks in high places were aware of a coming pandemic before the public got word. Programs were in place to prepare for warfare against a pandemic. However, the next set of legislators dismantled the programs. New tactics had to be established for the Disease War...and war it was.

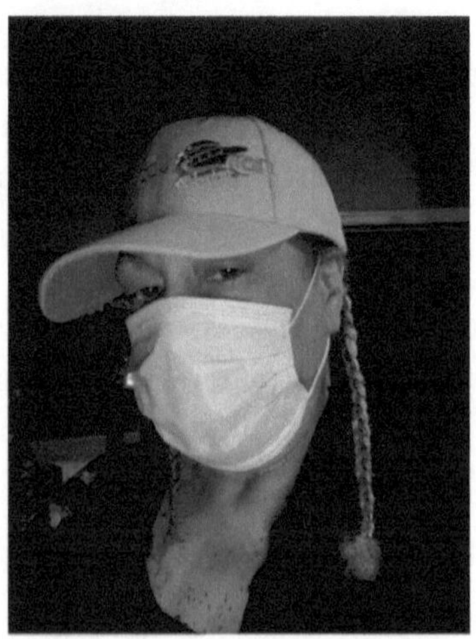

("A rose is a rose is a rose" = Things are what they are!) Gertrude Stein

To wear or not to wear became the question of the day! I chose to don that mask. I could bear being a little uncomfortable since it meant saving lives. I washed my hands, sprayed everything coming into my home, wiped doorknobs, and made sure that only masked people could enter and stay a distance from me.

So, what if I sweated under the mask in the summer? The benefits were important. I appreciated that heat during the winter.

It made sense to cover the lower face and wear rubber gloves since COVID was considered airborne and tactile. I didn't touch anything without wearing my blue rubber gloves. That included the mail and groceries. The virus was killing people all over the world at a fast rate. I was striving to not be one of them. It was a scary time.

Fights over wearing masks were alarming. Some said that wearing one infringed upon their civil rights. People who didn't want to wear them were angry. Others surmised that death was far more frightening than covering the face. The debates were consistent and unbelievable.

Wearing masks was not a new concept. Full face masks and those covering just the eyes and nose had been worn for holidays and parties for centuries. Thieves used them so that identification could be confusing. However, the Coronavirus brought on a new purpose for the mask: health.

Masks came in different shapes, sizes, colors, and decorations. Creating them generated a lucrative industry. The sewing machine business bloomed once again. The N95 masks were purported to be the best. However, there could be a runway modeling of the different colors, patterns, and shapes. Boxes of blue, white, and black seemed to be the most popular. There were masks that allowed for changing a white filtering pad to keep germs in or out.

My sewing skills were minimal. I was not inclined to jump on that bandwagon. Years ago, I was proud of the costumes with masks that I made for my husband and me to wear to a Mardi Gras party. The masks were made of red feathers to match the costumes. To my surprise, the outfits turned out to be pretty nice according to my friends. I never got the feeling that my husband was enamored with them. He agreed to wear his costume.

When we got to the party, none of the men were in costume. My husband was glad he wore a nice outfit under his costume. I did not. In haste, he took off his costume and put it in the car. My feelings were hurt! However, the compliments I received for my outfit assuaged that pain. Oh, how I wish I could fit into the cute red devil red costume today.

Halloween used to be my favorite holiday as a child. Even as an adult, I loved taking my children and their friends out for "Trick or Treating." I think it came about because when I was young, I would carefully plan my costume and mask. My Aunt Gladys gathered the family children to canvas my grandparents' neighborhood. We only moved the full- face masks down to our chins while walking, so we could see. We were identifiable among the throngs of candy beggars, because we were the only black family living in the Italian community. Plus, we were led by this tall, stout, cheerful woman who spoke Italian. My aunt was greeted with laughter, hugs, and "AHHH Gladeez!" The doors opened to sweep us in, and fill our bags with goodies, while my Aunt Gladys dined on food and wine. By the end of the night everyone was happy.

A couple of years ago, I had a different encounter with masks. I was the speaker at a women's Bible retreat entitled "Wearing Your Mask." The concept was hiding from God. Interestingly, my statement about folks wearing invisible masks to hide their feelings, brought signs of recognition. The reality of this concept hit home when I saw those people attacking the U.S. Capitol on June 6th. I surmised that they had been wearing invisible masks for many years and now their true feelings were televised. Their personalities and intentions were unmasked.

I am old. I am sick and I am black. That virus is looking for me. I surely do not want it to catch me. I have gotten all of my shots with the hope of saving myself and others. I would never forgive myself if I was the cause of someone's death because I didn't wear a mask. It would really upset me to cause my own death. Although I won't live forever, I can do my best to stay here for as long as I can. If wearing a mask can help, then that is what I will do. Wearing a mask is a small gesture with a big outcome. So, if I might be a little uncomfortable for a little while, it is for the greater good.

Dr. King once said, "The ultimate measure of a man is not where he stands in moments of comfort and convenience, but where he stands at times of challenge and controversy." In these defining times...I chose to wear the mask! It seems to be such a small thing to reap great rewards.

Lying Choices

As a child, Veronica was taught that telling a lie was deplorable. Her parents made sure that their children understood that telling the truth was important. They had a specialty waiting for liars. She had even heard that some children got their mouths washed out with soap for lying. She swore that was not going to happen to her.

They taught that...

1. When you lie, you have to remember the lie.

2. One lie leads to another lie.

3. Lies can lead to hurtful situations.

4. Lies put you in positions you might not want to be in.

5. In the long run, a lie will be exposed.

6. Once the lie is in the air, you can never take it back.

Veronica tried to follow these rules but there were slip-ups. It was not until she was an adult that she realized that everyone lies about something. If they say they don't, they are lying. There were times when she had to lie. At least four times a year she would intentionally lie.

1. Be good so that Santa will come to visit.

2. The Easter Bunny will leave you treats.

3. Put your tooth under your pillow for the Tooth Fairy! She will leave you a surprise.

Those were the fun lies. Then there is the work lie. Veronica called into work to say, "I am not feeling well. I think it might be the flu. I don't want to spread it." She'd sound as sick and weak as possible to generate sympathy. Deep in her heart she was sure the secretary knew she was lying, just like everyone else who wanted a paid day off from work. She liked to stay home and rest at least once or twice a year. This was a deserved day off. On those days she usually ended up doing housekeeping and running errands. She loved her beautiful home. However, working around the house was not her idea of resting.

Veronica usually used eight out of ten days of sick leave for sick or lying children and husband. She figured the other two were hers illnesses or to do with as she pleased.

On those days she didn't tell her family that she was taking a day off because her husband would line up chores, like taking his shirts to the cleaners, and the children would beg to stay home! Even her parents would want to spend some time with her. This was going to be her day of no responsibilities!

She thought about going to a spa, hiding in a funny movie, or shopping until she dropped. She felt that she might be seen in a spa, so that was out. A dark theater would be great. She could wear an odd outfit and a wig, but she settled for shopping in the city, away from people who would know her. She planned to take a train, shop, have lunch, shop again, and get home before school let out.

It was perfect. By lunchtime, Veronica, laden with packages, headed to a restaurant for her favorite meal, Chicken Marsala. Just as she nestled into a spot by a window, she glanced up and saw...

***

(Choose your own ending!)

Ending A: "Best friend!"

Just as she was about to tap on the window, she noticed that Paula wasn't alone. She was talking with a couple and they were all holding hands. As Veronica rose from the seat, Paula leaned in and gave them both a passionate kiss on the mouth. Veronica sat down, stunned. So, she wasn't the only one living a lie. Veronica had lost her appetite. Before she could gather her things to leave even before ordering, Paula appeared.

"Hello, sweetie, what are you doing in town? Shouldn't you be at work?"

Veronica couldn't speak. She sat down and gawked!

"Listen, I am not going to explain what you just saw. It is my business and I don't have to share it with you."

"What about your husband?" Veronica asked.

"He knows, so you don't have to feel guilty. I know you well enough to know that you wouldn't tell. I saw you and I would have acted differently. This is me and I don't apologize."

Veronica did not respond although she had questions.

As Paula rose to leave, she said, "Once you have calmed down, we will talk, but right now I have to get back to work. By the way, does your family know you are out here shopping like a crazy woman? Better hurry up or you will miss the train."

__Ending B:__ *"High school love, Sam!"*

Sam tapped on the window, smiling. Veronica beckoned him in. He approached, dressed in a tailored outfit from head to toe. Surprisingly, Veronica's love juices started to bubble! He kissed her hand! It was more than nice to see him. He was as handsome as ever.

"Do you mind if I order for us, my treat?" he said, and Veronica nodded.

"I'd like two White Russians, a Philly cheesesteak with fries, and Chicken Marsala for the lady."

She was impressed that he remembered.

They had a great time laughing and talking about old times. Sometime during the discussion, Sam expressed that he had never stopped loving Veronica. Now that he was divorced, he wondered if there was a chance to get back together. Holding her hand made it difficult for her to think.

"I know that you are married with a couple of kids," he said. "I have one of my own that I adore. We were young and college life was exciting. Maybe if we had gone to the same college, things would have been different. I have never gotten over you."

It felt good to hear this and Veronica did not pull away. Her husband never talked of love. This was upsetting and exhilarating.

She wondered, "Why she couldn't do both—see him on the side and keep her family. Then her mother appeared in her thoughts, saying, "A lie will always come to the light." Veronica had a decision to make. She had thought about Sam constantly over the years. She didn't need any time to think about it. She did not choose Sam.

Ending C: "...an extensive menu!"

The menu offered all kinds of delicious choices. Veronica stuck to her guns and ordered the Chicken Marsala. It was divine, so she ordered enough for her family's dinner.

On the drive home from the train, she spotted her husband's car. She remembered he said that he had an important meeting that day. Evidently, it ended early.

She had to stall him because she needed time to get home before he did! She called his cell to ask him to stop at the store to get some milk and bread. That is all she could think of at the time. No one ever questions getting milk and bread. She could see him shaking his head and flailing his arms about as he protested the stop. She knew he would do it, though.

It gave her just enough time to get home and pull into the garage to hide the warmth of the car motor and her packages. She would throw on some jeans and make sure her makeup was perfect!

The table was set and food was warming. Once he arrived, they immediately took the time to satisfy their lustful spirits before the children got home. That night the family had a lovely dinner of Chicken Marsala. All was right in the world.

Ending D: "...that time was passing too fast."

Veronica had to hurry through lunch to beat everyone home. After dining on her favorite meal of Chicken Marsala, she didn't have time to shop again as planned.

She bought a Mound candy bar to eat on the train in remembrance of shopping trips with her mother. She loved their trips to the city twice a year for school clothes and Christmas shopping. Her mother always bought her a comic book and a Mound on the way home. A tear formed in honor of those trips.

Veronica smiled all the way home. That stopped when she reached her house. It had been a great day until she spotted her husband's car in the driveway. It was disturbing.

She thought, "What in the world is he doing at home? Okay, now what? Think, Veronica, think!"

She was not going to take her packages out of the car. She was glad that she put them in the trunk; it was too late to hide them. Maybe presenting him with his new watch would grant forgiveness.

"Wait a minute," she thought. "Why do I need forgiveness? I am a grown woman, making a good salary. I am not frivolous—well, most of the time. Okay, so today I was. How long has he been home and why is he home so early?"

Veronica secretly touched the hood of his car as she walked by to see if it was warm. It was not. Evidently, he had been home quite a while. She couldn't get her thoughts together fast enough to beat his opening of the front door. When she saw his face, something in her stomach began to hurt.

He asked, "Where in the world have you been? I called your job. I called Paula and your mother. No one has seen you. I started to call the hospitals, the police! You look okay! Are you okay? Do we need to have a talk? Are you seeing someone? What is going on?"

The lying had to stop at this point. Veronica decided to tell the truth. He was right. They needed to have a talk about why she felt she had to lie.

Second Chances

When she opened her eyes, she was standing in a flowering garden that reached to the horizon. Nestled in her arm was her cat, Melody. A lion and a lamb gracefully waited. Once they knew that she could see them, they began walking side-by-side down an unbelievably green, grassy path. Unafraid, smiling and with her Melody tucked in her arms, she took a step to follow them. The path felt as soft as cotton but firm enough to support the heaviest of weights. She wondered how that was possible. Her yellow gown, blown by a soft wind, trailed each step as if she was a famous singer on a stage with a fan blowing to present an alluring effect.

An assortment of birds flew above as if their mission was to escort her. An owl hooted from a nearby tree and a canary sang from a flowering bush. Their harmony could challenge the work of any gospel choir.

As she passed a baby-blue pond, she couldn't help but glance in. Water creatures colored by the rainbow looked back, welcoming her with their eyes as their lips projected kisses.

Then she saw her reflection. No longer was she a seventy-eight-year-old woman. She had suddenly lost at least fifty years of aging. She almost didn't recognize herself. Melody, a kitten once again, purred and licked her arm. It was startling. She liked it. Gladly she accepted the change and turned back to the path.

The lion and the lamb were no longer there. Instead, a grizzly bear and a fawn appeared on the path. She followed them as they ambled along until they reached a huge gate. It was covered in purple pearls. She remembered hearing that purple was the color of royalty. This must be a regal place. The gate was hugged by bushy green shrubs on each side. The grizzly and the fawn did not stop. They continued strolling past the gate but she stopped to get a good look. She wanted to take a picture but she didn't have her phone. She wondered, "What am I doing, wandering about without my phone? If something should happen, I can't call for help."

She approached the beautiful purple gates, wondering what was behind them. Everything so far had been beautiful. The creaking of the gate gave her a chill. A smiling being that could be classified as beautiful by magazines standards walked through the gate. Dressed in a velvet orange cape and with arms open, they said, "We have been waiting for you. Welcome! Are you ready to join us here for the time of your existence?" Unsure of what that meant, she held tight to her kitten and took a step forward.

The cloaked being held out their hands and said, "Welcome! You are on my special list!"

However, something didn't seem right. The kitten clung to her, grasping with her claws, and her purring turned into a growl. She wondered about the smiling being and stepped back. There was something that bothered her about that smile.

There was a strange hint of something burning on a stove. This place looked beautiful from the path. However, the music that drifted out from behind the gates was not comforting. Everything else had seemed lovely until this moment. She recognized the smell as barbecue and baked bread and suddenly she felt hungry. Yet there was a strange orange haze lingering beyond the gate that didn't seem inviting. She thought about it for a moment and decided to turn back to the path and see what was beyond.

"If you leave, you can never come back. Goodbye!" said the orange-caped figure. With a flip of the hand and a twirl of the body, the creature turned and went back through the gate, followed by a strange meandering shadow. As the gates closed, the music became thundering chords forced from an unknown instrument. Suddenly, flames reached above the gate as the figure disappeared. Although she heard those sounds as she walked away, she thought about Lot's wife and refused to turn around to look.

To her surprise, an elephant and a mouse who had been watching walked onto the path and began to head away from the fire. She decided to follow them. Her kitten purred, licked her arms, and snuggled.

A waterfall up ahead seemed to call her forth with music different from what she had just heard. A new group of colorful birds took the place of the others and flew above her, singing in harmony. She couldn't help humming their familiar song as she walked along. They passed two more gates along the way but their guides did not stop, so she continued to follow them.

When they reached a pond, she realized she hadn't had a drink of water throughout the journey, so she cupped her hand and offered some to the kitten. Then she reached in for herself. There was a sweetness in the water. It was refreshing.

Time did not seem to matter in this trek. She felt that wherever she was going, she would be on time. Finally, she spotted gates ahead. She wanted to run to them. These gates were covered in multicolored pearls. As the gates opened, a soothing music wafted from inside. A rainbow crowned the area behind the gates as they opened. She heard giggling as a smiling creature in a pink and blue cloak floated out from the opening gates and settled before her. Although it appeared to be both male and female, the beauty of their face molded into one. They spoke in such a soft voice, it almost sounded like a whisper.

"Welcome. We have been waiting for you for ages."
"You have been waiting for me?"

"Yes! It is with love and joy that I welcome you."

"Thank you!" she said, shaking.

"You have been watched throughout your lifetime, so we knew you were on the way. That may sound eerie, but it was with affection and protection. We are so proud of you. This journey may seem confusing, but you will understand later. Few make it to this gate. Before you can enter, I must inform you of something wonderful. Are you ready to receive this message?"

"Yes!" she answered, feeling sure and amazed.

"We are happy to announce that you are a candidate for angel status."

"Me?"

"Yes, you! Do you understand? Well of course you don't. Wait...there, I just put it into your mind. You will now under-stand what I am talking about. The Supreme sees and hears everything and is so happy to have you here."

"The Supreme? Ah, I see what you mean now."

"Good! You have often made us smile. You have been a kind and giving being. You remained true to your family, friends, and some strangers too. Not everyone does that!"

"Thank you! I am ready for whatever is before me. Can my cat—I mean my kitten—and I enter together? We have both gotten younger since we started this journey."

"Of course. She can come in, but she might have to wait for you. We have a special place for pets to wait for their best friends. Some call it Rainbow Bridge. They cross over into a world of love. It is wonderful. We make sure that they do not go through a spell of longing. They will think that you are still by their side. They get a chance to interact with other pets and enjoy their waiting time. Do not worry. She will be well cared for here until you come back."

"What do you mean, come back?"

"I know that sounds strange. We are not rejecting you. We want you here but there are a couple of things you may go back to work on."

"Did I do something wrong?"

"Nothing that you can't change. We have great plans for you, so take this as a helpful criticism. No one is perfect...well, not anymore. There was one. You just have a couple of teeny tiny things to attend to."

A tear formed in her eye. She wasn't sure why.

"First, your involvement in listening to people's personal business can be a problem. Being curious is fine but getting involved is a 'no-no.' That is not always a good thing unless you are being supportive. Your mother, your husband, and your children have mentioned this to you. They may have sounded harsh, but it was said out of love. Being curious is fine, but getting involved is not always necessary. You have to work on that. We realize that you mean well, but you often pass the help stage and move into becoming a 'busybody.'"

"A busybody?"

"Yes, paying too much attention to what others are doing in their personal lives can be a problem. That is fine for angels. Angels are trained to help. We get involved, hoping to help. That trait might serve you well later, but it is not a good trait to have as a normal person. Some things should remain private.

"You were given two eyes, two ears, and one mouth, not two mouths, one ear, and one eye. Comedian Flip Wilson used to say, 'Loose lips sink ships, honey!' Where do you think he got those words?

"Also, we realize that telling the truth can be difficult. Your second problem is being careful what you say and who you say it to. You must master that. In your attempts to make people feel good, you have not always given them the responses needed. Although you may not want to hurt someone's feelings, you have unintentionally done that in some cases. You have to figure out when it is right and when it's not. It's a judgment thing!

"We believe that knowing better means doing better. Let

me make this clear. Everything else looks good. Your good outweighs the bad and so you are welcome here. The Supreme has decided to give you a second chance at moving up the ladder. Don't take it for granted. This is a rare opportunity but it doesn't come without some choices. If you don't like them, you don't have to accept them. You decide which path to take. You can take advantage of this or not. It is entirely up to you. Either way, you will be here with us.

"Should you choose to take this offer, you will be reborn but with a handicap this time. Since this will be your second time around, you will have a challenge. You can choose to be born blind or deaf. Either one will allow your other senses to become stronger. In doing so, you will see the world differently. You will end up wiser and with more understanding of how to carry out your new position.

"For instance, if you become blind, you will be able to hear, taste, touch, smell, and speak better than ever before. You will notice sounds that you never paid attention to, like songs of the birds you sang with on the way here and the humming of the bees as they go about their necessary duties. You will hear water rushing like you did at the waterfall. You will appreciate all kinds of music, perceive meaning in different languages and their tones of voices. You will even understand the sound of cracks in the sidewalk and feel the pressure of the air on your face...things like that. It will be an amazing experience.

"Being deaf will allow you to see things differently, like the changing of the seasons, the expressions of paintings, and the complexions of the human soul. Reality will unfold differently and you will be able to interpret reactions truthfully. Your senses of sight, taste, touch, and smell will be exceptional. However, it will take intentional work to learn to speak again, and that will be a challenge. You will enjoy visual art, detect distinct colors of the rainbow, interpret people's expressions, and observe intricacies that you had never paid attention to before. You will write and paint masterpieces.

"Of course, the family that you will be born into will be specially selected. They will love and help you through the good times and the struggles. That is not to say that everything will always be easy. You will have to learn all over again how to live with dignity, grace, and a sense of right and wrong.

"You have a minute to think about this opportunity and make a choice. You can stay here now, you can always go back to the first gate, or you can be reborn. If you want to be reborn, choose one of the handicaps. Either will be a blessing to you. If you stay here, this second opportunity will be given to another deserving soul.

"I am looking forward to being with you along the way. Since I have such hope for you, I am stepping down for the moment to be your G.A., your Guardian Angel. As your G.A., I will be with you on the journey. Only you will know that I am there. If you go back and do well, you will become a member of the Angel Band. No, that is not a musical group. I can feel your respect for that honor.

"This is truly an opportunity of a forever lifetime. There will never be another chance. So, which do you choose?"

She hugged Melody, kissed her goodbye, and placed her gently on the ground. The kitten looked up at her, purred, and ran through the gates as they closed. Her favorite music encircled her, but she did not hear it. As she turned to head back the way she came, a camel and a hen led the way. With her yellow robe blowing slightly and a presence of something in white floating beside her, she smiled and followed them.

All Kinds of Junk

It was my time to move onto a new phase of life once again. If you live long enough, there will surely be times of change.

This was my time. My husband was only fifty-seven when he passed away. I had retired. My children were grown with families of their own. I was on my own for the first time in my life and I had decisions to make. Being the matriarch of the family put me in a position toward which I had not aspired. I accepted my new life and planned to make some sensible but fun changes. Moving was to be my first step! I had to get rid of a multitude of things accumulated over the years. I had a lot of junk among my treasures. This was physical and mental work! I decided to move from a big house to something that made sense for one person.

First I thought about purchasing a condo where I could live like I was on vacation. That seemed doable but I wasn't ready for that yet, even though I was fifty-five. It sounded too much like assisted living. I got the concept mixed up with a dependent living care facility. I was not ready for an old folks home. I found out that a 55+ condo was not that. With a realtor, I visited beautiful units but decided to wait a few years.

Tiny houses were getting a lot of advertisements on the internet. I always wanted a playhouse as a child but that never happened. So, I was intrigued by this concept while hoping that I was not reverting back to childhood. Tiny houses reminded me of playhouses. As a child, I used to take blankets and hang them across the clotheslines in the yard, get out my tea set, and dress up in my mother's hats, shoes, and pocketbooks. I would invite neighborhood children and my little cousins over to have a make-believe tea party under the tented blankets. My mother would provide cookies, little sandwiches, and lemonade. That was childhood fun. I connected tiny houses with fun.

I didn't need a lot of space now, and a tiny house might work. I suggested playfully to my daughter and son-in-law that we could temporarily remove the fence and gate at the end of their driveway to allow for my tiny house to be placed in their backyard. We could put the gate back up once the house was completed. They laughed with me, but I was serious. This was a possibility! I can't imagine their joy in having wonderful me living in their backyard.

My third option was a camper. I could travel around the country, see unique things, meet new people, visit old friends, and participate in different experiences. The Grand Canyon would be my first stop. That is exciting.

My husband and I once owned a Volkswagen camper and loved it. We took a lot of trips in that little camper. We even talked about overcoming the challenges of living in one later in life. Now that he was no longer here, I thought maybe I could consider it anyway.

One of my favorite camper ventures was when we rented a large camper for a trip to Cape Cod one summer. It slept eight and had everything we needed: a full kitchen, a large bathroom, and space to lounge. We packed up our bikes and even took my in-laws with us. Unfortunately, the gas prices exploded that year. We ended up in Cape May instead. It was closer to our home in Pennsylvania. The vacation was still wonderful.

Being safe as a single woman traveling alone in a camper could be a problem. My safety depended on me now. There was no one else to protect me from danger.

I figured that a camper could work spatially and financially. I could travel half the year. I might be able to coerce some friends to travel periodically. Then I could park it in one of my children's yards and live in it the other half of the year . Since I would be so close to family if I would be living in the backyard, we could be available for each other when needed. I could also have my privacy. However, after researching prices, the costs for a new camper did not fit my budget.

While researching, I remembered seeing a sign on a side street that read "All Kinds of Junk." One of the pictures on the sign was an old camper. I decided to visit that junkyard on a day when I had time to browse. I had never been to a junkyard before and hoped it would be interesting. Since I couldn't buy a new camper, maybe I'd find a decent one that could be repaired inexpensively.

My family and friends would be appalled at this idea, so I didn't tell them. I was avoiding questions like, "What if there is a tornado or a hurricane? What would you do? You might need to get a dog if you are going to travel alone. Are you sure this is what you want to do?" I didn't want to hear any discouraging words. I was still in the thinking process. I needed to talk with an unbiased soul.

On the day that I drove up to the junkyard, I had no idea what to expect. I passed through the gates of a high metal fence. Four well-kept buildings nestled on a path. Three were painted the primary colors (yellow, blue, and red) and one was a white home with black shutters. Interesting objects neatly decorated the entrance. The water squirting from a large ceramic fish in an artistic waterfall was welcoming. It was nice and not what I had expected.

Pete

A man, about 5'5" with a neatly trimmed white beard and wearing a ragged but large straw hat sat in a rocking chair on the porch of the white house. If he had worn a red suit, I would have guessed him to be Santa. He smiled with such warmth that I felt like we knew each other. I guessed he was about sixty-five years old. His handshake was firm and came with a warm welcome to what he labeled as one of the loves of his life, the junkyard.

"My name is Pete," he said. "Come on over!" He guided me to the porch of what seemed to be a freshly painted ranch-style home. We sat in rocking chairs as a number of cats relaxed in the sun and others traveled about as if on errands.

"This is quite a unique place," I said as my head twirled, trying to see as much as possible.

He responded with pride. "Isn't it, though? That was exactly my plan. My wife and I raised a couple of kids here with a few chickens and pigs at one time. She's a school teacher and the accountant for our business. Her skills keep us on track with taxes and bills. Thank God!" He laughed and slapped his leg. "So, young lady, why are you here at All Kinds of Junk?"

I felt complimented by the reference to age. I hadn't been a young lady, physically, in a long time. After I told him the purpose of my visit, he took me back to where the campers were located. We had to walk down a long path. Some of the cats walked part of the way and then veered off. Acres of all kinds of objects had been laid out in subdivisions. It seemed a mess at first but there were gravel paths that defined themed sections. I saw bathtubs and old sinks in one section. I even saw a few horses that must have once graced merry-go-rounds.

We stopped at an area with cars on one side of the path and campers on the other. The grass was high around the campers but I was able to look inside the four I chose to inspect. They looked like they needed the least amount of work from the outside. Surprisingly, the insides were not as bad as I had imagined, but they still needed too much repair for me to handle. I wouldn't know who to hire to do repairs or how much it would cost. Pete said that he would give me a fair price on any one that I chose. I really didn't know him and thought, "Yes, that is what all car dealers people say and you find out that the deal was really not a deal." However, there was something about this man that made me believe him. Maybe it was the Santa look!

Cleo

As I stepped away from the fourth camper, a long black snake wiggled out from under the front tire. I almost bolted.

Before I could scream, Pete said calmly, "Stay still. Cleo

is a bit touchy these days. She is about to birth some babies. Other than that, she's okay. She needs space when she is in that condition." I assumed he was talking about the snake and sighed in relief when Cleo disappeared back behind the tire as quickly as she had arrived. That's when I realized that Pete had not said she was harmless.

"I hate snakes—or, I should say, I am scared of them."

"No need to be bothered by her. Respect nature and it will respect you! Cleo is just trying to live and take care of her own, just like us."

I thought, if Cleo is pregnant, she didn't get that way on her own. There must be male snakes around and loads of their children. I turned toward the way we had come, trying to hide that I wanted to run. Pete got the message.

Jerry

As we headed back the way we had come, a crow fluttered above us and then landed on Pete's hat. The glare of the sun flashed before my eyes when I tried to look at Pete's hat. It took a while for me to see the crow sitting proudly and staring in my direction.

"Hello Jerry!" he said. The crow responded with a loud caw. "This is Jerry." He pointed. "That is his tree up there. He comes down to visit every now and then when he is curious. Just look him in the eyes and say softly 'Hello Jerry' and he will be your friend."

"Hello Jerry," I echoed, trying to look into his eyes. As Jerry tilted his head from side to side, his eyes followed me.

Once the three of us arrived back at the white house, he flew away. A couple of the cats met us near the house and accompanied us to the porch. Others were busy doing whatever cats do.

I was so curious about this place and had all kinds of

questions. I just knew there were all kinds of stories hovering around the place. So, I started with, "How long have you owned this business?"

"Oh, shy of about thirty years. Got it from an old geezer, my dad. It is easy living and can be historical. Some of the things here are probably worth quite a bit. If you are careful you might find things that are priceless. You'd be surprised to see the many people who troll through here periodically. Some are historians and professors. Some just like to find things to fix up. The people are interesting and I make lots of friends. A few come around periodically to just sit and chat.

"Folks are always getting rid of stuff. When relatives die, they are stuck with things they don't want or value. Remember that saying, 'One man's junk is another man's treasure?' I bet you've heard that before. Some of it is pretty good stuff and may need a bit of polishing. Some folks come searching for something specific, like a treasure hunt. They might not find what they are looking for, but they may find something else along the way.

"My buddy, Jerry, and his family will sometimes bring me things and drop them at my steps. Crows tend to like shiny things. They will steal them. Sometimes those things turn out to be valuable and I feel a little guilty because I know Jerry and his gang are thieves. So far I haven't had any problems with the police checking for things reported missing." We both had to laugh at that.

The Cats

He pointed to a rocking chair. "Take a load off. Don't worry about the cats. They won't bite cha!" I sat down. He went into the house to get lemonade. At first, I was apprehensive about drinking something in a junkyard, but I liked Pete and I wanted to give him a positive impression of me. Anyway, the glasses were sparkling clean and the drink was delicious.

He sat down with his drink. "My wife makes a fresh batch of lemonade every day. She knows that it is my favorite drink. Don't worry about my animals. Between the snakes and the cats, I don't have to worry about mice and rats."

I thought, "But what about snakes? Is there something that keeps them at bay?"

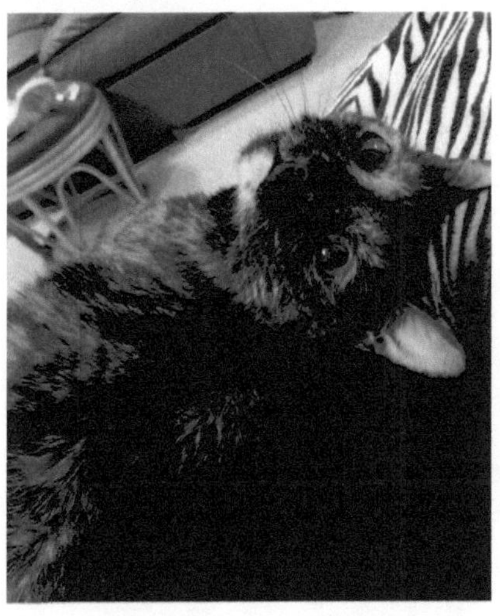

He continued, "The cats find food for themselves. I give them treats every now and then." Suddenly, a marble-colored cat jumped into my lap and got comfortable. I almost spilled my drink. I guess the cat sensed Sheba, my own cat, and my lap looked inviting.

"That's Susie. She is a Calico and she likes to meet new people. You can pet her. She doesn't bite and she enjoys petting. You must be special. I have never seen her do that."

As I caressed Susie, she purred. "What do you think I should do, Mr. Pete? I am really thinking about living in a camper. I may not be able to afford a new one but am not sure what it takes to fix up one of yours."

"Call me Pete, just plain old Pete. Everybody does. Here is my suggestion. You don't have to take it if you disagree. Find a used camper that needs a little repair and find someone to do the work. I know some folks in that line of business. You don't strike me as being good at repairs. Come back here if you need a name and parts. A lot of my business is with men who fix things. I must tell you that it's refreshing to see a gal out here interested in a camper. That is pretty unusual."

We sat on the porch talking all afternoon. I listened and

laughed at the old campers' stories. Pete had quite a few. They were funny, mysterious, love -related, learning experiences, and just plain interesting. He reminded me of the griots in Africa who carried the history of the people and their stories in their heads. They traveled from village to village, sharing information. Drums would announce their coming and people would gather for this special occasion. Pete's stories were just that good.

Pete and I became friends that day. I had come there for a camper but I got good advice, therapy, a new friend, and some entertaining stories.

I took his suggestion. He'd said, "Find folks interested in getting a larger camper for a growing family. They are probably ready to sell at a good price to get the new one for vacation time. Don't offer the top price for it. More than likely, they will come down but don't go too far down. Be reasonable. I don't know much about the little houses but research it real good before you step out there."

Decisions

There were loads of campers for sale. I settled in on a 2021 Forest River Salem FSX 260RTX on sale for $28,999.00. I planned to offer $28,000.00 and see what would happen.

However, I fell in love with a tiny house and dropped the camper idea. I found one perfect for me. After persuading my daughter and her husband to knock down part of their fence and extend the driveway back into the yard, my spot was secured.

Construction began. Almost everything was on one floor with two bedrooms, one bathroom, a living area, and a kitchen that housed full-size appliances. They would even make it a bit larger so that there would be a place for a double-decker washing machine and dryer. With a driveway up to my door,

I would be able to have my privacy and still be near family. I loved it!

Visiting Pete was next on my list. I wanted to let him know about my progress and thank him for his help. I also wanted to look through the junkyard to see if there were any great finds. I settled on a weekend visit so I could meet his wife. Since school was out over the weekends, I hoped she would be home. I wanted to invite them both over once my house was completed.

The Revisit

Early one Saturday morning, I drove out to the junkyard. It was surprising not to see Pete rocking in his chair or people walking about among the cats. I noticed a sign on the door that said "Closed!" His place was advertised as being open from 9 a.m. until 5 p.m. on Saturdays. I assumed working families would be out and about that day, but no one was there. Maybe they would be coming later in the day. But...

I spotted Jerry on the porch roof. He cawed at me. I looked him in the eyes and said, "Hello Jerry!" Jerry tilted his head from side to side, cawed back and flew away. I knocked on the door and a lady with long, beautiful curly white hair opened it. Her lovely face seemed a bit drawn as if getting over the flu or maybe COVID. That might be the reason no one was there. COVID had just been announced so I made sure to wear a mask. I pulled up the mask that was hooked to a chain around my neck, just in case.

Joyce

"Hello! May I help you?" she said. Her voice was muffled by her mask. I introduced myself a little louder than usual and explained that I had come to thank Pete for setting me on the right track. She smiled and invited me in or to sit on the porch. Although I was curious to see the inside of the house, I chose the porch. It was best that we stay outside.

"Don't worry about the mask. I did get my shot. Please, have a seat. We'll just sit a bit away from each other. By the way, my name is Joyce. I am not surprised that you are here," she said. "Everyone loves Pete. He told me that he had made a new gal friend looking to live in a camper."

I was glad that he put me in the friend category. "He thought that a camper was a nice idea but not what you should do."

While she was talking, I wondered why she didn't call Pete and tell him that I was there. Maybe he had COVID Maybe he wasn't home or taking a shower and couldn't come to the door.

"Pete is quite a character," I said. "He really helped me to make an important decision and he has the best stories. Is he home?"

"Well dear, Pete is...let me see, how can I put this? Pete is home. He is in his heavenly home. Pete died last week and I am not ready to open up the yard yet."

I was shocked. He had been in such good spirits when I first visited. "Died? What happened? Was it COVID?" Tears welled up in her eyes and she wiped them with a handkerchief that I hadn't noticed was in her hand.

In the Morning

"No, no! He was out taking a walk on the grounds. He did that every morning. When he didn't come back for breakfast, I went out to look for him. It was strange because he never was late for breakfast. I could hear the cats meowing. I had never heard them like that. It was like an alarm. I walked down the path, following their sounds. Some were resting on the campers and the cars. Once I approached, they stopped. I found my sweet Petey lying on the gravel path near the campers. Two long black snakes and some little ones slithered away when I ran up. The crows started cawing and flapping their wings. Pete had no pulse. I tried CPR but he was gone."

"Damn that snake!" I said. "I remember that snake."

His wife continued, "Yes. He called her Cleo. She was his favorite. Pete was friends with all of the animals. Even the bees didn't sting him."

"Cleo got him?" I asked.

"No, it wasn't the snake! I thought that Cleo was the culprit, too." She paused for a moment and took a deep breath. "The doctor said there were no snake bites. Pete had been hiding that he had heart problems. He knew how bad it was but he didn't want me and the children to worry. He had a massive heart attack and died instantly."

"I am so sorry."

"Thank you, dear. It was the way he would have wanted to go...out there on the grounds with his animals, and the doctor said he had no pain. His heart just jolted and stopped. Just like that!" She snapped her fingers. "He was a good man."

I responded, "Although we only met once, I knew he was a great man. I was really looking forward to letting him know about my decision and spending some time listening to more stories. I never realized how much I like to write until I retired. I write each night in a journal and it has taken off. I decided to write a book once my tiny house is completed. Right now, the packing and getting rid of stuff I don't need has taken on a life of its own. I thought about bringing some of it here, actually. I needed to talk with Pete, hear more of his stories, and thank him for helping me. I wanted to tell him that I had chosen a tiny house and invite him to come see it once it is finished. I chose a weekend visit so I could meet you. So glad I did. I would love for you to come over as soon as it is ready. Are you going to keep the junkyard?"

She answered with a smile. "I am! The children and I

decided that we love this place. There will be some changes, of course, but on the whole, we can't give it up. We don't make a fortune here but we do okay. With my retirement benefits and their help, I think things will meet Pete's approval. I know he is smiling down on us now."

The Partnership

It was time to bring up another reason for my visit. "I also came to talk to Pete about his stories. His stories would be perfect for my book. I got so involved in listening to them that I had to pull myself away that day."

"Yes, he was full of them," she said as she shook her head from side to side. "We should have recorded them, but between the kids, his sister, and I, we harbor quite a few of those crazy tales. We would sit out here on the porch in the evening and listen to him. It was better than television. Pete was the best storyteller ever, and I have heard quite a few. I even had him come to my classroom every now and then to share a tale during storytime. The children would clap as soon as he entered the room. He was a treat!

"We may not be as animated as he was, but you're the writer, you can put that in." She laughed! "I am sure my children will like this idea. It's wonderful! Pete would love it, even if some of his stories are questionable. The one about the ghost is pretty far-fetched. Tell you what! Why don't you come over and talk with us while your house is being built and then we can get some of his stories on paper? We'll sit out here on the porch. Telling his stories will help us get through this tough time and keep his memory alive. What a legacy! I am just thrilled!"

I sighed with relief because I wasn't sure how this idea would be accepted, especially since the family was going through a trying time. "Great!" I said. "I can't wait to get started. I bought a recorder for Pete's stories. Is it okay for me to use it?"

"Sure. That makes sense. There are so many of them. No one can write that fast."

"I think I'll call it *Stories from 'All Kinds of Junk?'*"

She threw her head back, laughed, and slapped her leg, just like Pete did. "Yep, that's a good title."

New Friends

Jerry cawed his approval from above and then flew away. Suddenly the cats came from everywhere and settled just beyond the porch like children ready for Pete's Storytime. Bees moved about the flowers near the porch and I thought I saw Cleo slither into a bush. This time I was not afraid. Susie the Calico purred, rubbed my leg, and found comfort in my lap once again. Joyce went into the house for some of my favorite lemonade. Suddenly, Pete's chair began to rock on its own and I smiled because I bet it was a sign that Pete approved.

> *The greatest discovery of all time is that a person can change his future by merely changing his attitude.*

– Oprah Winfrey

Chapter 5
Poetic Speaking

– Edgar Allan Poe

Eve's Point of View: Excuse Me!

Excuse me? All is NOT lost! We are still here.
Don't blame me, my brother! YOU...are your own greatest fear.
What? Oh no, Mr. First Man! God made no mistake.
He didn't put me here for me. I'm here for your sake.
You needed some help! I didn't ask to appear.
It was your decrepit soul that put me down here.
The Supreme just wants us to make things right.
My job is to see that all is done, in spite...
Of the messes that we tend to create.
Accept it, Brother Man! This right here is YOUR fate.
Come on now! You knew better! You didn't have to take a bite.
So don't you go blaming me, 'cause...I'm up for this fight.
You were told not to touch the fruit on that particular tree.

I didn't even know about it. It was your job to make me see.
When there is a mess up,
Who is there to clean up? ME.
When there is a need to perk up,
Who builds all the egos up? ME.

Don't look at me that way. What in the world would you do?
Honey, if there was no me, there'd probably be no you.
Hump? You think you can survive on your own?
Evidently God didn't! Can't make it by yourself, surely never alone.

These leaves aren't the best. Try them on. See what you think.
Can't wear them too long, but if you like my look, give me a wink.
So, you'd better get smart and know I am a blessing.
Sweetheart, I know you like me...and that's not just from guessing.
Time is of the essence. There's lots of work to be done.
If you stop brooding and be nice, maybe I'll squeeze in a little fun.

The Slide

"You can do it. It's Electric."

Every woman in the place
Had a smile upon her face,
And as I checked the room
They looked like roses in their bloom.

Some were up and some were down.
Drinks and food were all around.
All the women in the place,
Knew they had no time to waste.

No need waiting for a chance
For someone to come to request a dance.
Once they heard that line dance beat,
It was time to get up on their feet.

Rhythmic hips swayed to the sounds,
Men watched, some joined the rounds,
Skirts swished this way and that.
Fingers snapped and feet would pat.

It was finally time to part-tay!
Playing cards and eating hardy.
Claps echo melodic sounds,
Dancing queens donning salon crowns.

As the turntable spilled out its guts,
Folks leaped quickly right out of their ruts.
Suddenly, "Electric Slide," somebody yelled.
Mysteriously, the dance floor swelled.

Tall, short, skinny, and P-H-A-T.
One lady was even wearing a hat.
It was The Slide that took over the room,
The joy that grew didn't come too soon.

Even the floor moved with a freeing beat.
No one thought about taking a seat.
This was the jam that everyone knew.
Young and old stopped in mid-chew.

No man was needed for "The Electric Slide."
Each female was given a chance to glide.
Watching the bodies move was such a treat.
Droplets of sweat proved they were all in heat.

The song said, "You can do it. It's Electric."
While each toe proved a rhythmic geometric.
"Boogey, Woogey, Woogey," sang the voice.
It looked like the bodies had no choice.

They were swept into a magical whirlwind together,
Like a musical hurricane, almost like the weather.
"Some say it's mystic. Come let me take you on a party ride,
You can't resist it, and I'll teach you the Electric Slide."

So The Slide it was for a moment in time.
It gave the people an era sublime.
And that is such a wonderful thing,
To leave troubles behind and to get out and swing.

Every woman in the place
Had a smile upon her face,
The spirit of the dance is a freeing spirit in each ear.
It forces a warmth of togetherness that is easy to hear.

If you watch the dancers when the song is through,
You can see that a positive message remains there too.

"You can do it. It's Electric."

My Drum

I dance to the beat of my own drum!
It raps out rhythms that
Ignite my soul with energy
And I point my toes to glad music.

I prance to the beat of my own drum!
It stirs my life's juices with vibrancy,
Controlling all of my being
And causing my joy to swell.

I trance to the beat of my own drum!
It exudes a selfish high that
Blinds me to all negatives
And swallows all of my stillness.

I Dance,
I Prance,
I Trance,
To the beat of my own drum!

The Laundresses 1940s - 1960

(Dedicated to Entrepreneurs)

My Aunt Nance spelled her name N A N C with an E;
She was both an employer and employee.
Her days were laundry based with business tactical nights,
She worked hard to make sure that all her workers got their rights.

A smart business owner knew the success of order receiving,
So she made sure of a positive demeanor. Sometimes it was deceiving.
With a business sense assured that approval always pays well,
She knew that laundry talents and personality encouraged her sell.

"Separate the whites. Put the darks in those baskets.
Don't overload that machine. It will surely blow a gasket.
Put all of those colored pieces in one of those separate piles,
And stop checking out the items according to their styles.

Mrs. Murphy's clothes are folded sitting right over there,
But Mrs. Caine's special order is back there somewhere?
Just make sure that those are separate. Keep them far apart.
Come on now. Get to steppin'! Ya'll know how to work real smart.

On the shelf is my special detergent. Yes, that's the one I made.
I'll even barter that soap, if I can get a decent trade.
Keep the garments tossing and turning, 'cause in no time at all,
The eight loads will be done. Hey, Sarah answered that call.

Make up that good starch for Mrs. Cannon's man.
His shirts have to be as stiff and white as we can.
Look in the ice box, take them out right away.
Sprinkle, press, hanger the shirts, and don't commence to play.

Elsie, change that water now and rinse out all those stains.
Frances, that bucket is heavy. Don't you get the back strains.
Turn that handle slowly and crank that wringing dowel.
Wait, is that the dye from Mrs. Crandall's red towel?

Gotta rush it up a bit. Lucy, Frances, Elsie, and Louise,
Start the ironing right now, and no gossiping, if you please."
"Girls, did you hear about that brand-new handsome man?"
"Yeah, he is so cute. It looks like his skin is the color of sand."

"I heard tell that Mary Louise just had another set of twins."
"She surely needs clothes for her kids and a lot of safety pins."
"Did you hear the solo that Pastor asked Mamie to sing?"
"Girl, it was awful. All off key, loud, and everything."

"Miss Nance, sheets are ready for the mangle."
"Louise, come here. Help me get out this tangle.
Where is Mrs. Lear's stuff? It has got to be ready.
She's pulling up right now, look at her walking all unsteady.

I guess she had too much of her favorite red wine.
Wonder why she drinks so. Her clothes are sure fine.
Go out and help her up those steps, please, Mable.
Hurry, Louise, and grab her stuff off of the dining room table.

Finish up that ironing and get away from the door.
I'll deal with her. You know she'll be trying to take a tour.
Corral her in the living room. Right now, right away.
She is so nosy and always has something negative to say.

Good afternoon and how are you today, Mrs. Lear?
Your clothes are all ready. They are all sparkling right here.
Here's your receipt. Everything's written down and thank you.
Oh no, not next week, Mrs. Lear! I will see you in two.

Well, ladies, it's getting dark and everything is done.
Thank you for working hard. You always make it fun.
So, go home, get some rest. Tomorrow's another day.
No worries, it's Friday. Yes, you will all get your pay."

As the ladies depart in different directions,
They laugh...they hug, and exchange some reflections,
From a day filled with washing, folding, and pressing,
Thinking, "Thank God for this job, Miss Nance is a blessing."

"Wake up!" (1968)

I was nestled contentedly, reaping smiles of nice dreams.
Feeling cuddled by love and safe from my screams.
Suddenly, out of nowhere, a bright light came on.
It invaded my eyelids. I wished it was gone.

Like sharp searing rays from a too brilliant sun,
My battle for rest was lost...I knew it was done.
Confusingly ejected from a justified slumber,
I squeezed my pillow tightly and stuck my head under.

I hung on to my pillowed lifesaver just a little bit longer,
But I gave up the battle; the light was much stronger.
I had no idea where in the world I was.
This wasn't my home, and what was the cause?

A tall woman in white with a matching cloth crown
Appeared at a door, cuddling a very strange sound.
The white-clad figure spoke. "Good morning!
It's wake-up time."
Walking forward with a smile, she looked so sublime.

The clock on the wall showed it was only 3 a.m.
It was still dark from the window. This must be a scam.
Who would wake up someone at this time of the morning?
It was a grinning woman who was somewhat alarming.

Sane people are sleeping, of which I was one.
Maybe it was a prank and she was just having fun.
Suddenly at my side she seemed to give poise,
With the small bundle in her arms, making such a loud noise.

"What in the world's going on?" I shouted out loud.
When I glanced down at her package, I suddenly felt proud.
She handed it over with, "Here you go. It is time."
"Time," I reacted. "For what?" But I knew it was mine.

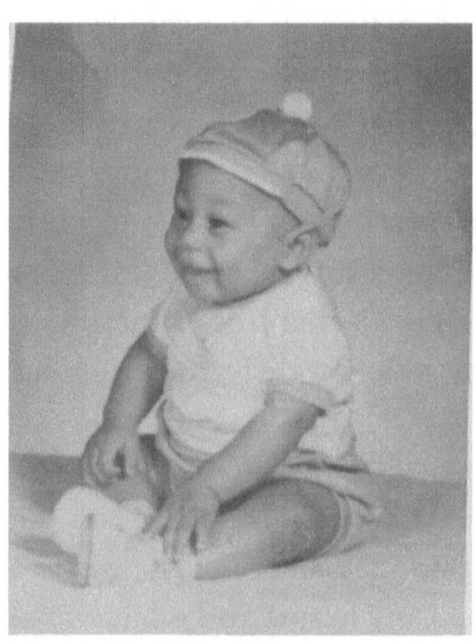

YOUR baby is hungry! He put on quite a fit.
Nothing's wrong with those lungs. He's fully equipped.
Baby, what baby? Oh right, I'd just had a boy.
My terrified heart almost exploded with joy.

"Wait just a minute, who eats in the middle of the night?"
"Your baby does, that's who, so don't put up a fight.
Every four to six hours is your special time to feed."
"No one told me about this unbelievable new deed."

"Four hours?" I questioned. "You have got to be kidding me."
"No one ever told you?" "No," I said. "So please let me be."
After unloading the bundle, she walked out of the door,
Saying, "Ring when you're finished. Tonight, this is my floor."

Then I pulled back the blanket to look at his face.
Oh, he's so tiny and cute, and then I saw a trace...
So sweet, so soft! What a strange thing to see.
Although mostly his father, there was a smidgen of me.

Yep, he was mine all right and I'd better brace up
For the serious responsibility for my little buttercup.
Then my surprise turned to wonder. Just look at his size!
He grabbed hold of my thumb and blinked his gray eyes.

"Now what?" Look at those teeny tiny toes,
those cute little knees.
He's so needy and scary. There was no time to freeze.
Well, we made it through the many years of caring,
And we stumbled through times of guiding and sharing.

About six years later, out came another pearl.
She had a dimpled chin and a cute little curl
Right on the top of her tiny and delicate head.
A handful she was, active but not really bad.

Two children, Lord knows I was learning by chance,
But all through their childhood, there was a Mommy romance
With them, teaching them, loving them, enjoying them and so
Not only did they learn things, but I also had to grow.

Our years together flew by maybe a little too quickly.
I was there through the joys and when they were sickly.
Sports, music, dating, graduations, marriages, and such.
Grandchildren, parties, just enough struggle, but not too much.

So here we are today and the roles have reversed.
Now I am the demanding bundle hoping to not be a curse.
They will always be my babies but I know they use psychology.
When their lights go on and they wake up just for me.

Haiku:

Baby

Embryo holding
Uninhibited water gushers
Energy bursts.

***

Cicada (2021)

Crunchy chocolate
Protein dessert, cicada
You might like it.

Remembering Miss Classie Mitchell (1942)

We smile when we remember Miss Classie Mitchell!
Every time Miss Classie Mitchell walked by
The entire room would smile and sigh.
Just the plushness of her skin
Made grown men want to sin.

Her hips would sway from east to west.
Her looks forced women to look their best.
Encircling her head were magnificent curls
That framed her face in lingering swirls.
Classie's laugh could fill up a room.
Her scent out "aroma-ed" any French perfume.
Oh...her soul exuded grace and kindness
That bypassed her features and proved her fineness.

But Classie was not about herself and her looks.
Oh no! Some talks were proof of a love for books.
Everyone knew she was as smart as a whip,
And was always ready with a meaningful quip.

She befriended the women with gifts and her smiles.
She'd stop by their houses just to talk for a while.
They'd laugh and pray and sometimes have tea.
Classie made sure that each was at peace and feeling quite free.

We all knew she was special in almost every way.
A man couldn't harness her; could not make her stay.
For she wasn't about just doing good deeds.
This gardener, renown, was spreading love seeds.

Classie left this earth too soon, gone from us now.
But her virtuous thoughts still linger somehow.
Yes, classy...was what she was for sure!
For Classie was classy to her very core.

And so, we smile when we remember the mesmerizing Classie
Mitchell!

The Painting Calls Me!

(Dedicated to the Last Poets of the 60s)

The Painting calls me to my canvases like whippoorwills.
I escape into a landscape of mixed media, trying to save
humanity's artistic sanity.
I want no fame from the mundane critics who might classify
me as insane,
As I reach beyond presenting safe, directed, protected, and
respected images.
Like a runaway train veering off tracks, swerving around hacks
who back up accepted and protected thought, my rejected route
is often unexpected, even to me.

The Painting calls me and says, 'I dare you to reach out,
to teach and beseech the unknown...Not the preached
Standard of what is represented, cemented into someone else's
reality.'
Sometimes my corrections placate and duplicate the mandate,
but...
Sometimes my off-the-chain art forms bypass the norms, to
seek a society

That perceives demonstrative comrades in a creativity that is hopped up.
I am not pumped up on what is a trumped-up reality, long gone. That is not me.
Coping photography can be a step toward creativity but not MY final art form.
The Painting calls me and forces me to show portrayals of personal choices.
I hear voices in my head explaining the steeped in expected and protected.
But I express myself anyway...through things that I have to say in my own way,

In light of indifferences of intense debates. I must at least attempt...
To commence, realize, and present original creations to the nations.
I acquiesce to the brilliant stimulant of those who master their own creative fate. I respect that!

The Painting calls me. I must insist that my art is to state, debate, and not subjugate choice.
Picasso changed, rearranged his what was to his what is and what could be.
Grandma Moses didn't let age deter, neuter, or defer her intent to offer a pearl to the world.

I'll not bear shackles or be tackled by minds imprisoned without vision.
Sometimes, I try not to appease what is different or indifferent.
My flowers may not look like your flowers, even after hours of trying to get them there.
My bout has been with trying to be like those who hone their own style.
My trial is not to be judged by what was but to be appreciated for what is.

The Painting calls me to understand that…
And forces me to appreciate how to survive the never-ending art game.
That is not to say that someone else's creativity, believability is not right.
Each artist brings soul presentations to nations that might not be accepting, but rejecting.
Once upon a time, men painted these things and women painted those.
It was dictated…but clouds are not all the same.

The Painting calls me and scares me sometimes with,
'Be you! Make no excuses for what you see to be a tree,
What you create comes from your fate, your love, unfortunately your hate.
Fear not trials. Use them to be smarter about illustrations of a vision.
Trust your heart and depart with pride about what you lay out for the world to see.

Behold being bold as you earn the tags of older and wiser.
Then you can say… Let me share something special with you.'
My pieces are my treasures, created not specifically for financial reward but for mediating and viewing pleasures.
I hope you see what I see, too…or at least try to find something new there in that space.
The Painting calls me. It calls me. When I hear it, I cannot run and hide.
I simply MUST OBEY!

Let Me Be Me

(Dedicated to parents of LGBTQ+ children)

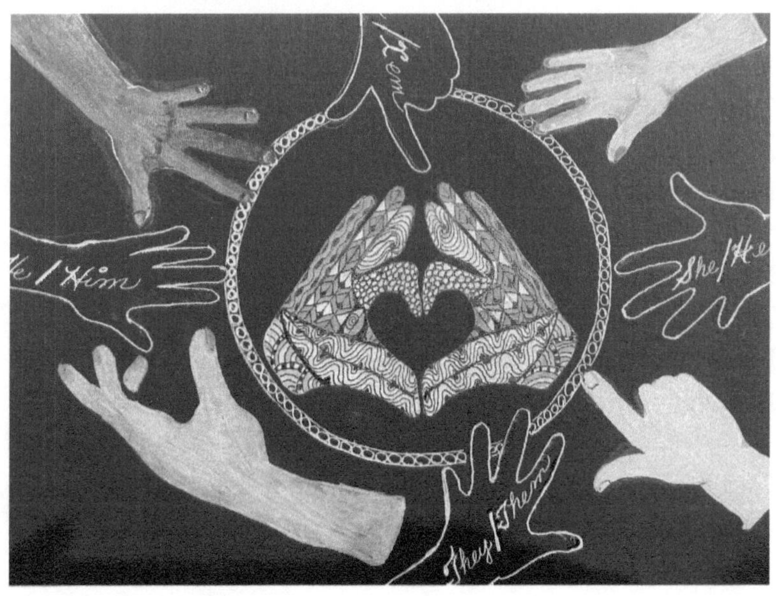

Seventeen years ago, I entered this world.
Unfortunately, I came in the body of a girl.
I'm really a boy and I hear what people say.
I pretend that it doesn't bother me each and every day.

One Christmas I got an American Girl doll.
I didn't ask for that gift...plus she had a weird smile.
There was a football, some skates, and a truck on my list.
An Easy-Bake Oven? Santa, why do you insist?

I begged for a Superman cape...please, Santa, please,
And some underwear to match would be "the bee's knees!"
At least that's just what my grandma might say.
She'd often take my hands, bow her head, and pray.

"Lord, please keep my grandchild safe, dear God.
From mean-spirited people who label her as odd.
Please keep the crazies far, far away,
Stop the hateful things they think and have the nerve to say."

My parents knew early. They seem to understand
That someday I could grow to be a good man.
Am I a she, a he, we, us, or they?
Does it really matter? Can't I live life my way?

I don't want to buy things with all of the girls;
They want to get perfume, lipsticks, and pearls.
I want Doc Martens. A skateboard works too.
Daddy, I don't want to go shopping. Can I hang with you?

I see some people staring. It makes me feel weird.
I wish I could hide behind a great big ole beard.
Others act funny or look slowly away.
Is it just me, or what they think I might say?

They don't even know me, why are they so mean?
I could use a big hug for my own self-esteem.
I am just another person, for heaven's sake.
I am a good person; I am not a mistake.

Wait a minute, they don't even know me.
Their prejudging spirits just won't let them see.
This is supposed to be a country created for WE!
Since you can be you, PLEASE, let me be me.

I Am From

I am from love.
I am from a God that says yes,
But sometimes says no.
Who "allowth" me to lie down is bleak pastures
And then "restoreth" my soul.

I am from loving, committed parents with
sometimes misunderstood convictions.
I am from those rich in mind, body and spirit
and yet poor in opportunities and respect.

I am from independent, strong, opinionated women
who fought not to be dependent.
I am from struggling men seeking dignity
In a world that too often rejects them.

I am from those famous and recognized for accepted tasks,
And those ignored for deeds that make positive differences.
I am from the godly who give,
And the devilish who take.

I am from the custodian, the chef, and the beautician store owner.
The gardener, blacksmith, inventor, mechanic, porter, and
housekeeper.
I am from the kind and the unkind...
From the educator, felon, administrator, minister, and healer.

I am from the gifts of prayers and thoughts of great minds,
The culmination of the people seen and unseen.
I am from the good and the bad,
The beautiful and the ugly.

I am from north, south, east, and west...
Allowing for understandings of regional pride.
I am from the beauty of combined cultures...
Designated by the multifaceted meaning of the word "race."

I am from the beauty of rainbow-provoked mindsets,
Which unite in respect for equality.
I am from lawmakers, judges, police, ministers, teachers, etc.
And from "lawbreakers," marchers, testimonial speakers,
captives, and so on.

I am from the Accusers and the Accused...
From the encouragers and the disillusioned...
From clarity and confusion.
From the caring, the uncaring, and the cared for.
From the uplifted and the downfallen.

I am from committed, sometimes misunderstood support
fighting for sanity while trying to render a moral compass.
I am from a God that says yes and sometimes says no.
I am from love.

Appendix A
Notes of Interest

Chapter 1. Historically Speaking

The Finale

(This story is created as a result of discussions, historical readings and documentaries.)

- "My story ends with freedom; not in the usual way, with marriage."

- "I can testify, from my own experience and observation, that slavery is a curse to the whites as well as to the blacks."

Life of a Slave Girl, an Autobiography by Harriet Ann Jacobs

***

The Trip

There were famous people on the Titanic but there were also the unknown. Their names may have been lost to history. This story introduces a family that boarded that ship. Created are unique circumstances that might have led to why they took that trip.

247

Joseph Philippe Lemercier Laroche (May 26, 1886 – April 15, 1912) was a Haitian engineer. He was one of only three passengers of known Haitian ancestry on the ill-fated voyage of *RMS Titanic.* He put his pregnant French wife and their two daughters onto a lifeboat. They survived, but he did not. Joseph's daughter, Louise Laroche (July 2, 1910 – January 28, 1998), was one of the last remaining survivors of the sinking of *RMS Titanic.*

Encyclopedia Titanica (2005) – Joseph Philippe Lemercier Laroche (ref: #486, last updated: 22nd September 2005, accessed 30th December 2022 19:16:27 PM). Joseph Philippe Lemercier Laroche: Titanic Victim

"LaRoche" is the title of a three-act opera by Atlanta composer Sharon J. Willis, based on his life and part of the 2003 National Black Arts Festival, premiering at the Callanwolde Fine Arts Center on July 18.

https://www.encyclopedia-titanica.org

***

The Queen (1626)

(The presence of the warrior queen is documented. This story combines her history with what could have happened.)

http://www.hup.harvard.edu/catalog.php?isbn=9780674971820

> *The fascinating story of arguably the greatest queen in sub-Saharan African history, who surely deserves a place in the pantheon of revolutionary world leaders.*

– Henry Louis Gates, Jr.

Snethen, J-1583-1663/. (2009, June 16). Queen Nzinga (1583-1663). BlackPast.org.
https://www.blackpast.org/global-african-history/queen-nzinga

Bortolot, Alexander Ives. "Women Leaders in African History: Ana Nzinga, Queen of Ndongo." In the Heilbrunn Timeline of Art History. New York: The Metropolitan Museum of Art, 2000.
http://www.metmuseum.org/toah/hd/pwmn_2/hd_pwmn_2.htm (October 2003)

***

A Survivor (1945)

(This telling is about the possibility of what could have happened to a survivor of the atomic bomb dropped on Hiroshima and Nagasakiiro.)

On August 6, 1945, during World War II, an American B-29 bomber dropped the world's first atomic bomb over the Japanese city of Hiroshima. The aim was to destroy Japan's ability to fight wars. The explosion immediately killed an estimated 80,000 people; tens of thousands more would die later of radiation exposure. Three days later, a second B-29 dropped another A-bomb on Nagasaki, killing an estimated 40,000 people. Japan's Emperor Hirohito announced his country's unconditional surrender in World War II in a radio address on August 15, citing the devastating power of "a new and most cruel bomb."

The radiation in Hiroshima and Nagasaki is on par with the extremely low levels of background radiation (natural radioactivity) present anywhere on Earth. It has no effect on human bodies. Nagasaki is perfectly safe for people to live in today. Not only is Nagasaki safe, but it is a lovely city.
https://www.icanw.org/hiroshima_and_nagasaki_bombings

<u>Memorial:</u> *"Each person had a name. Each person was loved by someone. Let us ensure that their deaths were not in vain."* – Setsuko Thurlow, survivor of the August 1945 atomic bombing of Hiroshima, Nobel Peace Prize acceptance speech, December 2017.

***

Not Quite a Bible Story: 200 BCE

Women during 1600 to 1700 BC were "...either held to be completely deceitful, sexual, innocent, or incompetent. Therefore, they were mostly withheld from positions of power or speaking their voice; males made decisions for them, and their lives were dictated by the men that ran the society. In many societies, women's primary roles revolved around motherhood and managing a household. During the course of their lives, women were dependent on their male kin, but they had different levels of power depending on their age and influence over male family members." (*https://sites.udel.edu.*)

Since there is so little written, Asenath's life has been surmised and presented by historians and playwrights to fill in the gaps of her life. Questionable plays were written and cartoons can be viewed on YouTube.

Was she the daughter of Potiphar's wife or the daughter of the Priest of On? No one seems to know. The only constant is that she was married to Joseph and bore him two sons.

One article provides a survey of the last twenty-five years of research on *Joseph and Aseneth*, a Jewish Greek novel probably written between the first century and the second century. This romance expands on Gen. 41-45 to narrate how Joseph and Aseneth met and later married under the auspices of Pharaoh.

Standhartinger, Angela. *"Recent Scholarship on Joseph and Aseneth (1988-2013)." Currents in Biblical Research 12 (2014): 353–406. doi. org/10.1177/1476993X14526968*

Lumpkinm, Joseph. *"A Love Story by Joseph Lumpkin."*

Standhartinger, Angela. "Recent Scholarship on Joseph and Aseneth (1988-2013)." Currents in Biblical Research 12 (2014): 353–406. doi.org/10.1177/1476993X14526968

***

Aunty's Flowers

Although the story is about a respected elderly lady, the back story is about a land settlement in the west.

Benjamin "Pap" Singleton was born a slave in Nashville, Tennessee, in 1809. Singleton escaped to Canada to gain his freedom, returning to Tennessee after the end of the Civil War. Seeking a better life for himself and for his fellow emancipated African Americans, he began his efforts to buy land in Tennessee for blacks to farm. His plan failed due to unfair prices set by white landowners. Singleton then looked to Kansas as a potential site for black emigration, organizing the Tennessee Real Estate and Homestead Association with his business partner, Columbus Johnson. This company founded the Dunlap Colony in Morris County and a short-lived settlement in Cherokee County. Although his company did not create many successful colonies, through his advertisements he did help thousands of Exodusters relocate to Kansas, leading to his name as "Father of the Exodus." Singleton also organized a political group called the United Colored Links and later in life he promoted black colonization.

Benjamin Pap Singleton: Kansas Historical Society, Kansas Memory, *https://www.kansasmemory.org/item/333. Item Number: 333, Call Number: B Singleton, Benjamin *2, KSHS Identifier: DaRT ID: 333*

Reeves, Matthew. "Singleton, Benjamin 'Pap.'" *Civil War on the Western Border: The Missouri-Kansas Conflict, 1854-1865.* The Kansas City Public Library. Accessed Wednesday, January 5, 2022 - 18:49 at *https://civilwaronthewesternborder.org/encyclopedia/singleton-benjamin-"pap"*

***

The Voyages

What Really Happened to the *Speedwell*?

<u>*Rumor 1:*</u> Members of the crew later confessed that the *Speedwell* had been sabotaged by order of its own captain. In refitting the ship before leaving Holland, they had supplied her intentionally with masts that were too large in order to get out of his contract. Reynolds and his crew had been hired by Thomas Weston, the merchant adventurer who orchestrated financing for the expedition, to remain with the colony for a year so they could use the ship. Captain Reynolds sabotaged the trip so that he could keep his pay, claiming it was no fault of his that the ship leaked, and then have it repaired and sold for his own profit.

<u>*Rumor 2:*</u> It was reported that the "cunning and deceit" was because the captain desired to get out of his commitment. Seeing that the ship was poorly provisioned and fearing that the "victuals" would run out before his contract did, the captain ordered every inch of sail unfurled, with the result that he soon had the excuse for turning back. Years later, a different rumor said that the Dutch wished to undermine English efforts to settle near the Hudson River, and "fraudulently hired" the captain to effect delays.

https://www.worldhistory.org/image/13077/embarkation-of-the-pilgrims/

Chapter 2. Theatrically Speaking

Telephone Face Offs

The FTC is the primary government agency that collects scam complaints. Report all robocalls and unwanted telemarketing calls to the Do Not Call Registry. Report caller ID spoofing to the Federal Communications Commission. You can report either online or by phone at 1-888-225-5322 (TTY: 1-888-835-5322). Apr. 26, 2022.

***

Please Don't Cut Down the Trees: (*Coronavirus Created a Toilet Paper Shortage?*)

Many attributed the shortage to disruptions in the supply chain. But it was actually a result of panic-buying, according to Dr. Ronalds Gonzalez, an Assistant Professor in the Department of Forest Biomaterials. https://cnr.ncsu.edu/news/2020/05/coronavirus-toilet-paper-shortage.

1. People resort to extremes when they hear conflicting messages.
2. Some react to the lack of a clear direction from officials.
3. Panic buying begets panic buying.
4. It's natural to want to over-prepare.
5. It allows some to feel a sense of control.

Andrew, Scottie (CNN Health): *"The psychology behind why toilet paper, of all things, is the latest coronavirus panic buy." Updated 5:14 PM EDT, Mon. March 9, 2020.*

***

Mary the Great

Mary Fields also known as Stagecoach Mary and Black Mary was an American mail carrier. She was the first Black woman to be employed as a star route postwoman in the United States. She worked as a mail carrier from 1895 to 1903.

One of the toughest women ever to work in a convent, "Black Mary" earned the respect and devotion of most of the residents of the pioneer community of Cascade, Montana, and enjoyed more freedom than most white men. (*George Everett Wild West Magazine* in February 1996.)
en.m.wikipedia.org

"Star route." *Merriam-Webster.com Dictionary, Merriam-Webster, merriam-webster.com/dictionary/star%20route. Accessed 18 February 2020.*

Blakemore, Erin. *"Meet Stagecoach Mary, the Daring Black Pioneer Who Protected Wild West Stagecoaches." History.com, A&E Television Networks, 14 September 2017.*

***

Box Story- Jennifer Irene Brown

The State of Homelessness in the U.S. 2021

- The average life expectancy of a homeless person is just 50 years.

- 39.8% of homeless persons are African-Americans.

- 61% of homeless persons are men and boys.

- 20% of homeless persons are kids.

- 42% of street children identify as LGBT.

- New York City has one-fifth of all U.S. sheltered homeless.

- The homeless problem is on a downward trend.

- Permanent housing interventions have grown by 450% in 5 years.

https://policyadvice.net › insurance

***

Did History Ignore?

Two women on the United States Women's Track & Field did not gain a hero's treatment given to other athletes. They were slated to participate in the 4x100 meter relay but for some unspoken reason were replaced by runners who performed slower that either Louise Stokes and Tiyde Pickett at the trials. They watched as the team captured the gold, robbing them of their chance for glory. That omission from the medal books is one of the reasons that they are forgotten in the story of African American sports groundbreakers.

Smithsonianmag.com

Both Tidye Pickett and Louise Stokes were included in the film storyline, "Olympic Pride: American Prejudice written by Deborah Riley Draper."

"Stokes and Pickett were only celebrated in their communities; they were symbolic of hope and the end of segregation. History deliberately forgets their trailblazing efforts."

https://www.historyheroblast.com/historyhero/louise-stokes

https://www.smithsonianmag.com/history/sports-history-forgot-about-tidye-pickett-and-louise-stokes-two-black-olympians-who-never-got-their-shot-glory-180960138

***

FMG, Female Genitalia Mutilation

While data on the mortality of girls who underwent FGM are unknown and hard to procure, it is estimated that 1 in every 500 circumcisions results in death.

Dec 31, 2021 — "It's a tragic case and, in a way, shows how many more people like her have died or are suffering, because the majority of cases are unreported."
https://www.theguardian.com › global-development › dec

***

The Continuous Nightmare

Although both adults and children experience recurring dreams, children may experience them more often than teenagers or adults. In one study, 35% of 11-year-olds reported having had a recurring dream in the past year, compared to 15% of 15-year-olds.

Children also have their own familiar plotlines, such as confronting characters from fairy tales, although themes like falling, being chased, and car accidents are also common. Children are less likely to have positive recurring dreams, though. They have significantly more recurring dreams that inspire a neutral emotional response.
https://www.sleepfoundation.org/dreams/dream-interpretation/recurring-dreams

Chapter 3. Personally Speaking

My Quadrangle - A Place to Remember

Cheyney University of Pennsylvania has changed locations, names and the curriculum since 1837. It began as a farm school for Colored Youth 12 miles north of Philadelphia, PA and grew over the years. It can be listed as the first Historically Black College & Universities. Richard Humphreys, a Quaker, left $10.000.00 to start the school.

"I've learned that your campus friends become a kind of family; you eat together, take naps together, fight, laugh, cry, and do absolutely nothing until you can't remember how you ever lived without them in the first place."
https://www.tuko.co.ke/355649-touching-college-memories-quotes.html

"Like anyone who graduates from university, you're leaving familiar surroundings, a comfortable environment, your friends, and everything, and you're starting fresh. It can be pretty daunting."
https://www.tuko.co.ke/355649-touching-college-memories-quotes.html

***

The Indigenous

"The first paths to freedom taken by runaway slaves led to Native American villages. There, black men and women found acceptance and friendship among our country's original inhabitants. Though they seldom appear in textbooks and movies, the children of Native and African American marriages helped shape the early days of the fur trade, added a new dimension to frontier diplomacy, and made a daring contribution to the fight for American liberty."

Katz, William Loren, *Black Indians: A Hidden Heritage*

"Learning about your history and heritage can help you understand how you became who you are. In fact, having a historical perspective of your heritage can serve as a guidepost and it often provides information about what you can expect in the future."

The Importance of Knowing Your Heritage –
yourheritagefilm.com
https://yourheritagefilm.com › the-importance-of-knowi...

Free Genealogy Sources

My Heritage Free Trial	National Archives	FamilySearch
Ancestry Free Trial	Library of Congress	Chronicling America
Cyndi's List	Free BMD	Freedman's Bureau
Ancestry Free Indexes	Internet Archive	Ellis Island
DeadFred	USGenWeb	Castle Garden
MyHeritage Family Tree Builder	New York Public Library	David Rumsey's Historical Maps
AfriGeneas	Find A Grave	Reclaim the Records

***

First Kiss (Sexual Abuse/First Love?)

"You are right to question this type of romantic behavior at this early age," says Dr. Kristin Carothers, a psychologist with the Child Mind Institute in New York City. "It is age-appropriate for a 10-year-old to be curious, but limits should be established for physical touch. Kissing and other behaviors are more developmentally appropriate behaviors for teenagers who are of dating age."

https://yourteenmag.com/health/teen-sexuality/how-old-for-kissing

***

Bottles & The Environment

Truth: With the development of mass-produced bottles, crimp capping, and mechanized bottling at the end of the 19th century, increasing amounts of beverages were sold for consumption. The bottles were expensive to produce, so bottlers used a deposit-refund system to ensure that consumers returned the bottles, and embossed the bottles with their logo and name as a means of claiming ownership.

Busch, James. *Second Time Around: A Look at Bottle Reuse.* Cleveland: American Public Works Association, 1991.

Currently, the following states have bottle bills and will pay you for recycling your glass bottles. They are California, Maine, Massachusetts, Michigan, New Yori, Oregon, Vermont, Hawaii, Iowa and Connecticut. The state will pay 5 – 10 cents per bottle.

Tomra https://www.tomra.com

***

What Goes on In the Beauty Shop
Stays In the Beauty Shop

"As a therapist who tries to be open-minded, I believe there is value in sharing your thoughts and feelings with hairstylists— even if they haven't been trained in mental health issues. The truth is that many of the people we listen to the most haven't had any mental health training at all (Oprah, anyone?), but their experiences have taught them an awful lot about human behavior. Similarly, hairstylists spend hours listening to clients and often have helpful feedback to share.

The ultimate point is to talk openly about what's bothering you so that your anxieties don't negatively impact your life. My only hope is that you seek out a trained mental health professional if the emotional problem you're dealing with becomes a pattern and requires more time than a monthly haircut allows you."

Meyers, Seth, Psy. D. *The psychology of Hair Salons & Stylists: Therapy for Free, Psychology Today.* Posted July 2, 2012.

***

Lessons on the First Job

"The Fair Labor Standards Act," established in 1938, covers minimum wage, overtime pay, record keeping, and child labor rules for children under the age of 18, affecting full- and part-time workers in private industries and the federal, state, and local governments. The rules vary based on the age of the child and his or her occupation.

The FLSA child labor laws are meant to protect children's educational opportunities and prohibit employers from putting them in working conditions dangerous to their health or safety. The provisions include restrictions on hours of work

for children under the age of 16 and lists of occupations that are too dangerous for them.
https://www.thebalancecareers.com/list-of-employment-laws-2062282

***

The Skirt War (Mother/Daughter)

During the 60s and 70s, strict dress codes were established and followed in most schools. Some universities attempted to outline and enforce dress codes from the 50s and 60s, but these attempts failed. By the 1980s, youth from kindergarten to college were wearing nearly anything they wanted.

Inglish, Patty. *Young Fashion: Public School Dress Codes of the 1960s and 1970s*, Bellatory, Mar. 3, 2020.

***

Honeymooning: Fun, Fear & Fish

<u>10 Snorkeling Safety Tips</u> (by Snorkeling Around the World),
snorkelaroundtheworld.com was first indexed by Google in March 2015

Be confident in the water!	Learn to use your snorkel gear!
Find a snorkel buddy!	Follow the weather forecast!
Protect your skin from the sun!	Be fit and healthy!
Stay hydrated, but NO alcohol	Don't swim on a full stomach!
Don't touch marine life!	Stay close to shore!

***

Anniversary Dinner

Historically, the origin of the wedding anniversary can be traced back to the Holy Roman Empire. During this time, husbands celebrated their wives by crowning them on particular landmark years. Specifically, on the 25th anniversary, wives were crowned with a wreath of silver.

"Be devoted to one another in love. Honor one another above yourselves." (This Bible verse emphasizes the importance of commitment and loyalty, two important factors in a happy marriage.) Romans 12:10.

***

The Hospital Room

Topic 1 - Hospitals are institutions built, staffed, and equipped for the diagnosis of disease; for the <u>treatment</u>, both medical and surgical, of the sick and the injured; and for their housing during this process. They often serve as a center for investigation and for teaching.

Later during the COVID reign, the hospitals became places of hope that sometimes turned to despair. Beds were few because so many people were sick with the virus and at times there was no room for folks with other maladies. There was a fear that the virus was contagious.

Topic 2 - Types of Infidelity

- Physical Infidelity: Physical or sexual connection outside of the relationship.

- Emotional Infidelity: Emotional attachment or intimacy with another person.

- Cyber Infidelity: Social media has made it easier for people to engage in online messages, chats, forums, or groups with sexual content.

***

The Only One Upstairs (Alzheimer's)

What is the difference between Alzheimer's and typical age-related changes?

Signs of Alzheimer's and Dementia	Typical Age-Related Changes
Poor judgment and decision-making	Making bad decisions once in a while
Inability to manage a budget	Missing a monthly payment
Losing track of the date or the season	Forgetting which day it is, but remembering it later
Difficulty having a conversation	Sometimes forgetting which word to use
Misplacing things and being unable to retrace steps to find them	Losing things from time to time

*Alzheimer's Association –
https://www.alz.org/alzheimers-dementia/10_signs

***

An Encounter on a Marble Bench (Angelic Pause)

"It is far more common for angels to appear in as humans than wearing wings. Often an angel will appear as a human because the angel wants to offer assistance-a good Samaritan who changes your tire, or a fellow shopper who helps you pick the perfect outfit for a meaningful event. The best way for angels to work is in public around other people unnoticed. Maybe an angel appeared to you as another patient in a hospital waiting room, Maybe an angel appeared a stranger who spoke kind words or a hand to hold while you waited for news on a loved one's condition or some test results of your own and when you turn around, there is no sign of this stranger. Angels who appears as humans often have very kind eyes and a peaceful, calming energy. They are remarkably helpful and usually don't say much but what they say is very poignant.

Richardson, Tanya Carrol: *How to Tell if You've Encountered an Angel in Physical Form*

> *Let mutual love continue. Do not neglect to show hospitality to strangers, for by doing that some have entertained angels without knowing it.*

– Hebrews 13:1,2

Chapter 4. Relatively Speaking

It is Time

"The problems of the Great Depression affected virtually every group of Americans. No group was harder hit than African Americans, however. By 1932, approximately half of African Americans were out of work. In some Northern cities, whites called for African Americans to be fired from any jobs as long as there were whites out of work. Racial violence again became more common, especially in the South. Lynchings, which had declined to eight in 1932, surged to 28 in 1933." (Library of Congress)

https://www.loc.gov/classroom-materials/united-states-history-primary-source-timeline/great-depression-and-world-war-ii-1929-1945/race-relations-in-1930s-and-1940s/

***

Dear Diary, "As-Salaam-Alaikum"

"Thirty-nine-year-old El Hajj Malike El-Shabazz was killed today. His pregnant wife and three daughters were sitting on the front bench. My heart hurts for them, for us and for the world. He was shot numerous times while speaking at the podium in the Audubon Ballroom, 3940 Broadway at West 165th Street in the Washington Heights neighborhood of Manhattan, New York City. It has been eight months since the speech he gave in Harlem. Now his voice is silenced by bullets."

https://www.biography.com/news/malcolm-x-assassination

***

The Innocent

What do you do if your husband gives you an STI? Here are some ideas for handling the conversation.

1. Imagine that your roles are reversed.

2. It's best to be direct.

3. It's best to be honest.

4. Let the conversation proceed naturally.

5. Don't push your partner to make decisions about sex or your relationship right away. ...

6. Encourage your partner to ask questions.

Studies have established that women have a higher biological risk for contracting STIs and HIV than men, with a higher probability of transmission from men to women than vice versa.

Coombs R W, Reichelderfer P S, Landay A L. Recent observations on HIV type 1 infection in the genital tract of men and women. *AIDS* 200317455–480.
https://www.ncbi.nlm.nih.gov › articles › PMC2563883

***

A Mask Is a Mask: ("A rose is a rose is a rose" = Things are what they are!) Gertrude Stein

Wearing a mask helps prevent the spread of COVID-19 by containing the droplets that are released during speaking, coughing, and sneezing.

New research suggests that an added benefit of wearing a face mask may be that it encourages people to physically distance themselves.

Healthline.com:

Shmerling, Robert, (MD), Senior Faculty Editor, Harvard Health Publishing; Editorial Advisory Board Member, Harvard Health Publishing. (January 15, 2022.) Masks-wearing protects against illness from viruses that travel through the air- not just VOVIC-19 , but also colds and flu. Some people worry that masks trap carbon dioxide (CO2) or limit the amount of oxygen you inhale, but that is not true. As you breathe out in a mask, CO2 escapes, as you breathe in, you receive oxygen

***

Lying Choices

Launched in 1979, "Choose Your Own Adventure" children's books became popular. The concept offered the reader choices on itinerary but also allowed them to see the outcomes of their choices. The discussions in classrooms were the catalyst for multiple discussions and debates. Students enjoyed the ventures but also developed unique ways of thinking that lead to compromises on trains of thought.

***

Second Chances

Question: What is an angel?

Thesaurus.com:

1. One of a class of spiritual beings; a celestial attendant of God. In medieval angelology, angels constituted the lowest of the nine celestial orders (seraphim, cherubim, thrones, dominations or dominions, virtues, powers, principalities or princedoms, archangels, and angels).

2. a conventional representation of such a being, in human form, with wings, usually in white robes.

3. a messenger, especially of God.

4. a person who performs a mission of God or acts as if sent by God:

5. a person having qualities generally attributed to an angel, as beauty, purity, or kindliness.

***

All Kinds of Junk (Quotes)

Change

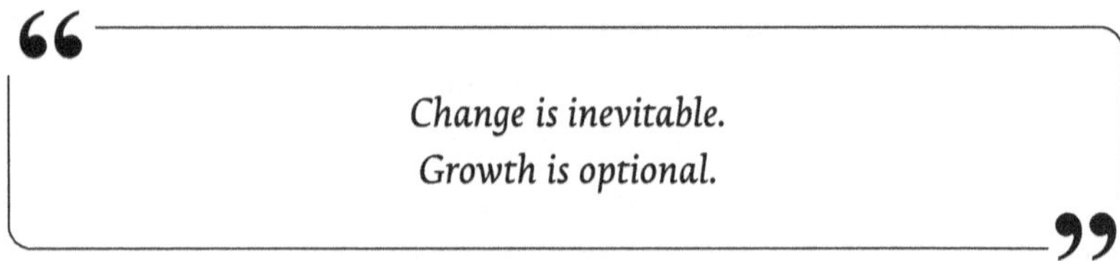

– John Maxwell

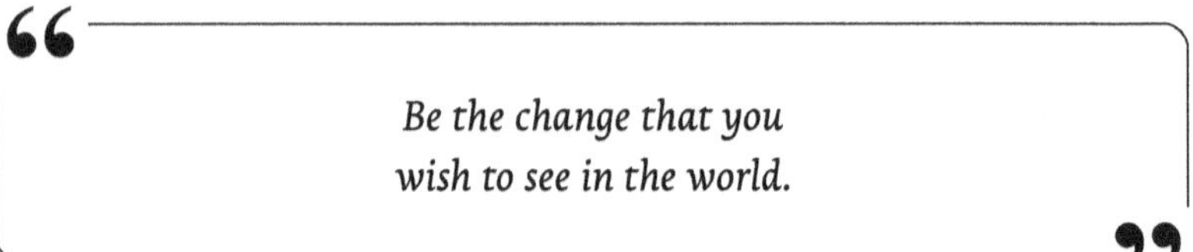

– Mahatma Gandhi

> The greatest discovery of all time is that a person can change
> his future by merely changing his attitude.

– Oprah Winfrey

Junkyards

- *"Going to a junkyard is a sobering experience. There you can see the ultimate destination of almost everything we desired."* Roger von Oech

- *"History is a pathetic junkyard of broken treaties."* Richard M. Nixon

- *"She can't help it,' he said. "She's got the soul of a poet and the emotional makeup of a junkyard dog." Stephen King*

Chapter 5. Poetically Speaking

Eve's Point of View

<u>Genesis 2:15-17 (NKJV)</u>

15 - Then the LORD God took the man and put him in the garden of Eden to tend and keep it.

16 - And the LORD God commanded the man, saying, "Of every tree of the garden you may freely eat;

17 - but of the tree of the knowledge of good and evil you shall not eat, for in the day that you eat of it you shall surely die."

<u>Genesis 3:2-3 (NKJV)</u>

2 - And the woman said to the serpent, "We may eat the fruit of the trees of the garden;

3 - but of the fruit of the tree which is in the midst of the garden, God has said, 'You shall not eat it, nor shall you touch it, lest you die.'

In Genesis 2 it would seem the man was alone when he was given the command because in the next verses after the command, God expresses the loneliness of the man, but in Genesis 3 when Eve was having a discourse with the serpent, she uses the word "we" which is inclusive of her and the man as having received the command directly from God.

***

The Slide

Line Dancing gives women and men who enjoy dancing an opportunity to do so, since it does not require a partner. It gives everyone a chance to dance.

According to the Urban Line Dance History website, this version of line dancing can be traced back to the late 1950s and early 1960s, with the rise of The Madison. Dave Bush Jr. was the "godfather" of urban line dancing and created many different dances in his 66 years.
https://www.youarecurrent.com › 2023/04/10 › getting-i...Apr 10, 2023

"The Electric Slide" is a four-wall line dance set to Marcia Griffiths and Bunny Wailer's song "Electric Boogie." Choreographer, pianist, and Broadway performer Richard L. "Ric" Silver created the dance in 1976 from a demo of the Bunny Wailer recording,

***

My Drum

Written with respect for risk takers...Katherine Johnson, Beyonce, Octavia Butler, Marie Curie, Shirley Chisholm, Ellen DeGeneres, Gertrude Ederle, Oprah Winfrey, Ada Lovelace, Hillary Clinton, Annie Oakley, Rosa Parks, Sacagawea, Sally Ride, Jackie Moms Mabley, Harriet Tubman, Sojourner Truth, Malala Yousafzai, etc.,etc., etc.

***

The Laundresses

Twenty years after slavery was abolished, thousands of black laundresses (who had been labeled "washer women") went on strike for higher wages, respect for their work, and control over how their work was organized. They worked long hours and their wages ranged from $4 to $8 a month. They threatened that it would shut the city down. They then established a uniform rate at $1 per dozen pounds of wash.

More black women worked as laundresses than in any other type of work. There were more laundresses than male laborers. Only a small portion of white women worked for pay, and the average white family could afford the services of at least a washerwoman. Laundresses worked mostly in their own homes or in their neighborhoods with other women. They worked outside in the shade when weather permitted or inside, hanging clothes on a line or all over the house to dry.

They made their own soap from lye, starch from wheat bran, and washtubs from beer barrels cut in half. After working all day, they delivered some. Gallons of water were carried from wells, pumps, or hydrants. Then, after hanging the clothes to dry, the women would iron, using heavy irons. In the end, the strike raised wages and proved the black female workers to be instrumental to the economy.

Hunter, Tera W. *To 'Joy My Freedom: Southern Black Women's Lives and Labors After the Civil War.* Harvard Press, 1997.

Greenfeld, Carl. *The Identity of Black Women in the Post-Bellum Period, 1865-1885. Binghamton Journal of History, Spring 1999.*

***

Wake Up

Motherhood is an "on the job" learning experience. Some mothers never inform their daughters about life situations, such as menstruation, having a baby, and menopause. Some mothers may give too much information too soon. For instance, I never knew that I had to feed a baby around the clock.

As I grew in my mothering, I realized that mothers are totally winging it! They don't know everything and in some cases, natural circumstances can be a good teacher. There is no blueprint to parenting! They do everything they can to be the best that they can and still make mistakes. Prayer can be helpful!

I found out that when you think you finally know what you are doing, life throws a curveball and all you can do is try to catch it, hit it, or run out of the way. Being an adult is challenging.

As for me, I'm learning and making it up as I go along—just like my mother did.

***

Haiku

(Haiku is a Japanese poem of seventeen syllables, in three lines of five, seven, and five traditionally evoking images of the natural world.)

Cicada - Billions of Brood X cicadas emerged in 2021, making a lot of noise. Cicadas are predicted to begin the first or second week of May. Their lifespan is four to six weeks above ground. They'll begin to die off in late June and into July. But there may be a few stragglers that linger far into the summer. They appear every 17 years.

Cicadas have been around since the age of the dinosaurs.

"They can't hurt you," said Elizabeth Barnes, exotic forest pest educator at Purdue University. "People tend to worry that cicadas will bite, but they don't have the mouthparts to do that." (Apr 29, 2021)
https://www.cicadamania.com › cicadas › do-cicadas-bite...

***

Remembering Miss Classie Mitchell

Positive people can be easily recognized. It is time well spent to let them know they are appreciated. Here are some *"Characteristics that cause someone to stand out in a crowd."*

Friendly	Confident	Independent
Intelligent	Good Manners	Sense of Humor
Empathy	Healthy	Open Minded
Forgiving	Has Goals	Strong
Do Not Obsess Over Looks	Honest	Know their Worth

***

The Painting Calls Me

The Last Poets are several groups of poets and musicians who rose in the late 1960s African-American Civil Rights Movement. They were one of the earliest influences on hip-hop music. Critic Jason Ankeny wrote: "With their politically charged raps, taut rhythms, and dedication to raising Black consciousness, the Last Poets almost single-handedly laid the groundwork for the emergence of hip-hop."
https://en.wikipedia.org › wiki › The Last Poets

***

Let Me Be Me

On November 2, 1969, Craig Rodwell, his partner Fred Sargeant, Ellen Broidy, and Linda Rhodes proposed the first Pride march to be held in New York City by way of a resolution at the Eastern Regional Conference of Homophile Organizations (ERCHO) meeting in Philadelphia. Lesbian, Gay, Bisexual, and Transgender Pride Month (LGBT Pride Month) is celebrated annually in June to remember the 1969 Stonewall riots, and works to achieve equal justice and equal opportunity for lesbian, gay, bisexual, transgender, and questioning (LGBTQ) Americans.

***

I Am From

(Personal accountings.) "I Am From" poems are a type of list poem, where the writer uses the repeated refrain "I am from" to make a list of what they are from, not limiting themselves to being from a literal place, but thinking more broadly about how they are from their experiences. George Ella Lyons first wrote "Where I am From" poems by looking deeply into her own childhood to pinpoint things that make her unique. Lyon is able to lay out a roadmap to understanding herself. (Emma Baldwin)

en.m.Wikipedia.or

Behold, I stand at the door and knock. If <u>anyone</u> hears my voice and opens the door, I will come in to him and eat with him, and he with me.

– Revelations 3:20

Appendix B
Paintings & Photographs

Chapter 1. Historically Speaking

The Finale (1864)

File: *Slaves cutting the sugar cane* - Ten Views in the Island ...
Copyright: Public Domain, from the British Library's collections, 2013

The Trip (1912)

Juliette and Joseph Laroche and their two daughters Simonne and Louise.
Courtesy W. Mae Kent (public domain image).

The Queen (1626)

Queen Njinga meeting with Portuguese Governor Joao Corria de Sousa,
1622 (public domain image).

Blackpast.org/global-african-history/queen-nzinga-1583-1663/

A Survivor (1945)

Lilly Photography by Sandra Wilson).

Not Quite a Bible Story (100 BC)

"In Prayer" painting by Sandra Wilson.

Aunty Sue's Flowers (1862)

Flowers painting by Sandra Wilson.

Benjamin "Pap" Singleton, ca. 1880. Courtesy Kansas Historical Society (public domain image).

Voyages

Windmill Photograph (Bruges, Belgium) by Sandra Wilson (2019); *Embarkation of the Pilgrims*, Robert R. Weir (Public Domain), *U.S. Capitol Rotunda Created: 1844 date QS:P571,+1844-00-00T00:00:0.*

(Original image by Robert R. Weir. Uploaded by Ibolya Horvath, published on 05 November 2020. The copyright holder has published this content under the following license: Public Domain. This item is in the public domain, and can be used, copied, and modified without any restrictions.)
https://www.worldhistory.org/image/13077/embarkation-of-the-pilgrims/

Chapter 2. Theatrically Speaking

Telephone Face-offs (Spam Calls)

"Telephones Through the Ages" painting by Sandra Wilson.

Please Don't Cut Down the Trees

Toilet Paper Container photograph by Sandra Wilson.

Mary The Great

Mary Fields, photographer unknown. Public Domain, https://commons.wikimedia.org/w/index.php?curid=.

The Continuous Nightmare

Mother/Daughter photograph by Sandra Wilson.

Chapter 3. Personally Speaking

My Quadrangle

Photograph, Carnegie Library (1909), Cheyney University, Pennsylvania, November 10, 2009 Public domain image, From Wikimedia Commons, the free media repository - (Original file (1,582 × 1,143 pixels, file size: 335 KB, MIME type: image/jpeg). *https://www.blackpast.org/african-american-history/cheyney-university-pennsylvania-1837/)*

What Goes In the Beauty Shop
Stays In the Beauty Shop.

House Photograph by Sandra Wilson.

The Skirt War (Mother/Daughter)

"The Skirt" ink drawing by Sandra Wilson.

Honeymooning

Scuba Diving License photograph by Sandra Wilson.

In Deep Water painting by Sandra Wilson.

Anniversary Dinner

Glass of Wine photograph by Sandra Wilson.

The Only One Upstairs

Family photograph by Sandra Wilson.

Chapter 4. Relatively Speaking

It Is Time

Portrait photograph by Sandra Wilson.

The Innocent

"Germ Beauty?" painting by Sandra Wilson.

A Mask Is a Mask

Sandra Wilson photograph by Sandra Wilson.

Second Chances

"Carnivorous Plants" painting by Sandra Wilson.

"Birds of Paradise" painting by Sandra Wilson.

All Kinds of Junk

"Sheena" (cat) photograph by Sandra Wilson.

Chapter 5. Poetically Speaking

The Slide

"Dancing Feet" painting by Sandra Wilson.

My Drum

"Musical Instruments of the World" painting by Sandra Wilson.

Wake Up

Baby photograph by Sandra Wilson.

Let Me Be Me

"Let Me Be Me Pride" painting by Sandra Wilson.

I Am From

"Family Crest" painting by Sandra Wilson.

Acknowledgments

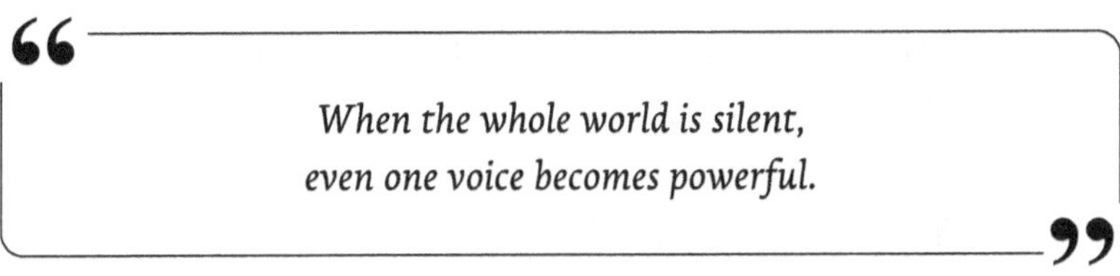

– **Malala Yousafzai**

To the cheerleaders who believe that my writing has value, this book is my tribute. They inspired the courage and tenacity it took to complete this work. My mother's voice resounds in my soul. Her serious and supportive demeanor provides a foundation that offers encouragement. Her mantra was "You can do it." My proud, strong, and reassuring father's voice stays in my mind and continues to provides a sense of security. Together my parents built a support system that has held through opportunities and pitfalls.

The compliments, support, and suggestions of my children, Dr. John Wilson III, Shawn Wilson Hill, and their spouses, Lisza Morton Wilson and James Hill, are important. I cherish the encouraging words from my cousin (SisterCuz), the late Sheila Wallace, and friend, the late Patricia Blue Williams. It is sad that they are not able to see the finished product. I am happy that they got a chance to hear some of my readings.

Cousins Sharon Burton and Sherry Burton Stein provided artistic support. They even found and treated me to venues for my presentations and then attended them.

I am grateful to friends who listened to and/or read some of the work. They are also my heroes and "sheroes." It reminds me of what the Bible says: "For without them there would be not anything made that was made."

Thank you to author and writing professor Susan Moyer for rewarding critiques and constant reassurances. I am grateful for my writing friends Doris Durrett, Trish MacDonald, and Gloria Petit-Clair for their comments and encouragement after listening to and reading some of my work. Gratitude goes to Charlotte Hartnett, Robin Watts, Brenda Demby, Sheila Hill, Wendell Whitlock, Cecelia Robinson, and my late brother John Slaughter for having faith in me and listening. Thanks to Author Charles Heller who guided me to his publisher when I was in the midst of wandering.

I am grateful to Beverly Yates, Cecelia Robinson, Michelle Bradly, Ronald and Denice Swann, Michelle Marcus, Natalie Robinson, Michele Mitchell, Nicola Kennedy, Karen Hicks, Monique Lester, Jacqueline Pelzer, June Blue, and Rhonda Benthall for attending my open mic performances (virtual/ or in person). There are a number of people who attended the readings that I did not know but who took the time to express their appreciation. That is meaningful.

I am thankful for God's guidance and for picking me up when I grew tired and disillusioned. When there was no one else around I could count on a heavenly source. I am forever grateful!

***

> *Behold, I stand at the door and knock.*
> *If <u>anyone</u> hears my voice and opens the door,*
> *I will come in to him and eat with him, and he with me.*

– Jesus Christ

About Atmosphere Press

Founded in 2015, Atmosphere Press was built on the principles of Honesty, Transparency, Professionalism, Kindness, and Making Your Book Awesome. As an ethical and author-friendly hybrid press, we stay true to that founding mission today.

If you're a reader, enter our giveaway for a free book here:

SCAN TO ENTER
BOOK GIVEAWAY

If you're a writer, submit your manuscript for consideration here:

SCAN TO SUBMIT
MANUSCRIPT

And always feel free to visit Atmosphere Press and our authors online at atmospherepress.com. See you there soon!

About the Author

DR. SANDRA WALTON WILSON, grew up in Willow Grove, Pennsylvania. She taught in the elementary schools of Abington (PA) and Endicott (NY); Montgomery Community College (PA) and Temple University (PA). She supervised teachers in the Reduced Class Size Balanced Literacy Program (PA) and was a Teacher Editor for a Silver Burdett Ginn's Science Program.

Sandra earned a B.A. in Elementary Education (Cheyney University, PA); a M.A. in Urban Education (Montclair University, NJ); a M.A. in Humanities with a concentration in Fine Arts (Arcadia University, PA) and a Ph.D. in Urban Education (Temple University, PA).

As a Deacon at Bethlehem Baptist Church (PA); Chapter and National President of Black Women's Educational Alliance, Inc.; NAACP Youth Director (Eastern PA); chapter officers in Alpha Kappa Alpha Sorority, Inc., (Phi Beta Omega and Psi Epsilon Omega), the Links, Inc. (Montgomery County, PA); and the National Association of University Women (Montgomery County, PA); and a Board Member of the Settlement School of Music (PA), she was involved in community.

Her paintings have been displayed in numerous shows such as the Women's Caucus for Art, Temple University, the

Bowie City Hall (MD), and the African American Museum of Philadelphia. Her writings appear in anthologies such as *HBCU Experience: The Book* and journals; and her play "We Are" was included in the first *International Journal of Black Drama (Temple University)*.

Sandra feels that her most important gift has been mothering her two children and watching them as they nurture her grandchildren.

***

> *And we all, who with unveiled faces contemplate the Lord's glory, are being transformed into his image with ever-increasing glory, which comes from the Lord, who is the Spirit.*

– 2 Corinthians 3:18